Limits

Susie Tate

For all the people who feel lonely in a crowded room.

Contents

1. Limits   1
2. Him   7
3. Thwarted ambition   18
4. Safe space   29
5. Ruin everything   42
6. That chick is weird   51
7. Absolute terror   61
8. Strong enough   69
9. Millie wuvs books, don't cha?   78
10. I think I love you, uptight lady   84
11. We'll see, baby   93
12. I know pain when I see it   108
13. Lamb to the slaughter   118
14. Professor X   129
15. Fuck all the men   138
16. Pathetic   144
17. This is me   152
18. Unique   161
19. At least try to be normal   172
20. "When... when do we do that again?"   181
21. You just wait until next year, right?   190
22. What did she have to lose?   197
23. Nothing you can't do   204
24. The stupidity of the Y chromosome   212
25. Yes, I trust you   219
26. You're not trying hard enough   229
27. Huge asset   239
28. You'd be surprised what people will believe   250
29. Endorphins   258
30. Nothing to do with us   267
31. Boundaries, schmoundaries   274

32. Every word, dear   284
33. All she ever wanted   291
  Epilogue   297

  Acknowledgments   309
  A Word on Anxiety   311
  About the Author   313

Chapter 1

Limits

MILLIE STOOD AT THE VERY BACK OF THE CLUB, HER EYES fixed on the stage. If she wasn't so terrified she would be smiling. But with her level of anxiety at being around this many people, that would be an impossibility. When Jamie had asked her to come tonight she'd been surprised. But then he had literally asked *everyone* who knew his girlfriend Libby to come.

Still, it was a surprise.

Millie was never invited anywhere. Nobody wanted the Nuclear Winter (she'd overheard that nickname more than once) around socially, she knew that. Even if somebody had decided to extend an invite, she would never usually have gone.

Millie knew her limits.

She knew what she could cope with, and this was way, way beyond them. Eleanor had been ecstatic that Millie needed something more casual to wear. They'd spent over an hour picking the perfect outfit. She'd even made a move to give Millie a hug after they'd finished, which Millie had deftly avoided. El was nice, but then El was paid to be nice. Millie imagined that most people would be nice if they were a personal shopper who took a commission from someone who didn't care about cost of clothes.

Money meant nothing to Millie, but wearing the right outfits did, and she did not trust her own judgement. Years ago, at the start of their interactions, Eleanor had tried to extract an opinion from Millie about the clothes she got her to try on, but she didn't bother anymore. Millie simply gave El the situation the clothes would be worn in, El had her try a few outfits, and then she chose everything for her – right down to her underwear. Millie knew that she herself had no taste. She knew that if *she* chose her clothes it would not be perfect, and appearing perfect was *very* important to Millie.

"Hey, Dr M."

Her head whipped round to see *Him* grinning down at her, his eyes twinkling with mischief. This man's eyes were always twinkling with mischief.

Pavlos Martakis was definitely beyond her limits.

As Millie was a radiologist and Dr Martakis a consultant surgeon, she managed to avoid him to a certain extent, but she couldn't avoid him completely and he'd always unsettled her an unreasonable amount. In a way he was her complete opposite: physically intimidating, likable, naturally attractive, extremely confident, sexually promiscuous (and very talented in that area, if hospital gossip was to be believed). Yes, he unsettled her, but more than that she got the impression that to him she was just one big joke. That he took an interest in her purely for his own amusement – like poking a turtle with a stick.

"Hello, Dr Martakis," she said in a tight voice, taking a small step back. She fixed her attention back on the stage and heard him sigh.

"Why don't you call me Pavlos?" he asked. When she didn't reply she heard another more drawn out sigh. Why was he wasting his time talking to her?

"You okay? You seem a bit tense."

Millie blinked. She wasn't really used to concern. It threw her for a moment.

"Fine," she managed to get out eventually. He was still studying her and she got the impression he didn't miss much. After a long pause, Dr Martakis finally broke the silence.

"Here." A drink was held out in front of her. She looked down at it but made no move to release the death grip she had on her handbag.

"I don't drink alcohol," she told him.

Dr Martakis burst out laughing, but when she kept on staring straight ahead it slowly died. "Bloody hell, you're serious. Why on earth not?"

"Well the latest evidence suggests that the interaction of alcohol with primary and secondary targets within the brain causes alterations in gene expression and synaptic plasticity, that leads to long-lasting alteration in neuronal network activity." Out of the corner of her eye Millie could see the pint that had been making its way to Dr Martakis' mouth being slowly lowered.

"Jesus," he muttered. Millie's hands clenched her handbag even harder, and her eyes dropped to her white knuckles. This is what she did: take a perfectly happy, socially confident person and make them feel uncomfortable. It was her special gift. She closed her eyes in a long blink and counted in her head, just like Anwar had told her to, trying to slow her breathing. Dr Martakis cleared his throat. She thought he would move away but he just put his pint down on one of the high tables next to them.

"Okay, so, no alcohol. Can I get you something else?" he pushed, and Millie started sidling towards the exit she could see from the corner of her eye. To her annoyance he simply moved with her.

"No," she told him. "I'm fine."

A low sound came from deep in Dr Martakis' throat, almost like a growl. Millie took another step to the side.

"Do you know any words other than 'fine' and 'no'?" he gritted out.

Millie jerked in surprise and risked a brief moment of eye contact. He was watching her closely, his arms crossed over his broad chest. She suddenly felt very small and very intimidated. In general Millie kept most of her interactions with people superficial and free of emotion. As a consequence, she might not be liked but she encountered very few openly rude comments. The only experience she had to draw on was her hostile, critical parents, and she'd never been great with dealing with them either.

"Er..." She took a step back. The music had changed to another song now, and most people had already moved to the stage to dance. Millie had seen what she came to see: Jamie had proposed to Millie's one and only friend in front of the whole club (at least Millie considered Libby a friend – Libby probably only thought of Millie as convenient childcare). She had never danced in her life. It was time for her to leave.

"Bugger, that came out wrong," Dr Martakis said, moving with her and putting his hand on her forearm to stop her retreat. Her eyes flew open wide and she jerked her arm away violently, shooting him another nervous glance and taking another step back.

"Hey, hey, hey," Dr Martakis said, lifting both his hands in the air, palm up, in a gesture of surrender. Millie glanced around and breathed a sigh of relief when she saw that the nearest exit was now only feet away. This time when she moved, he didn't touch her, but he did spring forward and block her path. Millie took a step to the side and he moved with her. She focused on the exit sign and bit her lip.

"I'm sorry, that was rude," he said.

"It's fine," Millie told him before she could stop herself, and then watched his lips twitch.

"I really just wanted to ask you about speaking at the Grand Round."

"Oh," Millie said, breathing a sigh of relief. She was always much better if she knew the context of the interaction with another person. Now she understood. Dr Martakis wanted her to speak at the Grand Round. That was why he was talking to her. Whilst she felt relief to have his approach explained, there was a tiny part of her, buried deep, that was disappointed. "I can't do that."

"Of course you can," he said. "It'll be a great warm-up for speaking at conferences."

"Conferences?" The word came out strangled and Millie cleared her throat. "I won't be talking at any conferences."

"But you've made a big breakthrough, Dr Morrison. People will want to hear what you have to say."

"I've published my findings," she said, her voice still high and tight. "I... look, I just can't..."

"You can." Dr Martakis' face was set with determination. "I've set it all up for the week after next."

"No."

Dr Martakis blinked. "You can't just say an outright no, that's not—"

Millie could feel a ringing in her ears; she knew she was breathing too fast.

"My answer is no," she said through gritted teeth. The very idea of public speaking was making her come out in a cold sweat. She swallowed, glanced behind her to see another exit a bit further away, and she ran. On the way through she collided with a huge man covered in tattoos, who steadied her to stop her going down.

"Hey, what's up?" the giant asked, taking in her pale face and wide, fearful eyes. He looked over her shoulder. Millie could hear Dr Martakis calling after her. The huge man's jaw clenched tight and his eyes narrowed. "Don't you worry, miss," he told her. "I'll deal with this joker." Millie didn't wait to see what "dealing with this joker" might entail. As soon as the giant released her she was off.

She didn't stop shaking until she was in the back of a taxi five minutes later. This had been a mistake. She knew her limits. It was just that, recently, living within those limits had felt so very lonely. As the taxi took her all the way back to her boring house and her narrow life she felt a dull ache in her chest, but she didn't cry.

Millie never cried.

Chapter 2

Him

"Ki-Ki! Please!" groaned Libby, chucking a bread roll at Kira's head. "Can we not talk about *my* sex life. God."

Kira rolled her eyes. "Libby, it's not like I've been going through the dong-meets-foo-foo logistics or anything. I just think you guys should have a dirty weekend away. Maybe then you'd be a bit less vomit-worthy around us more sexually frustrated mortals. And you could do with a break. You know you could." Libby had only just recovered from a bout of pneumonia. There was real concern behind Kira's teasing.

"We are not vomit-worthy," Libby hissed in outrage.

"Uh, Lib," Pav cut in. "That would hold a lot more water if Jamie hadn't had his hand on your leg under the table for the last ten minutes, and if you hadn't sent him a dirty text just now."

Libby's face flamed bright red as Jamie jerked both his hands onto the table-top and swept his phone up into his pocket. "I did not send him a dirty text," she hissed, and Pav rolled his eyes. "I didn't, I just–"

"Okay, maybe not *dirty* dirty but I bet there were a few emojis involved."

"Yeah," Kira said, sitting forward in her chair. "You probably sent a couple of aubergines and a crazy ghost. Am I right?"

"Wh... what are you–?"

"Don't act all innocent you frisky little minx. You know exactly what I'm talking about."

Pav started laughing whilst Jamie's eyes were dancing and his mouth was pressed into a firm line. The filthy look Libby shot Jamie as his shoulders started to shake only served to increase the volume of Pav's merriment. He shook his head in his amusement and something caught his attention out of the corner of his eye. She was standing completely still across the canteen, and her perfectly made-up face was staring straight at him. It was her expression that surprised him.

Just for that moment she didn't have her standard uptight, aloof mask in place. Instead the corners of her mouth were tilted up ever so slightly and her eyes were warm. For some bizarre reason her expression seemed almost... longing. However it didn't take long for her to notice his stare. Her face shut down again and her eyes slid away as she practically ran over to the new coffee stand.

"Don't you think, Pav? Pav?"

"Er... what?" Pav replied, keeping his gaze fixed on Dr Morrison's rigid back. Kira huffed out a sigh.

"Don't you think they should be letting us babysit more? Hello? Earth to Pav?" she said as she waved a hand in front of his face.

"I'll... um, just be a minute," Pav mumbled as he pushed away from the table to stand up. "Anybody want a coffee?"

There was a long pause. "Pav you've just had a coffee. One that *I* bought for you seeing as you don't have the patience for it."

"Right, well, I've got a long list this afternoon, so a bit of a caffeine boost is in order. Ladies?" Libby and Kira looked down at their barely touched cups and then back at Pav with identical frowns.

"Wh–" Libby started, but Pav didn't catch the rest as he was already striding away.

"An Americano, please." For some reason Dr Morrison's soft voice ordering coffee gave Pav a weird buzz of excitement as he came up behind her.

"A what, dear?" Doreen was a lovely lady in her eighties who had served the teas and coffees for the last twenty years in aid of The League of Friends, a money-raising charity for the hospital. She and her cronies used to have a little hole in the wall with only tea bags and some milk. In a real pinch they would make you an instant coffee, but it would provoke a rather stern look. But a couple of months ago, since Costa had moved into the gym across the road, the management had decided to get The League of Friends up to speed with a state-of-the-art coffee machine that ground its own beans, frothed milk and made a massive assortment of coffees, all of which were listed above Doreen's head and none of which she actually knew how to make. Apparently Doreen and co. had undergone "intensive training", but this was certainly not evident in their customer service. After Pav had climbed over the counter, kissed a flustered Doreen on the cheek and made his own bloody latte last month, Jamie had banned him from any further ordering.

"She means black coffee, Doreen," Pav put in as he moved to stand inches from Dr Morrison with his hand nearly touching hers on the counter. He had just a brief moment to inhale the scent of her shampoo and some sort of expensive, subtle perfume before she took a startled step to the side away from him.

Damn it, Millie thought as she studied the jar of cookies in front of her and smoothed a non-existent wrinkle in her skirt. She *knew* she should have stuck to the Nescafé in the radiology department, but the lure of the new machine and the smell of everyone else's freshly ground coffees in the morning meeting had been too much for her. Generally she avoided the rest of the hospital as much as possible. She liked to stay on familiar ground. When she'd walked into the canteen and seen *Him* laughing with his friends, she'd actually been glad to have broken her normal routine. Whilst direct interaction with Him was stressful, being able to observe him from afar was one of her favourite things.

Of course he was always handsome; but with his head thrown back and his deep, rich laugh filling the air around him, he was so beautiful it was almost painful to look at. Dr Martakis fascinated Millie. He was the most uninhibited, charming, outgoing and *free* person she had ever encountered in her life. The way he expressed himself with his hands, his extravagance of movement, his familiarity with everyone (except her, obviously; Millie wasn't familiar with anyone apart from Donald, and he didn't really count): it was almost... wild, and it thrilled and terrified her in equal measure. So when he'd caught her staring, those dark eyes focusing intently on hers and the laughter dying on his lips, she'd skipped thrilled and gone straight to terrified.

What she should have done was leave immediately, but that would have shown weakness. Millie might actually *be* weak, but that didn't mean she had to *show* it. So, in spite of her heart beating practically out of her chest she'd made it to the coffee stand. Unfortunately Millie had not factored Doreen into the equation, but by the eighth time of giving her order she had seen the error of her ways.

And now He was right *there*. That was twice in one month she had been this close to him. Millie had only felt his body heat and seen his large hand next to hers before she heard his voice, but for some reason she'd known it was Him. Having put sufficient distance between them to keep control of her hammering heart, but not so much as to betray fear or weakness (she hoped), Millie resolved to try and ignore Him whilst Doreen bashed away at the coffee machine in slightly alarming fashion.

"I'll have a latte whilst you're at it, Doreen," he said, smiling across at the flustered, white-haired lady.

"You'll get what you're given, young man," she told him. "And stay on that side of the counter."

Dr Martakis chuckled, and the sound skittered over Millie's skin, making her shiver.

"You cold?" he asked.

She could see him turn fully towards her out of the corner of her eye, and sucked in a startled breath.

"No," she managed to squeeze out past her tight throat. It sounded rude and curt – exactly what he, and most other people, would expect from her. But for some reason this man was not put off. In fact, he chuckled. *Chuckled*, in the face of her Nuclear Winter. Nobody chuckled at Nuclear Winter; they ignored her, they left her alone – she did not make them chuckle.

"Well, I've been bloody freezing all day," he continued as if they were having an actual conversation. "The theatre air-con is buggering about. Had to wear thermals to stop my hands shaking."

"Uh…" Millie bit her lip, her eyes flicking from his tanned hand up to his thermal-clad arm. Something about the white material pulled tight over his muscular forearm caused the most weird sensation to sweep up from her stomach. Her heart actually felt like it had stopped for a moment, before it picked up double time.

"It's my Greek blood I guess," he said, and she blinked before taking another small step away. "Thanks, Doreen."

It was then Millie realized that her coffee was in front of her and she had inadvertently moved away from the cash register. Oh God, he was paying for her coffee! She watched in horrified silence as Dr Martakis handed Doreen a tenner and was given a twenty and some loose change back. The most ridiculous argument ensued, culminating in him forcing another tenner on a confused Doreen, leaning right over the counter to *kiss* Doreen on the cheek, and refusing any change. Millie watched all this with her mouth slightly open. That was until he turned to her and started moving forward. She sucked in a breath and skittered back, catching her hip on the condiment counter.

"Hey," Dr Martakis said softly, stopping his advance and holding his hands up. "Hey, you okay?"

"I'm fine," she croaked, then cleared her throat. "You... you can't pay for my coffee."

Dr Martakis' concerned frown melted away to be replaced by his wide, glamorous smile, showing his white teeth off against his olive skin. Millie's heart skipped another beat as she focused on his mouth, before quickly dropping her gaze down to her feet.

"I think I just did so... maybe you can get the next one?"

He was moving towards her again, and as her back was now pressed up against the counter, short of darting around him (which again would have revealed weakness and she had been weak enough around this man already) she had nowhere to go.

"The... the next one?" she muttered, frowning down at her coffee cup in confusion.

"Yes," Pav said as he moved right into her personal space and put his hand gently on her back to propel her forward away from the counter. "The next one. Like, tomorrow? You sort of owe me after that stunt you pulled at the club. I had some explaining to do to Mr Steroids on the door."

"I... oh, you mean the... the bouncer? I just–"

"Don't worry about it," Dr Martakis dismissed, waving the hand that was not at the small of her back. "I know Barry. We sorted it. Now, about that drink–"

"Wh... what?" she stammered, feeling the heat of his large hand on her back and moving faster to get away from it. That was until she couldn't move any further. He'd manoeuvred her over to his table before she'd even realized what was happening.

"Hi, Millie," Libby said gently, giving her an encouraging smile.

"Hey," Jamie put in, giving her a brief nod before he turned to Dr Martakis and frowned, probably confused as to why he'd dragged her over here. *That makes two of us*, Millie thought in bewilderment.

"Dr M.," Kira muttered, not bothering with an encouraging smile. Libby and Kira had both started as medical students at the hospital a few months ago and whilst Libby was kind, Millie was well aware how much Kira disliked her. Ironically, though, the feeling was not mutual at all. Millie thought Kira was hilarious and a little bit crazy. Unfortunately, when faced with big personalities and extreme extrovert behaviour, Millie tended to shut down. So any interaction she'd had with Kira in the past had been strained to say the least. The friendlier Kira was, the more dismissive Millie became and there was no way for her to stop it.

"Dr Morrison and I have been grappling with Doreen for

the last ten minutes," Dr Martakis explained smoothly whilst he pulled out a chair and gestured for Millie to sit down. Millie looked at his hand and up to his thermal-covered forearm before she glanced at his face, still sporting that wide glamorous smile. "Take a seat."

Her mouth dropped open and she blinked once. There was no way in hell she was sitting down.

"I think you're making Dr Morrison uncomfortable, Pav," Kira said, her voice uncharacteristically flat and unwelcoming.

"I... I'm not..." Millie took a step back and watched as Dr Martakis shot Kira an annoyed look before he skirted his chair to move towards her, causing it to scrape along the linoleum.

"Ta-ta, Dr M.," Kira said with a fake smile and a small wave. "Great chat, as always."

Millie took another step back but came to an abrupt halt as her back hit a solid wall of flesh. The coffee she was holding spilled over the edges of the cup and onto her hand. She barely registered the scalding pain.

"Shi – I mean, sorry, Dr Morrison," the large ODP (operating department practitioner) that worked with Jamie and with whom Millie had just collided said.

"It's fine," she said. "I... sorry..." She trailed off and turned on her heel to leave. As she weaved through the tables she put down her coffee cup; it was only half full now anyway and she couldn't exactly run back to the radiology department with it sloshing all over the place. Her hand started to throb as she rounded the double doors of the canteen and strode down the corridor at speed. Once in the safety of her office, she leaned up against the door and closed her eyes.

Donald was on leave today. It was bad timing. She needed him here. Shaking her head in an attempt to clear it, she took a deep breath and squared her shoulders. Needing Don was a bad idea. Needing anyone was a bad idea. Millie knew she had to rely on herself. Her hand throbbed again and she rolled her eyes. If she hadn't scuttled backwards like a terrified rabbit she wouldn't have run into that ODP and she wouldn't have burnt her hand. She moved away from the door, and was just about to start running some cold water into the small sink in the corner when a loud staccato knock caused her to jump about a foot in the air.

She knew who it was before his head appeared around the frame. That knock could only belong to someone as larger-than-life as Him. She contemplated hiding under her desk (it wouldn't have been the first time – she'd tucked herself in behind the front panel more than once before to avoid people) but there just wasn't time to sufficiently squash herself into the available space, and the thought of how ludicrous she would look if caught made her break out in a cold sweat.

"Hey," Dr Martakis said as he stepped into the office as if it was his own. Millie would *never* enter someone else's space unless specifically invited. She marvelled at how confident, pushy and... and *rude* this man could be. Then, after entering her office without permission, he proceeded to casually stroll up to her, stand way too close and take both her hands gently in his. "Ah, bugger," he muttered as he moved her right hand into the light to see the red burn marks over the back and fingers. "Let's get this under some cold water."

He propelled her forward to the sink by her elbow, turned on the faucet and then held her hand under the flow. Millie's whole body had gone rigid with shock as soon as he put his hands on her. And now, with her back to his front and his arms around her to hold her hand under the tap, she felt like she couldn't breathe. There was the instinctive fear she had when in physical contact with anyone, but this was mixed with a far more worrying and foreign feeling, almost like flying; kind of what she imagined it would be like to take drugs. Her ears were ringing and her heart was hammering in her chest.

"It's pretty red but hopefully it won't blister," he murmured behind her ear, and she could feel his breath on her cheek. "Jesus, what are all these bruises?" Her sleeves had ridden up and the inner surface of her forearms were showing. "What the –? Who did this to you?"

Millie dropped down and ducked under his arm, then dashed across the room, putting her office chair between them. He spun around to face her with a bemused expression on his face. She gripped the back of the chair and kept her eyes focused on her desk.

"Dr M?" he called, and she flinched. "Okay, I'm going to move away from the sink now, all right," he told her as he started walking backwards to the other side of the room and Don's desk. "I'm sorry I crowded you, but can you please put your hand back under the water?"

Millie blinked down at her hand, which started throbbing again as her adrenaline receded. She glanced at Dr Martakis out of the corner of her eye; then, with as much dignity as possible under the circumstances, she walked to the sink.

"Will you keep it under the water?"

Millie never cried. Tears did not work for her when she was a child. Instead of crying her throat would close over almost completely, making it impossible to speak. Thus, a distressed Millie was always, always an entirely silent one. So, with no other option, all she could do was nod her head whilst she stayed focused on her hand under the running water.

"I'm going to go now, okay?" he said cautiously, and she nodded again.

After the door closed behind him, part of her was weak with relief, but the other part, the part that had experienced that rush when he was near her, that part felt such an acute sense of loss it was almost painful.

Chapter 3

Thwarted ambition

PAV SHOVED HIS HANDS IN HIS POCKETS AND FROWNED AS he made his way back to the canteen. He'd been so distracted that he'd left his phone on the table. Yes, he was normally a disorganized bastard, but that level of inattention was rare, even for him.

"What was all that about?" Jamie asked as Pav approached the group. They'd all finished their lunches and were starting to collect their things together.

"Is she okay?" Libby's face was awash with concern. To Pav's knowledge, Libby was the only other hospital worker who did not seem to hold any animosity towards Dr Morrison. Dr M. had even looked after Libby's little girl in the past, which was a shock in itself, seeing as people in general did not seem to be the radiologist's forte. As Libby was a medical student and a single mother (well, not quite so single any more thanks to Jamie), Dr Morrison's help had been a much-needed lifeline – but it was still a bizarre choice of childcare in Pav's opinion.

"I didn't mean to piss her off so much that she'd scald herself," Kira put in, shifting uncomfortably on her feet. "You know I can't control my mouth sometimes. It's just that she can be *such* a mega-bitch."

Dr Morrison had an unfortunate but well-earned reputation around the hospital for her cold manner and her ability to make you feel stupid when you requested a scan. Consultants like Pav and Jamie took that sort of humiliation on the chin, but it was a bit mean-spirited when it came to students like Kira. There had been a couple of times over the last month when Kira had come back from the radiology department with a pale face and without her usual relentless banter. Pav knew that Kira's confidence clinically had been knocked recently, when she'd failed an anatomy viva, so the last thing she needed was for Nuclear Winter to make her feel even more substandard.

Pav reached for his phone and tucked it into his back pocket.

"Is she okay?" Libby asked, a small frown marring her forehead.

"She's fine," he told them with a confidence he didn't feel. His mind flashed back to the red burn marks on her hand and the bruises he'd seen on her forearm, and his stomach tightened. "Maybe you could go check on her though Libs? You seem to be the only one she's comfortable with."

Kira snorted in agreement.

"You know, Ki-Ki," Pav said after a moment, "I'm not sure she means to be a bitch. Maybe she's just... shy."

"You think?" Kira's forehead was creased in a frown and her head cocked to the side so that her long red hair fell over one small shoulder. "I have to say she's pretty high up on my list of People Who Need a Slap With a Wet Fish."

Libby sighed. "I've told you all before," she said in an exasperated tone. "You don't know Millie. She's got... issues."

"Yeah, well, you're bang on there," Kira muttered, and Libby shot her an annoyed look.

"She's really good with Rosie, Kira. But you've got to be a bit less..." Libby paused and looked up at the ceiling before she shrugged and focused back on Kira with a small smile, "...you."

"A bit less me?"

"Yes. I think you intimidate her."

"*I* intimidate *her*?" Kira rolled her eyes. "Her heart is carved of ice Libs. I doubt any human could intimidate her."

"Just give her a chance."

Kira paused. "Well... I guess she did call me to sort you out when you were ill. She can't be a complete robot."

"I think we should all make a bit more effort with her actually," Pav cut in. "I've certainly got to try and get her on side if I want to get her to present at the Grand Round."

Pav *needed* to talk Dr Morrison around. So far she'd refused to even consider speaking about her research in public. Pav knew this because, as the Director of Surgery, he was the one who received the emails from conferences, when they had no luck with her. Apparently she'd turned down every one of them. Pavlos could not understand why anybody would turn down that opportunity. He himself would give his right arm to present his new surgical technique for minimally invasive prostatectomy. Knowing this, and desperate for Dr Morrison to speak at his conference, the organizer of the European Urological Association meeting had contacted Pav last week with an offer of a slot to speak to the main lecture hall, *if* he could convince Dr Morrison to take a slot as well. So far her study had only involved orthopedic and urology patients; both specialties were vying for who could convince her to talk first, and Pav's assistance would give the urologists the edge. The conference was in six months. Pav had told the organizer "no worries".

"Millie needs genuine friends, Pav," Libby said with more than a hint of reproach in her voice. "Leave her alone if you're just trying to get her to speak at that bloody conference you're always on about." Pav had told them all about the stalemate he was involved in with Dr Morrison. Libby had been adamant that he not push "Millie" too hard to present.

"You've no chance, mate," Jamie chuckled. "Even the legendary Pavlos rays of supercharm won't be enough to warm up Nuclear Winter." Libby punched Jamie in the arm.

"Don't call her that," she snapped. "And Pav, I'm serious about you leaving Millie alone. Jamie's being a dick, but he's right about the conference; there's no way she'll do that."

We'll see, Pav thought as he clenched his jaw in frustration. Thwarted ambition was not his style. *We'll just see.*

MILLIE'S BODY TENSED AS SHE HEARD THE FAR SOFTER knock on her door.

"Millie?" At the sound of Libby's voice she sagged slightly in relief but also a little, tiny bit of disappointment. It was official: she was losing her mind. Her office door was pushed open and Libby's head appeared around it, followed by Rosie's underneath.

"We've come to fix your hand," the five-year-old bossed as she pushed her way into the office and planted her little feet wide with her hands on her hips. Her bright blue eyes, so similar to her mother's, were sparking with determination and she shook her dark curls behind her shoulders. Rosie had turned five last month. Millie knew that her party had been at Jamie's house, as she had been invited – another surprise. Of course she couldn't go. Apart from anything, she'd known He'd be there, and after the club incident Millie was avoiding Him at all costs. Something that had backfired spectacularly today.

"You, young lady, have come to watch. *I've* come to check

on Millie," Libby said, trying to gently draw Rosie to the side. The little girl, however, was not in the mood to be pushed aside. She shook off her mother's hand and moved to Millie, climbing up into her lap and putting her strong little arms around her neck, before giving her a squeeze. Millie swallowed past a lump in her throat as she closed her arms around the warm curled body. Since she'd been babysitting for Libby (at first it was in the mornings so that Libby could go to the ward round before the hospital nursery opened, but Rosie had since started school, which meant Millie was now only allowed the odd evening babysit) she had become used to Rosie's affection. The only reason she'd even become sort-of friends with Libby was because Rosie had marched into Millie's office a few months ago after Millie had refused a scan request from Libby, and asked her straight out why she was "being mean to my mummy?". Libby had been mortified – she'd been trying to keep the child hidden behind the door whilst she asked for the scan (as a single mother and restricted by the nursery opening times Libby hadn't had much choice), but Millie had been enchanted by the child from the start.

In fact, now she looked forward to the evenings Libby needed babysitting so much it was almost pathetic. The casual affection she found so difficult with other people came easily with Rosie. Maybe because the social cues Millie found impossible to interpret with adults were easier to read with this child; there was no artifice, no small talk, no double meanings. Everything was clear and on the table. Affection was genuine. Millie had no idea why the little girl had taken to her so much, but she was not going to turn her away. In the company of this child Millie almost felt normal, something she hadn't experienced in a long time – if she was honest there was never really a time when the word normal would have applied to her.

"Right, now you can fix her hand, Mummy," Rosie further

bossed as she released Millie and slid off her lap. Libby rolled her eyes but smiled at her daughter.

"Can I see?" she asked Millie.

"Listen, my hand's fine. I don't–"

"That's not what Pav told me, Millie," Libby said gently, and Millie let out a breath at the use of her Christian name. Everyone except these two and Don called her Dr Morrison. She absolutely hated it. It meant a lot to her that Libby called her Millie. Even her parents wouldn't use the shortened version of her name, preferring instead the more formal Camilla.

Libby sucked in a breath as she prised Millie's hand from her lap and turned it over. "Sh..." Libby glanced at her daughter, whose ears had pricked up in preparation for a swear word, "... sugar, that had to have smarted, hun."

Millie blinked. Endearments were not something she was used to either. From childhood they had been few and far between. Libby's beautiful, make-up-free face was frowning down at Millie's burns. Her short messy hair looked like she'd run her fingers through it about a thousand times already today. The way she looked and acted was so natural and carefree it made Millie feel stilted and repressed. No doubt Libby had a two-minute shower in the morning, brushed her hair, flung on whatever she had to hand and that was that. It made a mockery of Millie's own ninety-minute routine: her obsessional need to be wearing the perfect outfit, for her appearance to be flawless, faultless.

"Jesus, we need to get this looked at by plastics."

"No." Millie pulled away her hand and leaned back in her chair. Libby's head tilted to the side and her forehead creased in confusion.

"But I think–"

"No plastics. It'll be fine." Millie knew what would happen if she saw a burns specialist. They would dress her hand in such a way that it would be rendered pretty much useless. Her right hand. They would then tell her to contact someone to look after her whilst the hand healed: a friend, family – someone to stay with her. She wouldn't be able to work.

"Millie, please–"

"*No plastics.*" Millie stared at Libby, her mouth set in a thin stubborn line, and Libby sighed.

"Okay, but let me dress it at least. I have iodine and gauze."

Millie hesitated but caught sight of Rosie's concerned little face. For a five-year-old she saw way too much.

"Yes," Millie said, slowly uncoiling her hand and laying it back on the desk for Libby to see. Making sure a medical student left her free use of her hand would be a lot easier than a fully qualified plastic surgeon. "I... um, thanks," Millie muttered. Accepting kindness was not her strong suit, but then she hadn't really had that much practice.

PAV WAITED.

He could be patient when he needed to be and he got the feeling that with Dr Morrison he needed to be very fucking patient. That didn't mean he wasn't keeping tabs on her. Pav knew just about everyone in the hospital and he had his sources in the radiology department as well. Dr Morrison hadn't taken any time off with her hand, which, whilst annoying, did not entirely surprise him.

What did surprise Pav was the tightness he felt in his chest when he thought of her using a burnt hand to click through her images, or the way his stomach had hollowed out when he'd seen her bandaged hand in the urology MDT and her flinch of pain when she used it to open up her laptop. He wasn't quite sure why the thought of Dr Morrison in pain should create such a visceral reaction in him, but there was no mistaking it was there. He reasoned that maybe it was because he had indirectly been the cause of it. If he hadn't propelled her over to their table and pushed her out of her comfort zone she wouldn't have been hurt in the first place. No doubt guilt was playing a part then. There was a healthy dose of anger too, which also surprised Pav. He was generally a pretty mellow guy. But the thought of Dr Morrison pushing on to work through her pain and not resting her goddamn dominant hand made him want to smash something.

Normally if Pav thought that somebody was being stupid (and in his opinion working with your right hand after sustaining a second-degree burn was right up there), he would make his view known fairly rapidly, and, more often than not, pretty loudly. But he'd already pushed Millie into a corner, not once but twice, with disastrous consequences, and for once in his life he needed to employ a bit of subtlety. So, he waited until he knew Don was back in the office from his holiday to approach her. That was about as subtle and considerate as Pav got.

"Hey, Don," he said from the doorway of the office. Out of the corner of his eye he watched Dr Morrison jump in her chair before she settled back down and focused on the screen. At a glance she looked perfectly composed, but Pav could see how rapidly her chest was rising and falling, and how white her knuckles were as she gripped her mouse to click through the scans. "How were your hols?"

Donald turned in his chair and narrowed his eyes on Pav before flicking a concerned glance over at Millie. "I went to Bognor. It rained. What do you want, Stavros?"

"Don, come on." Pav forced out a good-natured chuckle: the stubborn old man knew his name by now. Don just crossed his arms over his chest and raised one white eyebrow. Pav sighed. "Look, I'm actually here to talk to you if that's okay, Dr Morrison?" He watched her blink at the screen but no response was forthcoming. He tried again. "How's the hand?"

"Her hand is fine," Donald snapped. "Now, what is it you really want, son?"

Pav rubbed the back of his neck and then extended the journal he was holding in his other hand. Don glanced down at the front cover and smiled. "Millie? Why didn't you tell me about this? Bugger me, it got into *The Lancet*! I can't believe it."

Dr Morrison turned in her chair and, still avoiding eye contact with Pav, reached for the journal that was now in Don's hands. He passed it across and she laid it reverently in her lap, staring down at it and then touching the featured article title, "CBT and Surgical Outcomes: The Psychology of Recovery". A very small smile tugged at her perfectly painted lips before she masked her expression. She looked up at Don.

"I didn't know it was coming out this month and I–"

"You never said it was getting into *The Lancet*," Don grumbled through a smile so wide Pav thought it might split his face. "My Millie," he said softly, reaching for her hand and laying his wrinkled one on top, "changing the face of medicine." Millie rolled her eyes.

"Don't be ridiculous, Don," she mumbled, a blush creeping up under her foundation. "It's just an idea. Hardly groundbreaking. And Anwar had just as much credit, maybe more."

Don snatched the journal away and started flicking through it. "Ha!" he said triumphantly as he poked the page with his finger. "It says right here that this has the potential to be the biggest advance in post-op recovery in the last decade. It says that in the Editor's letter. You can't argue with the Editor of *The Lancet*."

"You would, Don," she told him, her small smile back in

action and her eyes soft on her colleague. "You would argue if they hadn't said that about me, if they'd said it was rubbish."

"Well," Pav broke in, and Dr Morrison flinched again as if she'd forgotten he was even there in her excitement, "the fact is that this is a breakthrough, and as Surgical Director I can assure you the hospital is fully behind you attending whatever international conferences or meetings you need to."

Pav let that hang there for a minute as he watched Millie bite her lip. He knew very well that she had no intention of going to any international conferences. Over the last month he'd had more emails from organizers all over the world, and he knew that she was continuing to turn them all down flat, each and every one. One of them was to Hawaii, for fuck's sake. Was she mad?

"That won't be necessary," Millie told him as she spun her chair back around to her computer monitor and started scrolling through images again.

"Listen," Pav said, making a fairly rubbish attempt to soften his tone, "you can't just ignore all this. At the very least you're going to have to present it to the rest of the hospital–"

"No."

Don sighed. "Millie maybe you could just–"

"Don, *no*."

"Dr M., look..." Pav spoke to her stiff back. Other than a small flinch she did not acknowledge his presence. "You have to present this stuff. You–"

"Talk to Anwar," she said, still not making any eye contact. "He did all the CBT. He'd be–"

"*You* set up the study!" Pav's voice was raised in frustration. "Most of the CBT that the patients did was online in a computer program *you* created. I can't just get the psychologist to talk about it on his own. That's ridiculous. It's *your study*."

"No!" To Pav's shock, Dr Morrison's normal, controlled

tone went up a pitch and she actually slammed her hand down on her desk. Unfortunately it was her injured hand. He saw her wince in acute pain as she snatched it from the desk and hugged it to her chest. That dreadful hollow feeling was back again as he watched her in pain. Why was she so bloody stubborn?

"I think, Stavros, you'd better leave." Donald was out of his chair now and drawing himself up to his full height (which unfortunately for Donald only came up to Pav's chest); but the steely look in the old man's eye and the disapproval in his expression had Pav backing away to the corridor.

Chapter 4

Safe space

"Dr Morrison?"

Millie's stomach clenched, not only because, yet again, it was Him, but also at that formal greeting. Despite being used to it, the small rejection that the use of her surname elicited always cut her deep, every single time. The worst thing was the awful awareness that the situation was her own damn fault. She'd been too unfriendly to too many people for too long, and had never invited any sort of informality. And now she found it upsetting, as if the people around her went out of their way to maintain that extra distance by using the formality of her surname. No other doctor in the hospital, probably the whole trust, was as disliked. It was two weeks since he'd confronted her with *The Lancet* and Millie had hoped he would have given up trying to convince her by now.

"Yes," she replied, not taking her eyes off the computer screen.

"Listen," the deep voice continued. "I know you're busy, but I would really appreciate it if you could afford me the courtesy of looking at me when I'm speaking to you. I might only be a surgeon, but I *am* a consultant at this hospital too."

Millie blinked at the screen and her hands balled into small fists. The feel of her nails digging into the skin of her palms helped to calm her racing heart and slow her breathing, but only just. She didn't correct him. She knew that most of the hospital thought she was a consultant. It was easier for the management that way. At her last placement she had been acting as a registrar and it made everyone involved very uncomfortable.

Millie passed the radiology exams before she even started the radiology training programme. Once the college found out that she was only a second-year doctor at the time they had wanted to take the exam away from her, but the fact that she achieved an unheard-of perfect score on all tests made this more than a little tricky. Nobody had ever completed the postgraduate exams without getting a single answer wrong. She was a phenomenon. At the highest level it was decided that the last thing they wanted was to lose Millie from their specialty, so they allowed her to count her exams but made her start at the bottom of the training. That had worked for the first couple of years, but as she became a senior registrar it became more difficult. She knew more about radiology than any of the consultants she was working with. She picked up errors in reporting that had been missed by the most experienced radiologists. Working beneath people she intimidated, if only unintentionally, had been very difficult; eventually the consultants couldn't hack it.

So a solution was reached. She would be transferred to a different hospital, instated in her own office, which she would share with a consultant who could supervise her and guide her, but who wouldn't be intimidated by her knowledge base. That consultant was Donald. He was seventy-two, unfailingly calm, incredibly perceptive and ridiculously kind. He had seen through Millie's cold indifference almost immediately. He was her only real friend.

It made sense for the rest of the hospital to think Millie was a consultant. She did Don's on-calls for him under his extremely loose supervision (Don had no intention of doing any on-calls any more). Without her, the consultant rota would fall apart. And she got through twice the amount of reporting as any of her colleagues, so they could hardly demote her back to first-year trainee: they needed her.

She forced her hands to relax in her lap and turned in her chair to face Dr Martakis. Her eyes rose to meet his gorgeous, dark ones for a split second before she focused on the far safer territory of his shirt collar and heard him let out a loud sigh.

She could feel the panic rising up to her throat and tried to swallow it down. Millie was not good with people, but this man... for some reason this man terrified her. It may have been to do with him being the most beautiful human being she'd ever seen before, or his manner: totally uninhibited, completely at ease with himself and others, quick to smile and laugh – the complete opposite of Millie. He fascinated her, although in much the same way a hawk would fascinate a tiny field mouse: with a good amount of fear and awe.

Well, he wasn't smiling now. In fact, his mouth was set in a grim line and a muscle was ticking in his jaw. Feeling the hostile vibes fill the room, Millie scooted back slightly in her chair and kept her hands coiled into fists to stop them shaking. Thankfully the burn had healed enough that she didn't need the dressing on anymore.

"C..." she cleared her throat and swallowed down her anxiety. "Can I help you, Dr Martakis?" For the last two weeks Millie had been successfully avoiding Dr Martakis. To the extent that at the last urology MDT she hadn't even glanced at the coffee he'd put in front of her on the conference table (despite the fact it smelt amazing and she'd been having to survive on the terrible instant stuff in the radiology department for the two weeks before – there was no way she was venturing to the canteen again), and at the end of the meeting she'd raced past him without acknowledging his greeting. Millie was willing to admit that might have come across a little... weird, and a lot rude. She doubted Dr Martakis was used to being blanked by anyone. Donald had done a lot of the Dr Martakis fielding as well. Twice he'd effectively barred the man from coming into the office, and once he had managed to keep a straight face when Millie hid under her desk.

"My medical student came to you to request a perfectly reasonable scan twenty minutes ago." He paused and Millie decided to keep her mouth shut, adjusting her gaze to the centre of his chest, then wishing she hadn't when she took in the way his broad muscles filled out the shirt he was wearing, something she would never normally notice with other men. The sight gave her an unfamiliar swooping sensation deep in her stomach. Almost as though she was falling on a roller-coaster.

"Hello? Dr Morrison?"

Millie startled in her seat. Her perusal of his chest seemed to have scrambled all functioning neurons. Which for her was an almost unheard of occurrence.

"I'm sorry," she said, her voice high and tight. She cleared her throat again but knew the tightening wouldn't fade, not whilst He was here. "I don't know whi–"

Dr Martakis let out an annoyed huff and crossed his arms over his chest. More negative vibes filled the room and Millie shrank back into her chair.

"I'm not surprised you don't remember the request, seeing as you didn't even spare the medical student in question a single fu–" he looked away and took a deep breath in an obvious attempt to reign in his temper, "a single glance to acknowledge her existence."

Millie managed to stop herself flinching at the near-use of the f-word, but only just. It wasn't that she was offended by swearing itself: only that the words were so harsh, so confrontational. Millie was not good with confrontation. Not at all.

"I... Are you talking about the IVU that was requested?"

Where was Don? Millie thought to herself. He should be back by now; she knew Irene had packed his lunch today. How long could picking up a bag of Wotsits (something Irene's strict food rules did not allow) take?

"Yes," he bit out, and it was clear from his tone that his patience was fraying. "And you know what: yes, okay, it's not always appropriate for a medical student to request a scan but... Jesus, you could at least have the courtesy to look at her when you dismiss her from your exalted presence. Maybe explain why you won't do the scan for us. They do have to learn somehow you know. I presume you were a medical student once?"

Yes, Millie had been a medical student once, but she'd been nothing like *that* girl. Kira was full Technicolor high-definition, to Millie's dull, black-and-white persona. She always intimidated Millie and put her on the defensive. But this time Kira had changed tactics, being so friendly it was almost unreal: she smiled and chattered and *sat* on Millie's *desk*, apologizing for the "coffee incident" when that wasn't even her fault; the strange girl had even offered Millie a custard crème in order to "butter you up, you cheeky badger".

Millie dreaded her on-calls more than anything. If you were the starred consultant for the day you had to be available to discuss scans and investigations for patients. Thankfully most of this could be achieved over the phone, but sometimes junior doctors (rarely medical students) would venture down into the bowels of the radiology department to actually discuss a scan face to face.

Dr Morrison's a.k.a. Nuclear Winter's reputation as a stuck-up bitch was now firmly ingrained, mostly because Millie had a tough time making eye contact with the doctors that sought her out, and she often communicated non-verbally with just a curt nod if the request was reasonable. However, if the request was unreasonable or another investigation was indicated, she had to speak, and her anxiety normally made her voice tight, coming across as if she was angry and not terrified. Millie was good at her job, her suggestions were always correct; had they come with an encouraging smile, a bit of banter or a glimmer of friendliness, then the doctors she corrected would have thanked her. As it was, the fact she often changed requests and couldn't manage casual niceties had earned her a pretty unsavoury reputation.

Millie had certainly not known what to do with Kira's rampant friendliness, so she had withdrawn into her shell. The warmer Kira was, the colder Millie became. She barely spoke to her. Eventually, as was normally the case with Millie's social interactions, the other woman's smile had faltered and she had started to look uncomfortable. This was all the more excruciating as Millie would put money on the fact that it was very rare indeed for this particular girl to be uncomfortable in any situation. It had to take a really socially inept total bitch to make her appear so.

That's what Millie had been.

She'd been a bitch.

And whether intentional or not, she still took that on as her fault. She was the one who had insisted that medicine was what she wanted. It would have been easy to bury herself in the safe world of quantum physics or mathematics, but she'd known that if she went down that route, if she allowed herself to hide away in the backroom of some university or major company with them just being happy that she was producing results and supporting her hermit ways in order for her to continue doing so, she *knew* that she would lose her chance to be normal. She would lose her chance to really be a part of something.

The patient interactions Millie could handle: those followed set lines, set protocols, she knew the boundaries, the rules, and could work well within them. She could even communicate effectively with patients – not that that was always an essential part of radiology, but when it was required Millie could take a history, break bad news, reassure patients. It was interactions like this one now that she fell down on. She simply didn't understand the rules. And like it or not they were an essential part of being a doctor: you had to be able to interact with your colleagues.

Millie hated the fact that she'd made Kira feel uncomfortable. That she'd dimmed that girl's light for even a short time. Not for the first time it made her reconsider her decision. Maybe she should be festering away in some lab somewhere? At least then she wouldn't be able to upset anyone.

THIS BLOODY WOMAN IS NOT TO BE BELIEVED, PAV thought as he tapped his foot with impatience. Kira – *Kira* for Christ's sake – had come back to the ward with a blank expression after her run-in with Nuclear Winter. He knew that she felt bad about what had happened in the canteen and wanted to give Dr Morrison a chance; hell, Pav had been the one to encourage her to do so. When Kira explained what had happened earlier, she'd clearly been embarrassed.

Kira, *embarrassed*.

And she hadn't smiled since. Kira was always smiling; it was like some sort of disease with her. Okay, Pav knew she could be annoying, but the way Miss High and Mighty Reader of Scans treated her was totally out of order. And worse, it made Pav feel guilty – not an emotion he was particularly familiar with, or one he enjoyed overmuch. Kira was still low on confidence clinically since failing her anatomy viva, and he was the one who had suggested she go down to discuss the scan with the on-call radiologist. The fact he was scrubbed in theatre and they were a junior doctor down on the team was a big factor in his decision, but *come on*. Couldn't this bloody woman even discuss the options with Kira? Instead of point-blank ignoring her? Add in the fact that Dr Morrison had been avoiding him for weeks now, and the time she'd cut him dead in the MDT meeting, giving that smug twat Lucas the chance to smirk behind his back, and Pav was furious.

"Right, well," he said, gritting his teeth as he noticed she still hadn't bothered to actually maintain eye contact with him for more than a few seconds. She was sitting there in her perfect pencil skirt and pristine white blouse, with immaculate hair (not a mousy strand out of place) and expertly applied make-up, lording it over his medical student. For fuck's sake, she was lording it over *him*. He hadn't worked all this time to become a consultant surgeon just so snooty know-it-all radiologists could look down their noses at him. "I'm here now and hopefully you can discuss the options with *me*."

"The best investigation would be a CT urogram as the patient has a history of atopy and is taking beta blockers, giving him an increased risk of allergic reaction to the dye we use in the IVU..."

All this information was imparted in an almost bored monotone and directed straight at his right upper arm.

"How did you even know the patient's medical history? You can't–"

"Instead of looking at Miss Murphy I was looking at the screen and had drawn up his details after she said his name. We are now linked to System One GP records. He had a reaction to shellfish recorded on the 12th of May 2003 whilst he was a patient in Derbyshire."

"But..." Pav scratched the back of his head. "But there aren't any allergies in his–"

"It wasn't recorded as an allergy by either the hospital or the GP. It was mentioned in a pre-assessment for an appendectomy."

"But Kira was only down here for a few minutes. How could you have gone through all the notes in that amount of–"

"I read... um... fast... Very fast."

"Well, okay but that still means–"

"Your patient is in the scanner."

"What?" Pav did not like being on the back foot. He prided himself on being a step ahead of most people, usually using his charm and humour to achieve whatever he wanted. "How did you–?"

"I ordered the scan after Miss Murphy left."

Pav clenched both his fists by his sides, reining in his formidable but normally dormant Greek temper. "Could you not have *told* Kira that was what you were going to do? Don't you think that might have saved her and me some time?"

He watched Dr Morrison sitting motionless on the chair for a few seconds before she gave an almost imperceptible shrug. He'd been running around like a blue-arse fly trying to sort out this patient, and after Kira told him the scan had been refused he'd been distracted for the crucial last half hour of the nephrectomy he was doing, and all this bitch could do was shrug?

"Right, well, thanks for that information, Dr Morrison," he bit out. "And please don't worry, in future I won't *dream* of sending anyone less than registrar grade to request scans or ask advice."

She was still motionless, but now her attention had turned back to her computer screen. He rolled his eyes and muttered "stuck-up icy bitch" under his breath as he stomped out of her office.

Pav had thought he'd been pretty restrained when it came to that particular confrontation with Dr Morrison. Unfortunately he underestimated how loud his voice in anger could be, even when spoken under his breath; but he did see her visibly flinch as that verbal blow hit home. What he didn't see was her shoulders sag in relief as he left, or the repair job she had to do on her wrists later that night. Pav prided himself on his ability to read women, but with Dr Morrison, as was so often the case for her in the hospital, he'd failed miserably.

He may not have been able to read Millie entirely, but he found that over the next few hours he could not get that flinch out of his mind. He joked with people, he was cheeky, he teased, but he was *never* openly rude. What had pushed him into being such a wanker? The lack of eye contact had wound him up, coupled with her obvious reluctance to even talk to him. But was he such an arrogant twat that he needed every female he came across to fawn all over him?

Evidently, yes.

Sitting in his office at the end of the day, his hands went up into his hair and he tore his fingers through it in frustration. Bloody hell, he would have to apologize. He pushed away from the desk and stalked out into the corridor towards the radiology department. When he reached Dr Morrison's office it was just Donald sitting at his desk, grumbling under his breath at his computer screen.

"Uh... hi, Don," Pav said, smiling at the older man and walking into the room to stand beside him. "I'm looking for Dr Morrison."

"Millie?" asked Don, his eyebrows shooting up into his hairline. "She's not on call now, son. Colin took over at five. It's all on the rota."

"I know... I wasn't looking for her to..." Pav trailed off and one of his hands went to the back of his neck. "I just need to speak to her. I think maybe earlier I..."

Don stopped tapping away at the keyboard of the computer he appeared to be locked out of and turned to face Pav, narrowing his eyes in suspicion.

"What did you say to her?" he asked. Pav knew Don as a jolly chap. The quintessential picture of a benevolent white-haired grandad. Always smiling, always open and friendly. Well, he wasn't looking benevolent now, and he definitely wasn't smiling.

"I think there may have been a misunderstanding and I..."

"Millie left two hours ago."

"Oh, right, well..."

"Do you know that today is the first time she has *ever* left work early?"

"Uh..."

"I don't know what you said to her, but the best thing you can do now is leave her alone."

"I just want to speak to–"

"Leave her alone. This office is her safe space. I'll not have some arrogant, jumped-up surgeon take that away from her."

"Safe space? What are you–?"

"Ugh... look, I've got to visit the urinal for the five hundredth time today, damn prostate. By the time I come back I want you out of this office. You understand me?"

"Yes, sir," Pav said as Don strode past him with surprising

speed, considering he looked like Gandalf's older cousin. Pav watched him go with a frown. As he looked across to Dr Morrison's desk an uneasy feeling settled over him.

"Safe space"? What on earth did the old man mean by that?

Pav walked over to the desk and absently lifted one of the stone paperweights, which were the only decoration the sterile area contained. When he put it back down, slightly out of its perfect alignment, he must have knocked the computer mouse, because the screen of the terminal suddenly lit up. There was an open Word document in the centre and the name at the top of it caught his attention. It was addressed to Elizabeth Penny.

Pav had never been very good at minding his own business. And Libby was his best friend Jamie's girlfriend after all. He leaned in to take a closer look. It was outlining the ongoing payments for a grant, a very substantial grant: one that must have given Libby financial freedom. Pav knew that Libby had only recently hung up her stripper shoes. He'd assumed that she'd finally decided to let Jamie support her and her daughter in some way whilst she was still a student. Now that he thought about how fiercely independent Libby was, he realized that was unlikely. This grant was life-changing for her.

Pav frowned. How had Dr Morrison got hold of this? Pav knew that Dr Morrison used to look after Rosie a few early mornings a week when Libby was on the surgical rotation so she could start when the other students started at seven thirty. Apparently the little girl had hung out in Dr Morrison's office with her for an hour until the hospital nursery opened.

Millie wasn't the only one with a quick mind and a high IQ. Pav couldn't think of any reason why she would have a copy of this letter unless she was the one who'd written it. He filed that piece of information away. He had succeeded in alienating Dr Morrison completely that afternoon (so much for his legendary charm rays); he was going to need all the ammunition he could get if he was going to have any chance of changing her mind about public speaking. He had another six months to do it in before the conference.

No problem, he thought to himself as he strode out of the department.

There was nobody Pavlos Martakis couldn't talk around, given enough time. Nobody.

Chapter 5

Ruin everything

MILLIE STOOD AT THE BACK OF THE CHURCH IN THE shadows, prepared for a quick exit as soon as the ceremony was finished. This was the first wedding she had ever been invited to. El had, yet again, been ridiculously excited to pick out her outfit. Millie knew she looked perfect.

But she also knew her limits.

She would not be going to the reception. She would not be congratulating the bride and groom. It was enough to watch them from here, to see how happy Libby and Rosie looked, and to know that, in a small way, she had something to do with that happiness, not that she would ever let them know. Libby already took too much interest in Millie for her liking. Not many people looked beneath her cool exterior, not many could be bothered; but she had a feeling Libby was different. If she knew what Millie had done, she would no doubt double her efforts to draw her out.

Applause broke out when the couple kissed as man and wife despite the vicar not inviting them to do so. Millie knew that was her cue to leave. But she allowed herself a moment longer to watch their happiness. She even allowed herself a fleeting smile. Something caught her eye next to the altar and she froze, her smile dying on her lips. One pair of dark eyes wasn't on the bride and groom like the rest of the church; these eyes were looking directly at her, and, as always, they held way too much curiosity.

Pavlos Martakis was really becoming a problem. Since that day in her office a month ago he'd attempted to apologize more than once. Seemingly immune to embarrassment, he'd brought her coffees at every single weekly MDT and persisted in trying to approach her despite her continued rudeness. After the second week Millie had broken and taken a sip of the Americano he'd left in front of her. The bastard was smiling when he managed to catch her eye after that small victory, but it hadn't stopped her from polishing the whole cup off. By her calculation, she owed him fifteen pounds and seventy-three pence currently in Americanos. It was getting ridiculous.

She broke eye contact to take one more look at the gorgeous couple, then allowed her gaze to sweep over the congregation. The empty feeling that had been intensifying for the last few months grew almost crippling for a moment, but she pushed it down, like always, and turned her back on all the happy people around her to leave.

But, once she was standing outside the church, Millie realised that simply seeing Libby and Jamie get married would not be enough. She wanted just a *little* more. She wanted to watch them leave the church together, and she even wanted to shower some of the confetti rose petals she'd been given by one of the ushers at the start of the service on them. Although she knew that she wasn't responsible for the couple finally getting married, Millie liked to think that by taking the pressure off Libby financially (not that Libby knew it was her), she had had a small part to play. So she stepped back behind a few gravestones and watched the congregation file out.

The church had been packed so the crowd was huge. Perfect for melting into and remaining anonymous. Millie found crowds strangely comforting, as long as she was amongst them and not the focus of their attention. The wedding guests divided to surround the path out of the church and Millie joined the throng nearest the far gate. She merged perfectly, reminding herself to give Eleanor the most enormous tip next time she saw her. El would like that. It was some small compensation for the amount of time she had to spend with her; Millie was well aware of how boring and downright uncomfortable her company could be; the very least she could do was recompense Eleanor financially for it.

A cheer went up in the crowd as the couple emerged and Millie felt the corners of her mouth tip up, just a little. Jamie was carrying Rosie, with his other arm wrapped around his new wife, and all three were laughing. In Millie's mind the crowd melted away as she focused on them and the joy radiating from their threesome. When they were nearly at the gate she shook out her confetti to join the rest of the rose petals in the air. That was when Rosie spotted her.

"Millie!" Rosie shouted, wriggling frantically until she was set down on her feet next to Jamie and then plunging into the crowd to get through to where Millie was standing, open-mouthed with shock.

Rosie, Don and Gammy were the only people that Millie allowed herself to believe genuinely enjoyed her company. In Don's case he hadn't really had much choice in the matter, Gammy was family; but Rosie – now, Rosie had chosen *her*. She'd pushed her way into Millie's office one day when her mother was down in the radiology department asking for a scan and plonked herself down on Millie's lap. Millie didn't know any other children, but she knew Rosie was special. Gifted. Not in the way Millie had been gifted, not at the expense of her social skills or happiness. But in a way that complemented every aspect of her personality: that gave her higher emotional intelligence than most fifty-year-olds, leave alone five-year-olds.

"You came!" Rosie shouted when she was finally in front of Millie. Her arms went straight up in the air and she did a little dance on the spot before she launched herself at Millie's legs. For some reason the little girl looked like she had rolled in mud before the church service and had a couple of twigs sticking out of her hair. Millie felt her cheeks heat as all eyes swung from the newlyweds to her and she squatted down to Rosie's level. Rosie detached herself from Millie's legs to circle her neck with her little arms.

"You look so pretty," Millie told her, cuddling the small body close and letting that familiar warm feeling settle on her chest, despite the discomfort of being the focus of attention. "You've been bug-hunting though, huh?"

Rosie pulled back slightly and opened her little fist to reveal a centipede and a woodlouse. "They wanted to come to the church too," she explained. "Can you tell me their posh names?"

"This one is Armadillidium Valgare and this guy is Collinellidae. Okay? Now you'd better get back to your–"

"Rosie, what are you...? Oh, it's you." Millie looked up to see that Kira had made it through the crowd. She looked beautiful in her bridesmaid dress, her red hair containing a deep blue streak of the exact same shade. Kira was barely over five feet tall but Millie still found her ridiculously intimidating. Suddenly the light-beige silk outfit Eleanor had painstakingly selected felt dull and lifeless. "Rose-Pose, come on. Mummy and Daddy are waiting."

"I get a daddy now," Rosie told Millie, unwinding her arms from Millie's neck and skipping over to Kira to take her hand.

"I know you do," Millie said. "That's fantastic news. Statistically speaking, young women with father figures are more likely to complete higher education and less likely to conceive a child during their teen years."

Kira rolled her eyes. "I think she's a bit young to under–"

"I knows what she's sayin'." Rosie cut Kira off in an angry little voice.

"Of course you do, Squirt," Kira said, then turned back to Millie. "You're not on the table plan. You know that, right?"

"Yes," Millie replied, just above a whisper as she took a small step back.

"Libby was upset that you rejected the invite. It's just it's *really* difficult if people say they're not coming but then change their minds at the last–"

"I just wanted to see... I won't–"

"I know: you won't mingle with the commoners." Kira turned away after that cutting remark and started pulling Rosie along with her.

Millie huffed out a breath of relief as she watched them disappear in the direction of the bridal car. Then she started to weave her way through the crowd to get out onto the narrow street at the back of the church, where she had parked hers.

She was concentrating on her feet as she wound her way through the gravestones and onto the cobbled path, so she didn't notice the large obstacle in front of her until she was nearly on top of him.

"Woah!" Pav said, his large hands closing over her upper arms to stop her falling backwards. "Careful there. These stone buggers would give you one hell of a bruise on the arse."

Millie couldn't have spoken if she'd tried, so all she did was pull away and take a few steps back. She moved to the side to pass him, but he stepped in her way, blocking her *again*. He was wearing a morning suit but had already loosened the tie. He looked almost too attractive to be real. A sense of déjà vu swept over her. Why was this man always trying to get in her way?

"Listen," he said into the silence. She moved to the side again, and again he moved with her to block her path. "I want to clear the air with you once and for all. Okay?" Millie blinked and Dr Martakis let out a sigh before continuing. "I was out of order that day in your office. I might have been a little..." he paused and rubbed a hand over the stubble on his jaw in an uncharacteristic gesture of uncertainty, "... frustrated with the situation. And I wanted to come clean about something else, too. I *may* have knocked your mouse that day in your office a few weeks ago, and I *may* have seen a document on there mentioning Libby..."

Millie took a deep breath and forced herself to speak. The last thing she wanted was for Dr Martakis to start sniffing around *that* bit of scheming. He'd ruin everything.

"The Deanery sent some stuff through to me about her because..." she crossed her fingers behind her back, "because I'm on the committee for grant approval for the trust."

This was impossible for two reasons: first, there was no such committee, and second, Millie was not a consultant; even if she were, with her lack of basic communication skills she would have had nothing to do with the medical students anyway.

She must have been too flustered that day to close the file and shut down the computer properly, which just went to prove how out of character she behaved around this particular man. What Libby didn't know was that the university wasn't upping her grant at all, the money going into Libby's account every month was from Millie – but that was a fact Millie was intending to take to her grave. She didn't blame Dr Martakis for the suspicious look on his face. It wasn't like he could know that Libby's daughter was the first good thing to happen to Millie in forever. Or that looking after Rosie the few times she was allowed was just about the best thing in Millie's life, and that the fact Libby would trust Millie with her child meant everything to her.

Millie had money. She had *a lot* of money. But there was nothing to spend it on other than the charities she supported and the wardrobe Eleanor picked out for her. So if having a grant to complete her training and not have to rely on a man, or to strip for a living, would make Libby happy, then that's what Millie was going to give her. She couldn't offer the money directly – for one, Millie would never be that brave, and for another, Libby would never have taken it. But this way everyone was a winner – unless this interfering man standing in front of her blabbed about what he'd seen on her computer.

"Oh." Dr Martakis cocked his head to the side. Her gaze flicked up to his face briefly and she noticed him narrow his eyes. "Right. I suppose–"

"I've got to go," she blurted out, dodging round him successfully this time. To her annoyance she heard his heavy footfalls follow her to the small gate leading out onto the road. As she pulled back the latch and pushed it open, his hand shot out and held it shut. She could feel his heat at her back as he crowded her, but she was trapped between his body and the gate.

"You've got somewhere better to be?" he asked, and she could feel his breath on her cheek.

"Yes," she told him, realising too late how rude that would sound. "Move away. Now."

"Oh... right... sorry," he said, taking his hand off the gate and stepping back. She let out the breath she hadn't realised she'd been holding, and flew out onto the road.

"Whoa!" she heard him shout behind her, and then felt herself yanked backwards. A car shot past inches away from her feet and she staggered into the hard wall of his chest. "Christ. Are you okay?"

She could smell him: toothpaste, soap, aftershave and *man*. It made her head spin.

"I'm fine," she told him, and pulled away, this time safely onto the pavement. "Uh, thanks," she muttered at her feet, wondering what was the minimum required amount of time you had to spend with someone after they had saved your life. But of course she would never have been rushing out onto a road had he not been intimidating her, so it was not *entirely* her fault, not that someone as arrogant as Dr Martakis would ever apol–

"No... don't thank me. It was my fault," he said quickly. She started in surprise but then began to inch away again. "Look, Dr Morrison, I really did just want to say sorry for being a pushy arsehole, but I guess I just acted like a pushy arsehole... again. Could you... I mean... I..."

He was following her down the street now as she had started walking away in earnest.

"It's fine," she muttered, having at last reached her car. "You'd better get back." She attempted to force a smile, but, going by his frown, realised she likely missed the mark by a long way.

Home, she thought to herself, *limits*.

"Okay, well I–"

She slammed the door of her Prius, cutting him off, and then closed her eyes for a moment before she pulled away from the curb. Millie tried to resist the rear-view mirror, she really did. But just before she turned the corner her eyes flicked up. He was still standing there, his arms crossed over his broad chest and his head cocked to the side like she was some sort of complicated puzzle he wanted to solve. A challenge.

Millie didn't want to be a puzzle or a challenge. She wanted to try and live her life within her limits. Somehow she had a feeling Dr Martakis and his damn curiosity could threaten that.

Then again, she'd had years of experience blending into the background, making herself invisible, or at least unpleasant enough to be avoided. A man like him would forget about her in a heartbeat.

Chapter 6

That chick is weird

MILLIE LOOKED DOWN AT HER ARMS AND SIGHED. DEEP grooves where the nails had bitten into the skin marked her palms, and there was the familiar livid bruising on her inner forearm. She closed her eyes slowly, forcing her hands apart and taking a deep breath before she moved to the sink to wash them. The sting of the soap on her exposed knuckles was weirdly comforting as it cut through the fog of her anxiety. She looked up at herself in the mirror; all she could see was the dark circles under her eyes and the tight set of her mouth. It was a long time since she'd been this bad. She knew that she was going to have to do something. There was no way she could go through with the presentation.

There were things she simply could not do, and talking to a lecture theatre full of people was one of them. Talking to just one person was often a challenge for Millie, but two hundred? No way. There was literally nothing for it: she would have to speak to Him, again. Her hands shook as she held them under the hand drier and grabbed a small plaster from her desk. They were still shaking as she carefully applied it to her knuckle, and

51

then arranged her papers and keyboard symmetrically in perfect alignment, before shutting down her computer. Taking a deep breath, she smoothed the front of her skirt and started for the door, but stepped back as it swung open.

"Oh, sorry dear," Don said as she retreated further to avoid being mown down – their small office did not offer much room for manoeuvre. "Are you finished reporting?" He squeezed past her to get to his chair before muttering a few expletives when his computer wouldn't let him log in. Millie reached past him to grab the wallet he had slung on the desk and took out his smartcard.

"We have to use these *every time* we log on now, Don, remember?" she said gently, pushing the card into its slot and typing in his password (after a number of IT helpline call-outs with forgotten passwords it was now just easier for her to keep track of it for him). Don ran both hands through his white hair causing it to stick straight up almost as if he had been electrocuted, then smiled at Millie, the wrinkles at the corners of his eyes going into overdrive.

"What would I do without you, love?" he said, grabbing her hand and giving it a squeeze. Don might rely on her for all things technological (at seventy-four he was not keen to start learning all the new computer systems the hospital brought in) but she knew she owed him far more. Without Don she probably wouldn't have a real conversation with another human being for weeks on end.

Millie never said anything in meetings, the radiographers she worked with had long since given up any kind of small talk with her, and she avoided the rest of her colleagues like the plague. Sharing an office with Don was the best thing that could have happened to her. Don didn't intimidate her, he didn't expect too much of her. She could relax around him and she had been able to tell him about her limitations without him making her feel like a freak. She'd even, after weeks of persuasion on his part, been back to his house for dinner a few times and met his wife Irene, who was just as warm and understanding as Don.

Don and Irene were good people, kind people. The sort of people who tolerated someone as painful to be with as Millie. She knew that was why they pretended to like her.

"You know it's really the other way around, Don," Millie whispered. Don's smile faded as he frowned up at her.

"Listen, Camilla, Irene and I have been talking, and–"

Millie dropped his hand and turned to grab her handbag from her chair. "Sorry, Don," she said, cutting him off. Lately he'd begun trying to persuade her into trying to make some changes, and before he launched into one of these lectures he would always preface it with the fact he'd consulted Irene, as if she was the oracle of all things and this gave gravitas to his opinion. So far Millie had successfully managed to dodge the subject. "I've got to pop out for a bit."

"But it's ten o'clock," Don told her. "You hardly ever leave in the middle of a reporting session."

This was true. Millie was a creature of habit and routine; not in a funny, quirky way, but in a slightly desperate, trapped and terrified way. However, the fear of standing up in front of two hundred people was overriding that of breaking her routine for a morning. She had no choice; she *had* to talk to Him before it was too late, and she knew he wasn't operating right now, as he had just sent a consultant-wide email out about a reorganization of rotas.

"I know I'm bad but I can break my routine once in a while without too many dramas," she said, going for a confident smile, which was rather more shaky in nature. Don raised an eyebrow but kept quiet as she slipped from the room. Millie hadn't told Don about how she'd been backed into a corner over the last week. Dr Martakis had managed to get Dr Small, the head of the radiology department, on side to make her present at the Grand Round. Dr Small had implied that if she didn't, he'd have to think about moving her into the registrar office in order for her to "assimilate better". It was blackmail. He knew Millie wouldn't cope without Don.

Walking anywhere in the hospital was a challenge for Millie: eye contact, casual nods and smiles were simply not in her repertoire, so she mostly kept her head down or stared straight ahead. Nobody called out to greet her anyway; nobody really knew her – unless it was as "that prickly bitch radiologist" or "Nuclear Winter", both of which she still overheard on a fairly frequent basis.

So no, nobody attempted to interact with her as she walked down the corridor. In fact nowadays it was actually as though nobody could even see her, which, in Millie's opinion, was for the best.

You'd have thought the urologists would all have their own offices, but if anything they were more cramped than down in radiology, and He shared his office with two others. She paused at the door as a burst of loud, male laughter sounded from the other side. Before she could stop herself she took a step back into the middle of the corridor, straight into the oncoming traffic of a hospital trolley, which smacked painfully into her ankle, causing one of her high heels to snap clean off. The pain and the shock caused her to let out a very uncharacteristic scream as she collapsed down onto her side, spread-eagled across the corridor.

"Jesus Christ!" the porter shouted, reversing the trolley to release the heel of Millie's shoe. "Are you okay?"

Millie twisted over to her hands and knees. Her hair had somehow worked its way out of the perfect chignon to spill over her shoulders and into her face. This was literally straight out of one of her nightmares.

"Hey, love?" she heard the porter call more softly but closer this time. "Can you get up?"

She nodded at the floor, concentrating on slowing her breathing down. "I'm fine," she whispered, lifting her head slightly as she heard the ominous creak of a door opening, through which she saw two big, leather-clad shoes emerging from the office.

Pav opened the door and was about to step out when he saw the woman on her hands and knees in front of him. A porter was hovering anxiously over her, seeming unsure whether to help her up or leave her in her frozen position on the floor. Light brown wavy hair was covering her downcast face and spilling down the back of her fitted grey dress.

"I heard a scream," he said, crouching down in front of the woman and cupping one of her elbows with his hands. "Are you o–" The woman unfroze at rapid speed and pulled away from him violently, only to smack her head on the trolley above her.

Pav winced but made no more moves to touch her for fear the woman might actually knock herself out if she sustained another injury. He watched as she pulled herself up to her feet on the trolley with her back to him, then heard her whisper "Sorry" to the bemused patient, and "I'm fine" to the porter, before stepping back so that they could pass, and nearly stumbling into Pav on her uneven heels.

His hands shot up to enclose both her forearms before she could go down again. She tried to wrench away but another trolley was bearing down on them, so Pav had no choice but to keep hold of her. He dropped his hands once the trolley had passed, and then watched as she stepped away and turned in a small circle (hobbling on her one heel) until she was facing him. She pulled her hair back from her face and tucked it behind her ears. Wide grey eyes flicked up to his and she froze again.

It was Dr Morrison.

Dr Morrison, looking human for once. It was safe to say that under normal circumstances she was not his type in any way: perfect make-up, perfect clothes, never a hair out of place. Everything about her screamed uptight, and Pav was not into uptight stuck-up women. He liked women who smiled easily, who weren't afraid to get messy, who were friendly, easy-going. This was the first time Pav had seen her without that fucking roll thing firmly in place at the back of her head. She looked... different.

"Uh... hi, Dr Morrison," he said, stumbling over his words slightly, which was almost unheard of for him. "Are you all right? You must have taken quite a hit."

She was still staring at him, her lips parted and her cheeks flushed. She looked almost... cute.

"Dr Morrison? How hard was that bump to your noggin?"

She blinked slowly, her long lashes shadowing her cheeks for a moment whilst her face drained of colour. When she looked back up she no longer had any trace of cute in her expression; her mouth had snapped shut into a tight line and she seemed to be focusing on his shirt collar rather than his face.

"I'm fine," she snapped at his shirt collar, wobbling slightly as she balanced on one heel, then flinching away from him again when he went to steady her.

Gah! That bloody word again. He swore this woman could be lit on fire and she'd still be using it.

"Okay," he said, drawing out the word. "Is this about tomorrow?"

She nodded and her thick hair slipped over her shoulders.

"I... I..." She met his eyes briefly, then looked past him into his office. "I need to talk to you."

"Okay, well, come on in and we can have a chat." She hesitated; bit her lip before squaring her shoulders and moving past him into his office.

"Hey, Dr M., how's it hanging?" Jamie said from his desk, smirking at Pav.

"H-hello, Dr Grantham," she said, not even sparing him a glance as she hobbled into the room and then turned back towards Pav, who was now perched on his desk.

"I've told you to call me Jamie."

Dr Morrison didn't respond to that, so Pav decided to fill the awkward silence.

"So... Millie," he started, but paused as he noticed her briefly startled expression at the use of her first name. Somehow, in her present state it seemed more fitting than "Dr Morrison". But Pav would have expected annoyance, not bewilderment, in reaction to his use of it. "How can I help you?"

She cleared her throat and focused on his computer screen. "I can't do the Grand Round tomorrow. You'll j-just have to get someone else."

Pav sighed. "Listen, we've been through this before. I don't know why it's such a big problem. The Grand Round is fairly informal. It won't take up much of your time. And it's relevant to everyone. It's important, Millie."

Another flinch, this time accompanied by a small frown. Pav crossed his arms over his chest. He wasn't lying. Her research – her *published* research – was going to revolutionize pre-op care. Yes, okay, it was in his interest to get Millie to speak so that she would at least consider the conference. But it *was* important stuff and it *was* relevant to everyone. To be honest he was starting to lose patience with this woman. That was why he'd scheduled her to talk at the Grand Round without consulting her. Why couldn't she even be bothered to present it to her own hospital? The one that had helped her test and audit the bloody thing in the first place.

"If I just forward somebody else the slides, they could present it with Anwar instead. It doesn't have to be me, I mean–"

"Dr Morrison," Pav snapped, reverting to formality, seeing as the gentle approach was not working for him, "as far as I'm aware you've never presented *anything* at a Grand Round. Don't you think it's about time you did?"

"I'm not–"

"Why can't you spare the thirty minutes it would take, anyway?" he asked, straightening to his full height, which was nearly a full foot taller than the woman in front of him, who had given up balancing on her one heel and sunk down to stand on her other foot. "Would it kill you to participate for once?" He felt his frustration bubble up again and didn't seem able to tamp it down. There was something about being around this woman and not having her fully acknowledge him, connect with him, that was driving Pav insane.

"Pav, I think–"

"Shut up a minute, Jamie."

"I just can't," she said. "It's impossible, I–"

"It's not impossible," he cut her off again. "You're at work that day. Your head of department says you've no commitments conflicting with that time. I'm sorry but you're just going to have to–"

"Please," she whispered, meeting his eyes in her desperation, and he could have sworn that they were glassy with

58

unshed tears. He frowned and pushed away from the desk towards her, but she stumbled back. Pav held his hands up and retreated a step to give her the space she obviously needed. She was holding her bag in front of her almost like a shield. His frown deepened as he saw that her knuckles were white from her grip on the leather.

"Hey," he said, gentling his tone. "Are you sure you're okay? You're–"

"Fine," she cut in, her voice coming out in another bark. He watched as her eyes cleared of moisture and her expression turned cold. "I have to go." She turned towards the door. There was something so achingly vulnerable about the way she was hobbling across the room that Pav forgot her earlier reaction to him. He stepped over to intercept her before she could leave, and cupped her elbow.

"Listen, maybe we should..." His voice died as she wrenched her arm from his grip, stumbling again and nearly going down but gripping the door handle to steady herself. She straightened slowly, then focused back on his shirt collar.

"I've got to go."

"I don't think–"

Without letting him finish she pulled open the door, kicked off her shoes, snatched them up with her handbag, and ran out into the corridor. By the time Pav looked out after her she was gone.

"That chick is weird," Jamie said through a smile as Pav went back to his desk to grab his wallet; he was already late for his list that afternoon.

"Yeah," he muttered, shoving his wallet into his back pocket and rubbing the back of his neck. "Yeah, she is."

"Maybe you should let her off this presentation business," Jamie suggested. "Doesn't seem to be her gig. And you know what Libby says about Dr M. being misunderstood. That she's... well... sensitive... or something."

Pav frowned at the door, then shook his head. "She's not given me any *real* reason she can't do it, mate. It's not enough of an excuse that she just doesn't fancy it. We've all got to contribute from time to time. She needs to get over herself and quite frankly she needs to stop being so prickly and start becoming a team player. I mean, how long has she worked here now and everyone *still* calls her Dr Morrison? Get over yourself. Smile more, look people in the eye; it's not rocket science. Jesus."

Chapter 7

Absolute terror

MILLIE STARED OUT AT THE AUDIENCE AND SWALLOWED, her eyes flicking back to the laptop in front of her. There was still a low murmur of voices through the lecture theatre, but as she continued to stand there, saying nothing, silence slowly spread until you could hear a pin drop. A trickle of sweat ran down her spine as she cleared her throat, her eyes flicking up to the sea of faces before going back to the much safer territory of her laptop. She knew Anwar was behind her but she was too scared to turn her back on the audience to seek him out. Don had promised her he would sit in the front row, but she hadn't been able to pick him out, likely due to the fact that she only seemed to be able to manage looking up for a microsecond at a time. She gripped the sides of the lectern until her knuckles turned white, and tried to slow her breathing.

"I..." Her voice came out as a strangled squeak, about two octaves higher than was normal. She attempted another micro-glance into the audience and this time her eyes clashed with His dark brown ones, which she could see were clouded with annoyance under thick brows lowered in a frown. Millie was used to hostile looks, she knew she was not a person people warmed to, but for some reason the negative reaction from this man hurt her more.

After humiliating herself in front of him and practically begging not to do the Grand Round, she hadn't been able to face him again in person. She'd sent a few emails suggesting alternatives to her actually standing up to give the talk, but they had all fallen on deaf ears. Eventually she had given up and decided that maybe if she used some of the techniques she learnt with Anwar, *maybe* she could do it. He'd given her a couple of extra sessions to help her get ready for it. And he was going to give the second half of the presentation. She only had to talk for five minutes maximum; she'd look at Don on the front row instead of the audience; she'd remember to keep her breathing slow; she'd...

"I..." She tried to start again but her vocal cords still refused to cooperate. When she looked up her eyes caught on one of the cardiology consultants who had confronted her last week after she changed one of his requests to a more appropriate scan. A testosterone-fuelled cardiologist with a dented ego was a tricky beast to placate, and unfortunately Millie's social skills had been nowhere near up to the task. She hadn't missed his muttered "Nuclear bloody Winter" comment as he'd stalked out of the radiology department, and she could plainly see the satisfied smirk on his face now.

She looked back down at her laptop but the words of her PowerPoint presentation were blurring; all she could see were rows and rows of her colleagues, all with the same mocking smiles on their faces, all revelling in her embarrassment. A sick feeling swept up over her as she felt heat flood her face. Her stomach roiled and she took a shaky step back from the lectern, her hand coming up to cover her mouth. Pins and needles were spreading up from the tips of her fingers to her upper arms and the edges of her vision were closing in. She looked up, desperate to catch sight of Don, but instead her eyes snagged on His yet again. The annoyance from earlier was now replaced with confusion – and he had risen halfway out of his seat. Before she could look away everything went black.

PAV SURGED FORWARD WHEN HE SAW HER START TO FALL, but was too late to prevent the sickening thud of her head hitting the floor. What was that great big oaf of a psychologist doing, standing behind her and watching her go down with a shocked expression on his face? Bloody move, you idiot! Catch her!

When she'd first stood up and spared only a few aloof, cold glances at the crowd, Pav had been annoyed. Her obvious reluctance to speak to a group of doctors she worked with pissed him off. So, when her knuckles turned white as she gripped the lectern, her face flooded with colour, her chest rose and fell with rapid breaths, and a bead of sweat trickled down her temple, he'd been confused. What he would never forget was the unmasked terror in her eyes as she'd looked up at him that last time, or the way her face had drained totally of all its previous life and colour, before she sank to the floor like a puppet with its strings cut.

Pav knelt down next to her, tilted her head and lifted her chin, then lowered his ear over her mouth whilst he felt her carotid pulse in her neck. His own breath left him in a sudden exhale of relief when he felt hers against his cheek and his fingers registered the pulsing of her artery. He brought her far hand over to the other side of her face, lifted the arm nearest him up so it lay at a right angle to her body, and then hooked her under the knee across from him to pull her onto her side and into the recovery position.

She may have been breathing and her pulse may have been strong, but it didn't change the fact she looked... dead... the fine veins on her eyelids standing out against the still-pale skin covered in a sheen of sweat.

"Dr Morrison," he said, giving her shoulder a gentle shake and smoothing back into place a tendril of light-brown hair that had escaped her ever-present bun. "Millie?"

"Jesus Christ," a voice next to him said as whoever it was tried to push him to the side. "Sweethcart, come on. Talk to Don now."

Pav looked up to see Don Phillips's wrinkled face focused on Millie. The old man's features were soft with concern as he looked down at her.

"Enough of this nonsense now, Millie," Don told her, attempting a stern tone that was undermined by the concern threading through the words. "Who's going to get me back onto the system for reporting this afternoon if you're lounging around on the floor?" Millie's thick eyelashes stirred and slowly blinked open until she was looking straight at Pav. She stared at him for a moment before her brow furrowed and that dreadful fear from earlier started creeping into her expression.

"Out of my way, you big bloody idiot," Don snapped, giving Pav a surprisingly hard shove from the side. "You're the last thing she wants to see right now. Show's over, folks," he said to the gathering crowd around them as Millie proceeded to curl further into a ball on the floor and squeeze her eyes shut.

"Are you lot deaf?" Don shouted when the people around them were slow to react. "I said *bugger off.*"

That seemed to get everyone moving much more rapidly. Don shot Pav a furious look and jerked his head towards the door before softening his expression again and prising away one of Millie's hands, which were both clutched to her chest, to take it in both of his.

"All over now, love," he murmured, stroking the side of her head. "Can't stay here now though; think old Prof Binky's lecturing this afternoon and the med students might find a woman on the floor a touch off-putting."

Pav watched Millie's wide grey eyes blink a couple of times as she scanned the crowd around her. She was terrified.

"Now, now, Millie," Don said, his voice managing to be soft and commanding at the same time. "You focus on my face now. Nothing else. Understand?"

Once Millie was focused on Don, some of the fear leaked out of her expression.

"Right, you're going to stand for me now, love, okay?"

Millie let out a breath and closed her eyes but gave Don a tight nod. Everyone other than Anwar had moved back from her after Don's outburst, but they were yet to actually leave the lecture theatre. Pav felt a surprisingly strong wave of annoyance as he surveyed the curious people around him, a fair few of whom were rubbernecking to try and get a glimpse of the prostrate Millie. Nosey bastards.

"Right, clear off!" he found himself shouting. "You heard me: get back to work. Grand Round is cancelled."

There was a pause as the low hum of voices subsided following Pav's outburst. A few of the surgeons at the front gave him curious looks.

"Doors are at the back people. I'm sure you've all got things to be getting on with; if not I can always take another look at the consultant rotas."

That got everyone moving and after about ten minutes the lecture theatre was nearly empty. The only people left other than Anwar and Don were Libby and Jamie, who both made their way down to the front.

Anwar was kneeling in front of Millie actually holding her hands and talking to her in a low voice. For some reason the sight of her hands in Anwar's gave Pav an inexplicable feeling of annoyance.

"Millie?" Libby asked tentatively. Pav felt that wave of irritation again: Libby was on first name terms with Millie whilst he had barely ever received proper eye contact from her. He normally had a lot of time for Libby; she had after all managed to pull his best friend Jamie's head out of his arse last year. The bastard was a lot more cheerful since they got together, and even more so since Libby had married his ugly mug. But for some reason, at this moment, he just wanted her to leave. In fact, for some reason he wanted them *all* to leave and for *him* to sort out Millie.

"She's fine," Anwar said, not taking his eyes off Millie. "If I can just–"

"How do you know she's fine?" Pav cut in, his growing irritation showing in his tone. She'd just been unconscious for fuck's sake. She dropped like a bloody stone. What business did Anwar the psychologist have saying that she was fine. And bloody Don nodding along with him as well. The old man was just an image fiddler; he probably hadn't practiced any real medicine in over a century.

"Young man," Don said with what sounded like infinite patience, as if he was talking to a small, unruly child. "Anwar and I know Millie; you do not. Please step away and let me deal with this. Okay, love, you ready to stand? Then we'll walk to the office and you can do some reporting. Yes?"

Pav's eyebrows went up into his hairline and he shook his head in disbelief.

"You're going to make her *work*? After she's just collapsed?" he said, his voice rising with uncharacteristic anger. Jamie had stopped looking at Millie and Don in favour of Pav now, his eyes alight with curiosity. "Listen, move out of the way, you two. She shouldn't be walking and she needs to be seen in A&E. They can do an ECG, take some blood, do a proper work-up." Pav moved forward and knelt down at Millie's other side. Millie's wide eyes fixed on his for a moment like a deer in the headlights before she focused on his shirt collar.

"Pav," Libby called, her voice sounding panicked for some reason. "I don't think that's a–" He felt her small hand on his shoulder but shrugged her off to lean forward and slide one of his arms around Dr Morrison's shoulders and the other under her knees. As soon as his body made contact with hers and he lifted her a few inches off the ground (she weighed next to nothing), he knew something was terribly wrong. Her whole frame stiffened and she let out such a terrified shriek that it felt like it was tearing right through to his soul.

"Bloody hell," he muttered as she flung herself away from him to land back on the floor. Before he could move a muscle she had scuttled back at lightning speed into the furthest corner of the lecture theatre.

"I told you to let me handle it," Don said in a low voice as Anwar sighed.

"What... ?" Pav whispered, then broke off briefly to swallow as he looked across at the now trembling Millie.

"Millie." Anwar was now approaching her with his hands held up as if in surrender. Her eyes fixed on him and some of the anxiety leeched out of her expression. For some reason the fact that this guy could calm her when all Pav seemed to do was instill absolute terror made his gut tighten with annoyance. "Slow your breathing, okay? Get control of those thoughts. Come back to us."

"Right," she whispered, still focused on Anwar. "I..." Her

eyes flicked over to Pav but Anwar moved to block her line of vision.

"Try thought-stopping," Pav heard him murmur, then peered around the big guy's back to see Millie whisper "Stop" to herself. One of her hands had pushed up inside her other sleeve and Pav's mind flashed to the image of her bruised fore-arms. He made to move forward but Don's hand came up to his chest to stop him.

"What's wrong with her?" he asked in a low voice.

Don sighed. "I do not have time to explain everything to you, Stavros."

Pav didn't bother to correct him.

"All I can say is that she will be able to sort herself out, but she needs *quiet*, she needs her work, and she needs to be left alone."

"Pav," Jamie said softly, "he's right, mate. Let's leave them to sort it out." He tugged on Pav's arm, trying to get him moving towards the exit, but Pav stood his ground, staring at the trembling ball of human in the corner.

"Anwar and I'll see to her," Don told him firmly. Pav dragged his eyes away from Millie to look into Don's sincere, faded blue eyes, and he puffed out a breath. Jamie tugged on his arm again, a little more forcefully this time, and after a final nod to Don and a glance at Millie, he turned to leave.

Chapter 8

Strong enough

Pav peered through the crack in the door. Millie was sitting at her desk, staring at the screen in front of her with her computer mouse in her hand, steadily clicking through the images. After each one she would touch-type a report, click to save, and then move to the next image.

She did not stop to stretch, she did not take a drink or glance at her phone: nothing. Her eyes were glued to the screen in front of her and she was so still it was almost unnatural.

Soft footsteps broke the silence of the corridor and Pav glanced up to see Don standing across from him with his hands on his hips, his head tilted to the side and his eyes narrowed at Pav. Without saying anything Don jerked his head and then shuffled off in the other direction. Pav took it that he was meant to follow. His eyes flicked back to Millie, but she hadn't moved from her position, still typing and clicking through the images. His hand went to the back of his neck and he dropped his head to look at his shoes.

What was he even doing here? After being forced out of the lecture theatre, Pav had resolved to put the entire incident out of his mind. Millie's business was hers alone and it was clear that his help was not welcome. *Really* not welcome. Christ, she could have broken her back with how violently she'd leapt out of his arms when he tried to lift her. Women responding to Pav with abject terror was not something he'd ever experienced before or that he was super-keen to go through again.

But however hard he tried, he just couldn't put her out of his mind. After all, it was *his* fault she'd been up there in the first place. She'd tried to tell him that she couldn't do it. And now, whenever Pav closed his eyes, all he could see was that beautiful face draining of all colour before she sank to the ground like a ragdoll.

Since he'd witnessed that, Pav had been going over all his interactions with her in his mind, and feeling like a complete wanker. It was safe to say that Pav was *not* very good at being ignored. He was a centre-of-attention type of guy, always had been. And he was good with people, dammit! People liked him; they warmed to him. He was a funny son of a bitch. So, not being able to soften Millie up with one of his smiles (something he knew worked on the opposite sex), or even the inordinate number of coffees he'd waited *years* for Doreen to prepare before each MDT, had been extremely frustrating. And he knew he'd let that frustration show. More than once. Each time thinking that she didn't make eye contact because she couldn't be bothered to interact like a normal human. Not that she simply... *couldn't*.

Pav sighed as he backed away from the door and followed the old man, who was waiting at the end of the corridor for the lift to arrive. The doors slid open and both men stepped inside.

"I'm not sure what you think you're playing at, young man," Don cut into the silence once the doors had slid closed, "but my advice to you would be to stay away from Millie." The doors opened at the ground floor. "Good day," Don clipped before he strode out into the large atrium and towards the exit.

"Hey," said Pav, jogging after him (he might look at least a hundred and fifty but he moved like a teenager on crack). "Listen. Wait!" He caught up with Don and met the shorter man's quick strides with his longer ones. "I just... Look, I was worried about her, all right? It's not every day a woman collapses at a Grand Round I've organized. And I don't care what you say; she does need to be checked out physically. She went down like a stone. And... and you lot are making her work? Shouldn't she have gone home? What kind of sweatshop are you running down in radiology?"

Don sighed and his power-walking slowed to more of a saunter. "You're worried about her." It was a statement rather than a question, and Don fixed Pav with a curious stare. Pav threw up his hands and huffed out a breath.

"Well, yes, *of course* I'm worried about her. She collapsed, didn't she? I mean, that's enough to worry anyone."

"But you're the only one spying on her, hours later, eh?"

Pav rolled his eyes and shrugged. What was the old codger getting at? Don chuckled, seeming for some reason in much better spirits than he had been a moment ago.

"You still haven't explained why she's still here and why she hasn't been examined," Pav gritted out as he followed Don into the multi-storey car park. They came to a stop beside a low-slung sports car. To Pav's surprise Don beeped open the locks. He'd never seen such an incongruous pairing. Don sported elbow patches, for crying out loud. What was he doing driving around in an Aston Martin Vantage?

"Millie is a complicated girl," Don said carefully. "She likes... she likes control, and she sets all these... limits for herself that she thinks she has to live within. Everything for her is very restricted. If she's pushed out of her comfort zone too far, then..." The old man trailed off and frowned down at his car keys. "Well, let's just say what happened today is just the tip of the iceberg. She panicked, she hyperventilated, and, as you know from medical school, if you hyperventilate for long enough and fast enough your body will shut you down. In Millie's mind she'd gone beyond her limits and that triggered her anxiety. The only method she has to get herself back under control is the routine of work and the techniques she's learnt from Anwar. She's nearly gone through the entire department backlog of reporting today, and she'll go on until late evening. Eventually she'll feel calm enough to go home."

"Jesus," Pav breathed, shoving his hands in his pockets. "I didn't realize she was so..." He trailed off, unsure how to complete the sentence. He cringed when he thought back to how he'd treated her in the past. He'd actually taken some sort of sick pleasure from baiting her, thinking she was uptight and snooty instead of having the real problems Don was describing. "Okay, well, thanks for explaining all that. I'd better be–"

"She could change, you know." Don cut him off as he turned to face Pav fully, narrowing his eyes at his face. "Millie doesn't think she's strong enough, but she is. She's already achieved so much since she started with Anwar. Anyone who's been through... well, let's just say she's got it in her to change, to try for happiness. All she needs is a little push."

"Uh..." Pav trailed off, backing away from the car. He hadn't realized that Millie herself had had therapy with Anwar, although when he thought about it and what an advocate she was for CBT it made perfect sense. "Right, well... as long as she's okay – physically, I mean – then I guess... " He cleared his throat, becoming a bit uncomfortable under Don's steely gaze. Was the old bastard expecting him to be the one to give Dr Cray-Cray the "push" she needed? Turning to jog to his own car, Pav spared a quick glance and a wave over his shoulder at

Don, who was now leaning against his Vantage, watching Pav's retreat.

Whatever the old man thought, Pav was not going to get involved. He had enough on his plate, he reasoned, without adding a lost cause into the mix.

Even if his plans for presenting at the conference went up in smoke there was no way he would be able to take on someone like Dr Morrison. A sudden vision of a more dishevelled, more human-looking Millie in his office, with her hair down around her face and a blush on her cheeks, swam into his mind and he paused as he was about to pull open his car door.

She's set limits for herself, he heard Don's voice repeat. *She could change, you know. She doesn't think she's strong enough, but she is...*

Pav shook his head to clear it. The last thing he needed was that sort of complication.

"Okay, I'll admit it. I was wrong."

Pav looked up in surprise from his computer. His office door was open and in it stood a sheepish-looking Don. Pav put down the batch of CVs he was holding, grateful for the interruption. He hated paperwork. It was one of the reasons being Surgical Director was not working for him. Going through CVs for applications for his own specialty was bad enough, without adding in this shit.

"Whilst I generally enjoy others being wrong and me being right, you're going to have to be more specific."

Don pushed open the door fully and shuffled into the office before sitting down heavily in the chair opposite him.

"Please, make yourself at home," Pav told him with an amused smile.

Don took a deep breath. "She's not getting any better," he said, a frown marring his forehead and worry pinching his mouth.

"Okay," Pav said slowly as he sat up a little straighter and cocked his head to the side. It had been a week since the lecture theatre incident and still, even now, he found his mind wandering to Millie pretty much all the damn time. He'd done what Don had told him to do: he'd stayed away from the radiology department, away from her – but he couldn't get her out of his head. Something about her was pulling at him constantly. Maybe it was the vulnerability he could see under that cold shell, maybe it was the way her arse looked in those bloody pencil skirts she wore constantly – whatever it was he didn't seem to be able to control it. "And what does this have to do with me exactly?"

Don's eyes flashed and his mouth turned down. "Boy, if you're not interested in helping, I won't waste my time." He stood up; Pav got the impression he would have jumped up and stormed out if his stiff joints had allowed. As it was, the drawn-out process involving Don pushing slowly up to standing as the sounds of the crepitis from his joints filled the room along with his low-muttered "Buggers" gave Pav the opportunity he needed. He leapt to his feet and rounded the desk, blocking Don's exit before he'd even fully straightened.

"I'm sorry," Pav said, holding both hands up in a placating gesture. "I'm a smartarse. You'll get used to it." Don's eyes narrowed as he looked up at Pav, but the corners of his mouth pulled up into a reluctant smile. "Please, sit down." Both men went back to their chairs and Pav decided to turn on the charm, unleashing his mega-watt smile on Don.

"Save that nonsense, Stavros," Don said through a chuckle. "It's not me you have to impress, you big peacock."

"Peacock?" Pav's smile fell a notch and he leaned back into his chair. "What do you – ?"

"Pfft," Don said with a dismissive wave of his hand. "Don't think I haven't seen you strutting about this hospital, rolling over everyone in your path and getting your way. Youngest in the family, were you?"

Pav shifted uncomfortably in his seat and pursed his lips. "I don't think you came here to talk about me."

"No," said Don with a smug smile, taking Pav's non-answer as a yes. "I didn't." He paused and cleared his throat, looking down at his shoes for a moment before squaring his shoulders and meeting Pav's eyes with fresh determination. "So. Millie. She's... well..." He trailed off, staring beyond Pav and obviously searching for the right words. "As her supervisor, I–"

"Supervisor?" Pav sat up a little straighter. "Why does she need a supervisor?"

Don frowned across at him and sighed. "Ah, I thought you knew."

"Knew what?"

"Millie's... not a consultant."

Pav's eyebrows leapt up into his hairline. "What is she then?"

"She's a senior registrar."

Pav rocked back in his chair in shock and his eyebrows knitted together in confusion. "Why in the fuck is she acting up as a consultant then?"

"She's passed all the radiology exams, and when I say she's passed I mean she's got 100 per cent."

"What?"

"She didn't drop a single mark. Not one. Nobody has ever performed as well in postgraduate exams."

"Jesus."

"She knows more than all the consultants in the department combined. She had to act up. I supervise all her on-calls and her reporting, but we can't have her as a normal trainee."

"No, I'd imagine that would be... tricky."

"So, as her supervisor I've spent a lot of time with her. More than anyone, I think, even Anwar, and slowly she's let me in. I owe her a lot. I'd have to have retired a while back if it wasn't for Millie. But–"

"Why would you have retired?"

"I can't work all the new-fangled computer gubbins," Don grumbled. "Millie looks after all that for me now. But... well, you might not have noticed but I'm getting on a bit. Can't keep going forever. The missus has been on at me for a while about retiring. Wants to go on a cruise." He snorted, his face twisting in disgust. "What do I want to go around on a bloody great boat for? Damn fool idea. But women... well..." He paused and rubbed his chin, his mouth hitching up at the side. "Son, fifty years of experience has told me that it's best to just go along with what they want. The alternative is ugly, and my wife can drag that ugly out for *years*, believe you me." He shook his head and shuddered. "I forgot my mother-in-law's birthday party in 1979 – one pint led to another at the pub; anyway it was well into the eighties before she forgave me. Sure, day to day she was much the same, but I knew: little things: no pork scratchings on the shopping list, no black pudding with my fried breakfast – cruel and unusual punishment... for over five years. No, I know better than to piss the wife off. So that means a cruise and not long after that I'll have to retire. Millie needs to be able to... interact a bit better by then, and she needs... Look, she's a complicated girl and she's had a difficult time of it so far."

"What do you mean?" Pav sat forward in his chair, his eyes sharp on Don.

"That's her story to tell."

"She's not exactly an open book."

"Used to easy women are you, son?"

"What? No... I just–"

"Course you are. Bet you have them queuing up, a dandy like you."

"Hey! So, I'm a peacock *and* a dandy am I? Tell me, Don, did you come here just to insult me or did you actually have a point?"

"It's your bloody fault she's slipped back, you stupid sod!" Don exploded. "Months of work with Anwar and coaxing her out of her shell and you buggered it all up in five minutes flat."

Silence followed Don's outburst and a stab of guilt pricked at Pav's conscience. He had practically forced her up on that stage. She'd warned him that she couldn't do it. She'd pleaded with him, for fuck's sake.

"Okay, okay," he muttered, holding up his hand to Don, who had started to push up again from the chair. "Look, I'd like to help but I'm not sure how much I can do. If you hadn't noticed, she's a mite bit terrified of me."

"Millie's terrified of *everything*," Don came back. "I'm not saying it'll be easy. I know you've got plenty of friends around to help you out. All I'm asking is that you *try*."

Chapter 9

Millie wuvs books, don't cha?

"MILLIE!"

Millie turned in her chair and smiled. Rosie had run full pelt into her office and was standing in the middle of the floor with her arms straight up in the air. Millie didn't think there had ever been anyone who expressed this amount of delight in seeing her. Quick as a flash Rosie lowered her arms and flung herself into Millie's arms. Physical contact wasn't always easy for Millie. Her childhood certainly had not been filled with it, and as an adult her personality did not seem to inspire warm relationships full of affection. So touch wasn't something she was used to, and the shock of it usually caused her to flinch away (this ensured that anyone who did bother trying to be physically affectionate with her, which to be honest was very rare, was put off by her apparently negative reaction). But with Rosie she hadn't been given any option. The little girl was all about kisses and cuddles and there was no way Millie could have kept her at arm's length.

"You look sad," Rosie said, putting her small hands either side of Millie's face and squeezing her cheeks.

"I'm not sad," Millie lied as she closed her arms around the warm little body. "How could anyone be sad with you hanging about?"

The truth was that the hollow feeling Millie had endured to some extent her whole life was gradually expanding. She felt like emptiness was slowly pulling her under, sucking her down into a dark hole. Collapsing in front of the entire hospital had been mortifying. It was the ultimate loss of control, and Millie was all about control. It was like a slap in the face telling her to respect her limits, to get back in her box and live her narrow life. Punishing her for thinking she could function like other people.

"Hey, honey." Millie's eyes flicked to Libby at the doorway. She gave her a much smaller smile than she had given her daughter and was about to look away when she realized she wasn't alone. Kira was standing next to her, and, bizarrely, she was smiling too.

"Hi Dr M.," Kira said, still smiling, although it was starting to look a little forced. This may have been down to the fact that Millie could not seem to muster one in return; the Rosie-inspired happy expression had slowly faded when she noticed Kira in the doorway.

"Hello," Millie said, trying with all her might to get her mouth to cooperate so the ends would at least tip up; but her anxiety was getting the better of her again. She looked back at Libby. "How long do you need me to have her?" Libby and Kira exchanged looks, and then, to Millie's confusion, both of them moved into the room. Libby took Don's seat and Kira perched on Millie's desk.

"We've actually come to talk to you, Millie," Libby said carefully. Millie pushed her chair back a couple of inches, still with Rosie in her lap, and frowned.

"Oh... uh..." There was literally no reason why these two

could possibly want to talk to her – unless... She bit her lip. Had Libby found out about the grant? Surely Pav wouldn't have told her. He didn't seem –

"So, tonight? You free to come?" Kira's voice cut through Millie's thoughts and she realized she'd missed some sort of suggestion.

"Wh-what?"

"We're going out to the mess do tonight at The Nag's Head," Libby said. "Jamie's babysitting. We thought it might be fun." Millie thought about a crowded pub, filled with people who actively disliked her, and she shuddered.

"No." Her answer was short and forceful. She knew it sounded rude.

"Come on," Kira wheedled, seemingly immune to the rudeness. "It'll be a laugh. Few shots of tequila and you'll be well up for it." Millie opted not to inform Kira that she did not drink and the biochemical reasons behind it at that juncture.

"I just... I can't," she told them, pulling Rosie's hair out of her face and re-fixing the grip that had come loose.

"You could come and have supper with me and Jamie-Daddy," Rosie told her. Millie had noticed this gradual change to Jamie-Daddy and sometimes just plain Daddy over the last few weeks. The man in question always seemed to visibly swell with pride every time he heard it. "After you show me the my-crows again."

"Microbes, Rosie," Millie murmured, inching her chair forward so she could get at her mouse and opening the relevant file.

"Wanna see the flesh-eating one," Rosie demanded, and Millie filled the screen with streptococcus.

"It's not always flesh-eating, Rosie," Millie told her, wishing fervently that she had never gone through all the possible medical outcomes of a streptococcus infection.

"I know, I know. Impy-tiger."

"Impetigo."

"Hurty wee-wees."

"Urinary tract infection."

"Foo-foo stuff."

"Vaginal colonization with group b streptococcus."

Millie heard a muffled snort from across the room. When she glanced over she noticed that Kira's shoulders were shaking, her lips were pressed together and her eyes were dancing. Millie felt her face heat, turned back to the screen and took in a long slow breath. "Rosie... maybe we should do this later. I..."

She heard a small squeal and noticed Kira flinch before rubbing her arm and scowling at Libby, who was now standing right next to her with her hands on her hips. Libby transferred her attention to Millie, squatting down next to her chair.

"Okay, hun. You don't like pubs, right?"

Millie turned back to the screen and shrugged. Openly admitting her fear was showing weakness, and she was very sure that, with the events of the last month, she'd done quite enough of that.

"How about... " Libby trailed off and looked up at the ceiling, biting her lip.

"I've got it!" Kira shouted, and Millie flinched in her seat. "Babe, you're going to have to get used to my voice. I'm loud. And obnoxious. It's my thing." Millie had never been called *babe* by anyone. But if she was honest, it was a vast improvement on Dr M.

Libby rolled her eyes. "Only you would couch 'loud' and 'obnoxious' as qualities to be proud of, Ki-Ki."

"Give me a chance, Sugartits." Compared to Sugartits, Millie considered that *babe* wasn't too bad at all. "I'm talking about the book group."

"Uh... wh – ?" Libby started, and Kira shot her an annoyed look and gave her shin a subtle kick.

"Our *book group*, remember?"

"Er..." Another kick. "Oh! Yes, of course. Perfect!"

"Millie wuvs books, don't cha?" Rosie rather unhelpfully put in, and Millie clenched her teeth. Why did she have to tell this kid so much? She knew Rosie was gifted but she seemed to have the memory of an elephant.

"I..."

"That's settled then," Kira cut her off.

"Wh-what?"

"I'll come get you," Libby told her. "The next one's at... er... my house on Tuesday." Silence, and then Libby's hand landed on Millie's shoulder and gave her a gentle squeeze. "It's a small group," she added in a soft voice.

"I..."

"Right, come on, short stuff," Kira said, grabbing Rosie's hand. "We've got to drop you off with the big guy so Mummy can help me get wasted. Hey, there's a salutation to the moon we could go to on the way home."

"Kira, it's below freezing."

"So what?"

"We are not taking Rosie to break into Burgess Park and dance around with a load of middle-aged naked ladies."

Kira let out a huff as the threesome made it to the door. "Mummy is so *boring*, squirt." They continued bickering as they turned into the corridor. Rosie shouted out a quick bye and gave Millie a small wave as the others said "See you next week, Dr M.," and "Later, Millie." Millie watched them go from her chair with her mouth hanging open.

When had she agreed to join a book group? She blinked a couple of times. A vague feeling of being the victim of a hit-and-run swept over her.

After clenching her hands into fists and starting back on the reporting, she had herself back in control. She would just put them off. Then she would go back to hiding in plain sight. Nothing would change.

She frowned as she started typing the first report. Why did that fact not bring her relief? Why did it just make her feel even more empty inside?

Chapter 10

I think I love you, uptight lady

MILLIE SUBTLY TUCKED THE FIVE-PAGE BOOK REPORT SHE'D typed up the night before into her Mulberry handbag, which she manoeuvred under her feet. She rested her hands on her lap and fought to stop them from clenching into fists. Eleanor, who was sitting on a squashy chair opposite, gave her an encouraging smile and she tried to relax her shoulders. Something furry bumped her hand and then a huge, ugly dog's head came to rest in her lap. The animal smelt, she had droopy eyes, an inordinate amount of thick fur, and she seemed to produce enough drool to fill a small pond. Millie lifted a hand tentatively and stroked the large head, which was surprisingly silky. The animal didn't exactly fit in with the clean modern lines of Jamie and Libby's spacious semi in Wimbledon, but she seemed more than at home there.

"Oh God," said Libby, moving from the kitchen to shoo the dog away. "I'm sorry, Millie. I know she's gross. However much shampoo we use on her she still smells like a dead badger. Beauty! Come *here*." She hauled on Beauty's collar but the massive beast stayed put. She looked straight at Millie and almost seemed to roll her eyes as she continued to ignore the lady of the house.

"Please," Millie said, both of her hands now settling on the dog's head and into the ruff at her neck. "It's nice... I... let her stay where she is." Millie had never had a pet. She couldn't say if she was a dog person or not. All she knew was that she now felt less overwhelmed with her hands buried in this one's smelly fur than she had a moment ago.

Book group, it turned out, did not actually entail discussing *books*. Or at least most of the conversation had yet to veer anywhere near literature. There was a lot of wine involved (of which Millie had taken a glass, as she thought it might help her fit in), a fair amount of chocolate (this was something Millie did like, love even, but she was too nervous to eat), and an incredible amount of chat.

The group included Kira, Libby, Amy (Libby's sister-in-law), Tara and Claire (both strippers who worked with Libby). Eleanor had come with Millie for moral support. Millie had gone to her in a flat panic that afternoon. She had no idea what you wore to a book group. Casual was not easy for her. Eleanor (who, over the last few weeks, had insisted that Millie call her El) had for some reason been thrilled that Millie was going to a book group. She wasn't quite as excited as she had been about the wedding, but then again she had been pretty disappointed to hear that Millie had only gone to the service and not the reception.

So when El had smiled at Millie and given her hand a squeeze after she'd found the perfect jeans-and-sloppy-jumper combo for the book group, Millie had found herself blurting, "Will you come with me tonight?" As soon as the words were out she'd regretted them. El's eyes had gone wide and she'd been speechless for endless seconds. "I mean," Millie had put in to fill the silence, "if you like books and... look, don't worry. I–"

"Of *course* I'll come with you," El surprised her by saying, her face breaking into another wide smile. "I haven't got a book group. I'd love to be part of one."

Millie was still in shock that she'd agreed, but having El there calmed her nerves. El knew how hard this stuff was for Millie. But despite even El's help, Millie knew after the first hour that this was not going to work. She had no idea what to say to these women. The way conversation flowed effortlessly between them was a complete mystery to her. For so long she had weighed and measured every word she said against possible consequences and interpretations. So whilst the chatter filled the room she stayed silent, her hands sifting through Beauty's fur (and eliciting deeply satisfied snorts).

"I'm giving him a chance, okay? He's not all bad. Sometimes he can be really sweet," Tara told everyone whilst she fiddled with the stem of her wineglass.

"He beat you!" Claire said, and the room fell silent as Tara glared across at her. "How can you take him back? You should–" Millie snapped out of her frozen cocoon and for a moment she forgot herself.

"This man, he... he *physically* assaulted you?" Millie asked, surprising herself, but she was so shocked it just slipped out. Five sets of wide eyes swung to her.

Tara blinked. "Well... it was only the once and he just slapped my–"

"He put his hands on you in violence?"

"I guess, but he's changed now so–"

"A study in America showed that 62 per cent of domestic violence offenders reoffend within two years."

"Well–"

"And those were only the ones who were arrested, the actual figures are thought to be much higher."

"Look," Tara snapped, her face flooding with colour. "*You* might be able to get a nice bloke with your fancy worthwhile job and your perfect little outfits, but the likes of me–"

"I have *never* had a... 'bloke'," Millie put in, and Tara's mouth snapped shut. "I have never been in any sort of relationship. My 'perfect outfits' are all chosen for me by Eleanor who is my personal shopper and whom I have dragged along here tonight as she is the closest thing I have to a friend – apart from Don, but he's in the wrong age group and gender for tonight. Anwar's my therapist so he doesn't count either.

"And by stating that my job is 'worthwhile' you are implying that your own is not. I would question this hypothesis. I perform a function at work and I get reimbursed for my time; you do the same. We both pay tax, we both contribute to society; both of our roles are vital to the people who rely on them. You could argue that your role in society is even more valuable than mine in fact. I am paid by the state to work in the state-funded NHS. You are working for a business and encourage people to spend money in that establishment, thus stimulating the economy and improving the country for everyone. I presume there are also foreigners attending the club?"

"Well... yes, of course. We get the Russians, the Japanese, the Yanks..."

"Even better. You are bringing foreign investment into the UK. The tax you pay is out of the profits of the business; the tax I pay is money that has *already* been collected in tax to fund the NHS. In the grand scheme of things you are helping this country to recover from the economic downturn and in turn aiding the world's recovery. I... am not."

Tara's mouth dropped open and she blinked again. "I... well, I've never thought about it that way."

"No," Millie said, tilting her head to the side as she looked at Tara. "You have not, which has probably contributed to your lack of self-esteem."

"What makes you think I have low self-esteem?"

"It is the only reason you would believe that it is acceptable for an incredibly beautiful woman and a valuable member of society such as yourself to align herself with a genetically deficient male."

"Oh." Tara sat back in her chair and puffed out a breath. Everyone's mouths were open now and they were all staring at Millie. She began to feel uncomfortable and shifted in her chair whilst her hands tightened and her nails started digging into her palms. She had a feeling that this was one of the many times she had missed some sort of social cue and inadvertently offended someone.

"I think I love you, uptight lady," Claire declared into the room, her face lighting with a wide smile.

"Right on, sister," Kira put in, her fisted hand punching the air.

"Well said, Millie," Libby murmured in her ear, and squeezed her arm.

"You didn't drag me here," El told her, a frown marring her expression. "I wanted to come and I'm honoured you consider me a friend, right?"

"Oh," Millie blinked and for the first time in the longest while her face broke into a very small spontaneous smile without having to force it.

"Woah," breathed Tara. "Chicky, you need to do that more. You look about ten times prettier and super-young."

"How old *are* you, Millie?" Kira asked. This was the first time Kira had ever used Millie's Christian name.

"Uh..." Millie, even with her social dysfunction, knew that this was not an altogether polite question, but then she suspected that if Kira wanted to know something she just plain asked, polite or not.

"Ki-Ki, you are so bloody rude," Libby snapped, confirming Millie's suspicion. "You don't have to answer that, honey."

"It's okay," Millie told Libby – straight honest questions she could deal with. "I'm twenty-six."

"What?" Libby's startled voice responded. "That's only three years older than us."

"How is that even possible?" Kira asked. "You're a consultant."

"No, I – I'm not," Millie said, stiffening in her seat but letting the feel of Libby next to her and the fur under her fingers calm her nerves. "I just do the consultant on-calls and reporting. I'm supervised."

"What year are you in your training?"

"I've just started my fourth year of my radiology specialty training."

"But... but that means you've been qualified for five years," Kira said, her eyebrows drawing together in confusion. "You would have been..."

"Twenty-one," Millie said. "I was twenty-one when I qualified. I started medical school at sixteen."

"Jesus, so you did your A-levels early, huh?"

"Yes." Millie decided not to admit that she had actually done her A-levels at thirteen, *then* done a chemistry degree at Oxford, before she was accepted to medical school. She was well aware that this made her a freak. Going to school and university with kids five years her senior had not been easy. And she didn't want these women to look at her the same way everyone did back then. Libby's hand slid down from Millie's arm to her hand and gave her a squeeze. It was then Millie remembered a conversation they had had a few weeks ago with Rosie:

"Did you hear how cool Millie is? She can do any sum you ask her."

"That is cool, darling," Libby muttered.

"If only all children felt like you, Rosie, I might have had friends at school," Millie said, smiling down at Rosie as she pulled her mass of brunette strands into the sleek knot she always wore, then carefully straightened a couple of items on her desk so they were back in perfect alignment.

"What do you mean?" Rosie asked. "Why didn't you have friends?"

"Oh... I..." Millie froze, her eyes still focused on the desk. "Well, I am a bit... different, Rosie."

"You're a good different," Rosie told her, and Millie glanced at her briefly, flashing a small smile.

"I'm glad you think so. But at school they didn't think it was a good different."

"That's stupid!" Rosie shouted in affronted disbelief.

Millie smiled and squatted down in front of the small tower of rage that was Libby's daughter. "Most of the time I wasn't even with children the same age as me, so friends... well, making friends was tricky. Not everyone has a gift for this. Now, you – you are twice gifted: you can make friends and you can do maths."

Millie took a deep breath, then turned her hand in Libby's to close her fingers around the other woman's. When she caught her eye Libby looked startled for a moment but then she smiled so wide it looked almost painful.

"Right," Libby said, turning to the rest of the group. "It's late and we haven't even got to the book yet. I propose we make the book club a weekly thing – every Tuesday night. What do you say?" Everyone, including to Millie's surprise Eleanor, agreed.

"How often do you normally meet?" Millie muttered under

her breath to Libby. Libby paused for a moment and looked away.

"We'll do it at my place next," Tara chipped in, bouncing in her chair. "I'm going to set up a bonfire of all Mark's stuff. You guys can help me burn him out of my life." To Millie's shock Tara stood up from her chair, skirted the coffee table and squatted down in front of the sofa, before pulling Millie in for a tight hug. Millie stiffened for a moment, until Tara muttered in her ear.

"Thanks, babe. Thanks for making me feel... like I matter." Millie's hand that wasn't held in Libby's came up to give Tara an awkward pat on the back, after which Tara pulled back slightly, smiled right into her confused face and gave her a loud kiss on the cheek. "Right, I'm outta here, bitches. Got a double shift tomorrow. Need my Zs if I'm gonna be able to shake my ta-tas to stimulate this country's economy."

"Well, with that last boob job you'll certainly be stimulating something," said Claire, moving across the room to drag Tara away from Millie. "Good to meet you, hun," Claire threw over her shoulder as she pulled Tara to the door. Millie looked up and Claire met her gaze for a minute. To her surprise it was soft and warm. Up until then Claire had struck her as anything but. She winked at Millie and mouthed *thank you*, before turning the corner into the corridor.

"Woah! Loverboy and his sidekick Dick Doc," Millie heard Claire shout after the front door opened, and frowned in confusion. She had started to feel safe. Not relaxed, not comfortable, but safe.

"Ladies," the deep voice sounded from the doorway, sweeping her feeling of safety away. "Always a pleasure, despite the adopted use of Kira's infantile nicknames."

"Oh, you smooth-talking son-of-a-bitch," Millie heard Claire reply. "If my toast was buttered on the other side I would eat you for breakfast. Tara, put your tongue in: you're driving me home." Heavy footsteps echoed down the corridor and Millie flew into action, tearing her hand out of Libby's and grabbing her bag from the floor. The dog she'd been stroking for the last hour, however, had other ideas: Beauty's big body trapped Millie's legs next to the sofa and her heavy head remained in her lap.

"I've got to g–"

"Hey there, fellow book lovers." Pav's large frame filled the living room and Millie flinched. "So, what great literary works are up for debate today? Hit me."

"Don't tempt me, Willy Fiddler," Kira shot back as he flopped down into the seat next to her and poked her in the ribs.

"Argh!" she shrieked, retaliating by yanking his jumper down and pulling so hard on his chest hair it looked like she'd actually ripped it out.

"Hands off the merchandise," he said through a smile as he grabbed her hand, twisted it away from her body and poked her in the ribs again. It was then that he noticed Millie, and paused mid rib-poke. As soon as their eyes met Millie looked away. Of *course* Kira and Pav would be together. They were both so confident, so open and free. Them as a couple made complete sense. But for some reason her chest felt so tight it was a struggle to breathe.

Chapter 11

We'll see, baby

"EL," SHE MANAGED TO FORCE OUT. ELEANOR WAS watching Dr Martakis with wide eyes, as Millie suspected any self-respecting straight woman would; he was the most watchable man she had ever seen in her life. Right now he was wearing jeans and a dark jumper with the sleeves pulled up to above his elbows. The glance she had allowed herself of his muscled forearms was enough to hollow out her stomach completely. "El..." Her voice this time was slightly choked, but she managed to raise it above a whisper and attract El's attention. "I'm going to... I need to go. Will you be okay? I can't..." She trailed off and grabbed her bag closer to her chest, much to Beauty's disgust.

"Of course," El said, frowning at Millie with some concern. "No worries. I'll be fine. My car's just round the corner."

Millie closed her eyes in relief, before a deep voice shattered it.

"Hello. I don't believe we've met. I'm Pav," Pav said, standing from the sofa.

"Hi," El replied, a blush creeping up her cheeks as she shook Pav's outstretched hand.

"Thanks, Libby," Millie muttered as she attempted to rise from the sofa. But Beauty's weight kept her pinned and she stared at the dog in desperation, whispering, "I've got to go now. Could you... could you move your head... please?"

Beauty's answer was to bury her huge snout under one of Millie's arms and fling it out and away from her bag so that it settled on Beauty's head again. Millie forgot where she was and who she was with for a moment. She smiled, leaned over and buried her face in the fur at Beauty's neck. Beauty responded by licking the entire side of Millie's face, and Millie did something she hadn't done in possibly years.

She giggled.

When she sat back up the whole room was staring at her. She glanced over at Dr Martakis and, bizarrely, his eyes were slightly unfocused, his mouth hanging open. Millie blushed, and then gave Beauty one final squeeze before she managed to ease her legs out from their pinned position.

"Come on, girl," Jamie said as he stepped over to pull the dog away, having more success than Libby through sheer brute force. The dog grunted, head-butted Jamie's crotch, and then ambled away as Jamie cupped his manhood, stifling a scream. Millie was up and starting to edge towards the exit.

"Bye, Mils," Kira shouted from the other sofa, and Millie managed a small smile for her. "Dr M." had become a thing of the past over the course of the evening.

"See you next week, Millie," El said, taking a step to the side to see around Pav's large body. Jamie grimaced through his pain and waved at her as she passed him at the kitchen island, and her breathing started evening out as the front door came into view... until it was no longer in view.

"Hey," Dr Martakis said, his chest filling her vision. She

blinked at the corded forearms crossed over it, and swallowed, choosing to focus on his tanned throat. "You didn't say goodbye to *me*."

"Uh... bye," Millie whispered, giving him a small, rather pathetic wave; but he didn't move. She knew what happened in this scenario and was not about to perform some sort of weird dance to get round him in front of the others. Instead she took a step back – maybe there was another exit? She could jump out of the window.

"How are you getting home?"

"Why?"

"Why what?"

"Why do you want to know?"

Her eyes strayed from his throat to his chin and she noticed the corners of his mouth tip up as he shook his head slightly. "Why won't you tell me?" She took another step back and he took one forward.

"I'm walking."

His smile dropped and his mouth set in a firm line. "No, you're not."

Millie bit her lip and gripped her handbag even tighter; her fingers felt like they might snap with the tension. What was going on? Why didn't he concentrate on getting *Kira* home and leave her alone? And why was he issuing orders to her? He barely knew her.

She took a deep breath and decided to be honest.

"I don't understand," she told him, glancing over at the others on the sofas who were all focused on the exchange like it was completely fascinating. Millie was more confused than ever. "I am walking and I don't know... I don't know what that has to do with you." Her house was only a few streets over. It would only take her ten minutes to get back by foot.

"No," he said, his voice firm. "You're not walking home in

the dark. I'm driving you. As to what it has to do with me..." He trailed off and smiled, after which his voice softened. "We'll get to that bit later, okay?"

"Get to what later?" she muttered, then tensed as he reached out and put some soft pressure on her elbow to guide her forward. He must have felt her flinch because he dropped his hand, and instead swept it out in front of him, indicating for her to precede him to the door. Millie glanced at their audience again and decided her best bet was not to create a scene in Libby and Jamie's living room. Maybe she could get away from Dr Martakis on the pavement outside.

She shrugged and walked forward, quickly skirting him and his forearms and avoiding any sort of mind-scrambling eye contact. He was fast though, and by the time she made it to the door he had pulled it open for her. She charged out onto the pavement and turned left. Breathing a sigh of relief when he made no apparent attempt to stop her, she marched forward and let her shoulders relax. That was why, when she felt something brush her neck and fall onto her shoulders, she nearly jumped out of her skin.

"You forgot your coat," Pav said. She turned to see him standing just behind her, a smile on his face and his hands in his pockets. She looked down at her long cashmere overcoat like she'd never seen it before. What was wrong with her? Millie *never forgot anything*.

"Right, thanks," she muttered, shoving her hands through the sleeves and realising how biting the cold actually was. She tried to smile at him but was unsure of the results. Before she could make an even bigger fool of herself she marched away. Despite the fact she was now power-walking, Dr Martakis' long strides easily kept pace with her shorter ones and they carried on down the pavement together.

"I thought you had a car," Millie said after a full thirty seconds of silence.

"Yup." Back to silence again.

"Well... why aren't you driving it?"

"Did you enjoy the book club?"

"Wh-what?"

"The book club," Dr Martakis said slowly. "Was it fun?"

Millie thought for a moment. Did she have fun? Fun was not a huge feature of her life and never had been. Had tonight terrified her? Yes. Did she make a fool of herself? Well, no, unless you counted the corridor stand-off with Dr Martakis. She had enjoyed listening to the women's banter. She'd felt good when Tara thanked her. Libby had held her hand.

"Yes... I... I think so," she told him, and heard Dr Martakis chuckle.

"You only *think* you had fun? Well, they'll have to do better than that."

"What do you me—"

"What book did you talk about?" he asked as they rounded the corner. The pace they were going was starting to take its toll on Millie. Dr Martakis didn't even seem short of breath.

"We didn't talk about the book."

"I thought it was a book club?" Dr Martakis sounded as confused as Millie had been and she felt herself smile.

"I know, so did I."

They stopped at the crossing and she pressed the button before glancing up at him, still smiling as she thought about the book club that had no intention of discussing books. As soon as their eyes met he blinked and his mouth opened slightly.

"Jesus," he breathed as his gaze roamed her face.

"What's the matter?" Millie asked as she frowned and her smile fell. The crossing started to beep and they both moved away, breaking eye contact. Dr Martakis cleared his throat.

"Ha! I knew it. I bet half of them didn't even read it."

Millie shrugged and bit her lip as she finally turned down her road with Dr Martakis hot on her heels.

"I bet *you* read it though, didn't you?" he said, amusement lacing his tone.

"Of course," Millie said, heat hitting her cheeks when she remembered the report she'd typed up. She involuntarily held her bag closer to her side – she should have known Dr Martakis would notice. He noticed everything.

"You wrote notes, didn't you?" he asked, his voice now vibrating slightly with humour. "Come on, let me see."

Before she could stop him he had somehow managed to fish out the report from the front of her bag. They arrived at her door and she made a grab for it but he held it out of her reach. In her fluster she collided with his solid chest and sucked in a lungful of his clean scent: soap, citrusy aftershave, and man, all mingled into one glorious combination. She leapt back, her cheeks on fire.

"Stop it," she said, wrapping her arms around her middle and feeling like an idiot. Dr Martakis took one look at her face and sobered immediately.

"Hey," he said softly, holding out the papers with one hand and reaching up with the other to push a few strands of hair that had escaped from her ponytail behind her ear. She snatched the report back, before turning and racing up the steps to her front door. Her house was in a large Victorian terrace in an affluent area. If Dr Martakis thought that was strange he didn't say anything. As she extracted her keys from her bag and shoved them in the lock she heard his heavy footfalls jog up behind her.

"I'm sorry, okay? I wasn't making fun of you. I knew you wouldn't have gone unprepared to that group and I... I was teasing you. That's kind of my thing: teasing people."

"Don't worry about it," she said in a tight voice when she'd finally managed to turn the lock and heard him sigh. She was about to close the door in his face when his foot moved to block the solid oak in its tracks.

"I've thought about how you can repay me for saving your life at the wedding," he told her.

"Wh-what?"

"The other day – you said you owed me. Now I'm collecting."

"I don't understand."

"I've read *The Field of the Cloth of Gold* and I want to discuss it with you."

Millie glanced down at her report with the title in large letters on the front page, and then back up at Pav in confusion. "You want to talk to me about a book? Now? At eleven o'clock at night?"

"Yes." Pav's chin tilted at a stubborn angle and for a moment Millie pictured a beautiful little boy with dark hair and deep, dark brown eyes adopting the same stance, a boy used to getting his way and not willing to give up until he did.

"Why?"

"Love, please just let me in. Talk to me – we'll only talk about the book, I promise – then I'll go away."

Millie was still stuck on the endearment at the start of the sentence. She felt it roll over her like a warm breeze. For some reason she stepped back and pulled the door open.

"BUT IT DOESN'T HAVE TO MAKE SENSE," PAV ARGUED through a smile. "I think this guy is just fucking with us. He's a bus driver having a laugh at the snobby literary world for shits and giggles."

Millie's eyes flashed.

"That's crazy! There *has* to be a point. It's a historical reference."

Pav's smile grew wider. He'd been there for over an hour now. For the first twenty minutes Millie had been reticent in the extreme. It was only when they started discussing the book and he started deliberately baiting her that she started coming out of her shell. At this stage Pav doubted she even realised how she was reacting. It was like seeing a robot slowly animate into a living creature – and a fascinating, beautiful, intelligent, funny creature at that.

Her house was huge, and he'd yet to see any sign of any other occupants. It was decorated in surprisingly warm colours and had a homey feel despite the fact it was tidy to the point of being disturbing. The throw cushions on the sofa looked like they had been aligned with a ruler.

"Ah, yes," Pav muttered. "Let's refer back to the report, shall we."

He snatched the paper from Millie's side and flicked through to the third page. She made a lunge for it, with the very satisfying result that her body pressed against his as he held the pages away from her.

That small, tentative smile was back on her face and he sucked in a sharp breath. Before he'd seen her smile he'd known she was attractive in a cold, clinical, abstract sort of a way. Well-put-together was the most fitting phrase that sprang to mind. But when she smiled she became one of the most stunning women he'd ever seen in his life.

"Now, now, Dr Morrison. Just let me get to the relevant paragraph. I believe you said–"

"Don't call me that." Millie was no longer smiling and she withdrew back to her side of the sofa. Even worse, he lost the eye contact he'd been enjoying for the last half hour at least, as she looked down at her feet and tucked her hair (over the course of the hour her hair had worked its way out of its confines and settled over her shoulders and down her back) behind her ears.

"Hey," Pav said softly, lowering the report back down into his lap and leaning towards her to try to catch her eyes again. "What's up?"

"I just..." She trailed off and he noticed her hands clench into small fists again. The sight of her knuckles turning white and the tight set of her mouth made his chest clench. "Look, don't worry about it. I'm being silly."

"Don't call you what?" Pav asked, his head tilting to the side, and Millie sighed.

"Dr Morrison," she whispered. "Everyone calls me Dr Morrison. It's like they..." She made a visible effort to unclench her hands and rubbed them both down her legs. "It's like they want to keep me at a distance. Like they don't want to interact with me in any sort of meaningful way. And I'm so..." She shook her head and moved forward to stand. Just as she was rising from the sofa, Pav caught her hand.

"Okay, Millie," he said, tugging her back down to the sofa so that she was right next to him. Her wide eyes met his for a moment before she quickly looked away. "No more Dr Morrison, all right?"

Of its own volition, the hand that wasn't holding hers on the sofa moved up to touch a lock of her hair that was hanging by her cheek. It was so soft, like satin. He breathed in and the scent of her shampoo and some sort of complicated perfume filled his senses. "You have such gorgeous hair," he muttered.

"D-don't be ridiculous," she stuttered as his face moved closer, just a few millimetres from the side of her head. "I... I... It's mousy."

Pav felt like he was drugged. He literally couldn't help

himself as he closed the small gap and kissed her silky hair before taking a deep breath in.

"It's golden chestnut," he told her as his lips moved to the shell of her ear and she sucked in a shocked breath.

"That's a... a... another way of saying *mousy*," she whispered. Fear threaded through her tone but also something else... something like anticipation.

"Look at me," he said against her neck, and she shuddered. His hand moved from the side of her head to her cheek and he put steady pressure on it until he'd turned her face to look at him. His forehead rested against hers for a moment. "You could never be mousy," he muttered against her mouth, and then he kissed her.

She flinched at the contact and he slid his hand back through her fucking fantastic hair to the back of her head to turn her where he wanted her. His other hand moved across the soft material of her jumper from her stomach to her back. She was stiff in his arms for a moment before his mouth started moving softly against hers.

"It's okay, baby," he said against her lips. Somehow that flipped a switch. She melted into him as soon as the word *baby* left his mouth. Her hands, which had been clenched in her lap, now moved: one into his hair and the other onto his bicep.

Then she kissed him back.

This was not a confident kiss; it was not an experienced kiss; and God knows Pav had kissed more than his fair share of confident, experienced women. But it was, hands down, the most unbelievable erotic experience of his life. He hadn't even moved past first base but he was more turned on by this simple kiss than he ever had been before. So when she suddenly tore away from him and launched up from the sofa to run around it to the other side he was stunned and it almost felt like he was in physical pain.

"Baby, what on–"

"D-don't you *b-baby* me!" she cut him off, her face flushed with colour and her hair wild around it, which had the unfortunate effect of enhancing her beauty and making Pav's pain level ratchet up another notch. "Y-you with your 'babies' and your 'loves' and your st-stupid forearms."

Pav frowned. "My forearms? What on earth do my forearms have to do with anything?"

"I'm *not* your love though," Millie said, and her body started shaking as she stood her ground.

"Okay," Pav said, keeping his voice calm and level and standing slowly from the sofa. "Okay, let's go back to the beginning here. Tell me what I've done to upset you, all right? We'll work from there."

"I... I... you've scrambled my brain!" she threw out helplessly, and then wrapped her arms around her shaking body. Pav's chest clenched again and he held his hands up, palms forward in a gesture of surrender.

"Millie? Take a deep breath and slow down, okay? Can you come here to me and sit down again."

"N-n-no," she choked out, shaking her head furiously. As he watched the blood drain from her face, Pav had a sudden vision of that awful moment before she passed out in the lecture theatre, and he started to feel some real concern.

"Right, if you can't come to me, I'm going to come to you. Okay?"

"Don't come any closer," she shouted, her arm coming up to ward him off.

"It's okay," he told her, taking a few slow steps towards her, his hands held out in front of him like he was approaching an easily spooked animal. "Slow your breathing down, Millie, okay? Can you do that?" She closed her eyes and shook her head.

Somehow Pav knew he needed to get closer. He made it to her outstretched hand and moved forward so that it was resting on his chest. After a few beats, her hand grabbed a handful of his jumper and she pulled him forward. Pav took another chance. He wrapped his arms around her and moved her body into his with both her hands now resting on his chest and her arms pressed between them. "Breath with me, baby. Okay?" She let out a puff of air, and as his chest expanded under her hands she took in more air. After another minute their breathing had slowed right down, and she was no longer shaking.

"Is it safe to ask what that was about now?" he said tentatively as he stroked her hair.

"I like to do research," she told him nonsensically, her voice muffled as she spoke into the wool of his jumper.

"Uh... okay?" he said slowly, and waited.

"I'm not a spontaneous person. I make decisions based on an extensive knowledge of the subject matter."

"Right..."

She sighed. "All I know about you is that you are... I mean, you seem to..."

He gave her a squeeze. "I guarantee that what you think you know about me will be bad."

She pulled away from him then and he let her go back a couple of inches but kept his arms around her.

"I do not want to conduct a conversation whilst engaged in an inappropriate embrace."

Pav couldn't help it then: he smiled. "Inappropriate how?"

Millie narrowed her eyes at him and he barely held in his chuckle. "You shouldn't be holding me," she told him.

"Why not?"

"Urgh!" she growled out, her expression a mixture of frustration and confusion. "Because... because a man like you is *not* interested in a woman like me."

"What are you talking about?" Pav asked, his smile dying and a frown creasing his forehead.

"You know exactly what I'm–"

"No, Millie. I have no idea what's in your head."

"Is it like a sport to you?" she asked him, and his head jerked at the apparent change of subject. "A game?"

"What are you–"

"Because it's *not* a game to me, all right? And even if it was, I would have no idea of the rules."

"Millie, I'm not playing games with you. I don't know why y–"

"You... you call me *Nuclear Winter*," she blurted out, and Pav froze. "I know you do. I've heard it. And... and that time in my office... what you said..."

"Millie... I..." Pav trailed off and scrubbed both his hands down his face as his stomach tightened at the memory of what an insensitive prick he'd been. "I'm sorry about that nickname. I should have never used it." At this juncture he did not want to get into the fact that he was the one who had actually made it up; he didn't think that would do his case any good at all. "And that time in your office, I was angry," he went on. "I didn't know–"

"You didn't know that I was a... a freak," she muttered. "You just thought I was rude. If you'd have known I was a freak you would have felt *sorry* for me instead, which is even worse than thinking I'm an outright bitch."

"Millie, please listen to me," Pav pleaded, reaching for her, but she flinched away again.

"Kira!" Millie shouted, and he shook his head slowly.

"What about her?"

"*She's* the type of woman a man like you is interested in.

For all I know, you and her..." She trailed off and dropped her head down to rest it on his chest again.

Pav snorted. "Kira and I would kill each other in the first five minutes. Is that's what's in your head?"

Millie shrugged. "You're both so confident, you're both funny, social," she paused a moment before continuing in a barely audible whisper, "attractive, beautiful."

"And because of that you think we're together? I don't under–"

"You were *touching* her," Millie mumbled as she looked up at him, and he saw her face flood with colour. "People don't... well, people aren't like that with each other unless... I just assumed..."

"I mess about with Ki-Ki like I would an annoying younger sister, brother even, given the number of head-locks I've put her in – she's pretty scrappy. Don't you have any siblings?"

Millie bit her lip, flicked her eyes up to him and away again, but he felt her body relax slightly.

"No, I don't," she told him. With three older sisters, life as an only child was totally alien to Pav, but he'd assumed that for Millie it made sense. "That still doesn't mean that you and me... I mean, it's ridiculous... I'm not... Look, I don't know what's going on but I can't–"

"So," he cut in, and watched Millie's eyes flash. Finding her on switch and watching actual emotions flicker over her face was fascinating, "I'll show you how a man interacts with a woman who he does not consider his little sister, okay?" Millie shook her head, her expression morphing from anger to panic. "I'll pick you up tomorrow at eight and we'll start there."

"I can't tomorrow," Millie said, perking up considerably. "I'm busy."

Pav narrowed his eyes. "Doing what?"

"Er... I'm going out."

"On a date?"

"Y-you don't have to sound so shocked," she told him, her chin going up a notch. If possible he found her even more attractive. He decided to leave it for now.

"We'll see, baby," he said before kissing the tip of her nose and pulling away. The strategically placed "baby" had the desired effect. Millie was too dazed to offer any further objections. He smiled wide at her, then sauntered to her door. "Tomorrow then," he said as he pulled it shut behind him.

Walking back to his car in sub-zero temperatures was a ball ache... and he smiled the entire way.

Chapter 12

I know pain when I see it

MILLIE BALANCED HER LARGE TUPPERWARE IN ONE HAND whilst the other unwound her huge scarf, as she made her way through the chairs to get to Gammy's usual table near the front. It was one of the El Compulsory Accessories that Millie genuinely loved. She was glad that taking what was basically a small blanket and wrapping it around your neck like a nomadic Mongolian goat-herder was considered fashionable: it was so warm, and Millie hated being cold. She'd left her coat on the racks by the door, so she just had on a large jumper, which nearly came down to her knees, and her leggings. Her hair was loose and she wore very little make-up. This was one of the few places where Millie didn't feel the overwhelming need to strive for perfection, so she could have a break from her up-do and relieve the constant pulling on her scalp. She smiled as she saw Gammy sitting in her wheelchair at their usual table, her tweed suit, high-necked blouse and white hair all perfectly styled as always. But Gammy was distracted. Very distracted. Millie froze, the Tupperware slipped from her grip onto the table, and her blanket scarf dropped to the floor.

"Hey, Millie," Pav said cheerfully, pulling his chair back and skirting Gammy to retrieve Millie's scarf from the floor. "You okay? You seem a little out of it." Millie's eyes widened in horror. She shot an accusing glance at Gammy, who shrugged and beamed back at her.

"Stop scowling and give your Gammy a kiss, darling," Gammy bossed. Millie leaned down and brushed the downy, lined, beloved cheek with her lips and Gammy gave her hand a squeeze. When she straightened she could see there was a distinct twinkle in Gammy's familiar grey eyes.

"What a gentleman," one of Gammy's best friends, Doris, who was sitting the other side of Gammy at the table breathed, as Pav handed Millie's scarf back to her.

"Come and sit down, Mils," he said to Millie, ushering her around Gammy to sit next to him at the small table as if it were perfectly normal to be in an old people's residential home on a Friday night.

"What are you doing here?" Millie hissed, nearly jumping out of her skin as he pulled her chair right next to his so that their thighs were touching, and draped his arm across the back of it (a possessive gesture totally unnecessary in a community room full of – predominantly – ladies with a collective average age of over eighty). Millie felt her stomach hollow out. Her heart was hammering in her chest. Only Pav could turn a woman on in the middle of bloody Northpark Residential Home's games night.

"You've kept quiet about this one, darling," Gammy said, now beaming at Pav. "He tells us you two have been close for a while. And to want to come down for Bingo – well: a man who can appreciate a good sausage roll and wants to get to know a lady's grandmamma is a jolly good sort in my book."

Millie leaned forward and pinched the bridge of her nose. This was not happening. The last thing she wanted was for Pav to know that the only meaningful social interaction she had was in a goddamn old people's home. She'd prefer that he wasn't party to the very sad details of her narrow life. There were some subjects Millie studiously avoided, like anything to do with her family.

"I *love* Bingo," Pav said smoothly, winking at Gammy, who Millie could have sworn blushed. (To still be able to blush at the age of eighty-six was a skill in itself.) "Millie and I had a date for this evening–"

"We did not h–" Pav reached under the table and gave Millie's hand a firm squeeze. Her mouth shut with a snap and she lost the power of speech.

"But I had an interesting chat with Don this afternoon whilst you were at ALS training, Millie," Pav said, giving her a quick wink before he turned back to Gammy. "He told me *all* about the bingo and yourself, Mrs Morrison, and I couldn't have Millie missing out on this tonight."

"You can call me Gammy, dear," Gammy told him, leaning forward to pat his hand. "A friend of Millie's is a friend of mine." Millie's eyebrows went up. Gammy knew very well she didn't have any friends.

She scowled down at his large warm hand still resting on hers, and shifted in her seat.

Pav's upper body jerked forward suddenly. "Who's this laddie?" Lindy asked, withdrawing her stick from its position held aloft to poke Pav sharply in the back. Pav turned to look at the small lady. Lindy was a hundred and one years old. Her back was so stooped that even standing she was at eye level with a seated Pav. Her hair was bright red – well, at least the half that wasn't the grey roots coming through was, and she never took off her long thick woollen tartan coat.

"Hello, I'm Pavlos." Pav's smile was met by a fierce scowl from Lindy.

"What's this now? Ah dinnae ken you were courting, Millie-girl?"

"I'm not," Millie said through gritted teeth. "Pav's a... I mean, Pavlos works with me... well, not with me, he works at the same hospital as me and–"

"And we're courting," Pav put in. Lindy started making a rather alarming wheezing noise, which Millie eventually realised was her form of laughing.

"You're all bum and parsley aren't you boy?" Lindy said in between her wheezes, giving Pav another poke with her stick – this time in his shoulder.

Pav turned questioning eyes to Millie and she shook her head. Lindy's turn of phrase was not always easy to decipher and wasn't helped by her strong Scottish accent. She had used that particular assessment before to describe the new vicar – Gammy had told her it meant she thought he was a blowhard.

"Um... yes?" Pav answered, making Lindy wheeze all the more.

"Buck up, Millie-girl," she said once she'd recovered herself. "You're a long time deid you know, may as well have your fun with the fellas being a bonnie wee lass. "

"Lindy I don't think–"

"Och, you're a wee scunner all right."

"Er..."

"Now then, where're my shortbreads?"

Millie pushed Pav's hand off her thigh and stood up on shaky legs to get the lid off the massive Tupperware she'd brought, then dished out a couple to Lindy.

"Keep 'em coming, lassie," Lindy told her as she shoved at least five into her handbag. Finally satisfied with her haul, she turned to Pav again.

"A nod's as guid as a wink tae a blind horse," she told him.

Pav gave her a bemused smile but nodded his head slowly anyway.

"I'll remember that," he told her solemnly, received another poke in the shoulder, and then chuckled as she moved away.

"I've got to go and hand these around," Millie muttered, gathering up the large box after depositing a plate of shortbread on the table.

"I'll help," Pav said, moving to stand behind her – too close, as seemed to be his wont, and she felt that hollow feeling in her stomach again. "You baked these?"

"She won the National Federation of Women's Institutes South West division annual baking competition with her Victoria sponge," Gammy told him, and Millie rolled her eyes.

"Come on then, Mary Berry," Pav said, giving her a nudge and a smile before they moved off to distribute the shortbread.

Pav spoke to *everyone*. He brought the whole, normally dull and lifeless, home to life. One man should not be allowed to have that much charisma, it was almost frightening. Millie wasn't sure that Doris Gibbs, who was well into her nineties and had had a new pacemaker fitted last month, would survive the heavy dose of Pav-charm complete with kiss that she received on her papery hand. He was a health hazard.

"So," he said as they made their way back to the table through his many admirers. "Baking, huh? I wouldn't have pegged you as the cupcake type."

"Baking is perfectly suited to me," Millie muttered. "It's all about precision, maths really, and it's *dull*." She paused, then added: "Like me," under her breath.

They were next to their table now and the bingo was about to start. Still, he laid his hands on her shoulders and turned her to face him. She forced her eyes up to meet his.

"Is that how you see yourself?" he asked softly, pushing back over her shoulder some hair that had fallen forward. She blinked but didn't reply. His face moved closer to hers until all she could see was the dark brown, almost black colour of his eyes. She sucked in a sharp breath as his citrusy masculine scent filled her senses. It was like she was hypnotized – in the middle of a residential home of all places. "*I don't think you're dull. Nothing about any of the time I've spent with you has been in the least bit dull.*" As if to emphasize his point his shoulder was shoved from behind by Lindy's stick again.

"Ye mak a better door than a windae," she shouted at him. Pav smiled, not breaking eye contact with Millie.

"What does she mean?" he whispered.

"She's... um, she's saying that you make a better door than a window." Millie glanced over his shoulder at an irate Lindy. "She wants you to sit down so she can see the bingo caller." He smiled and his hand moved from her shoulder to grab hers, tugging her down in the chair next to him and keeping their fingers linked as the caller read out the first number. For a good minute Millie was transfixed by the sight of her hand in his larger one. When she finally looked up she noticed that the caller had had to repeat the number several times. All eyes were on the two of them, and Gammy was smiling so widely she was practically bouncing in her seat. Millie could feel the blood whooshing in her ears and she felt out of control.

But somehow, a small part of her, buried deep in the dark for so long, was working its way back to the sun, and a tiny part of that black hole of loneliness was filled.

And she was terrified.

"You really don't have to do this," Millie whispered, darting a furtive look at a grumpy Lindy, who was perched on Pav's passenger seat.

It was safe to say that tonight had been one of the weirdest evenings Pav had experienced in a while. But that was fine. In fact, strangely, he found that the whole thing had been more than fine. He'd been annoyed when Millie had declined his dinner offer, so he'd decided to saunter down to the radiology department that day and change her mind. When he found that Millie was at Advance Life Support training, he got talking to Don and subtly coerced him into spilling the beans about where Millie spent her Friday nights.

Some men might baulk at crashing bingo night at a residential home and being the only man in attendance. But if there was one thing Pav was good at it was brazening out a potentially awkward situation. By the end of the evening he had those women eating out of his hand. He jerked forward with another poke to his shoulder and sighed – well, *practically* all of them eating out of his hand.

"Let's get going, laddie," Lindy shouted, and Pav felt yet another sharp poke in his shoulder. He was of course used to women being in his car; but they were usually under the age of a hundred, and did not in general prod him in the arm with their sticks for no apparent reason.

"I... really, it's okay," Millie said, wringing her hands and frowning up at Pav with huge eyes. "I always take her home after bingo. It's no trouble. She's just being stubborn." It turned out that Lindy was not actually a resident of the home; she just attended bingo night. Her son brought her and Millie always took her home. But tonight Lindy wanted Pav to drive her and she wasn't taking no for an answer.

"I'm taking her," he told Millie, reaching up for her hands and pulling them apart to hold in his larger ones. She started in surprise (something she always seemed to do when it came to physical affection) and her eyes dropped from his to fix on his shirt collar before she swallowed. He moved closer, focusing on her lips, and heard her quick indrawn breath as she stiffened. "I'll see you tomorrow," he said, his lips a hair's breadth from hers. Before she could pull away he brushed his lips against hers in a barely-there kiss, which was broken when he received another poke in the shoulder. Millie used the opportunity to snatch her hands away and take a step back. Pav grinned; he'd take her retreat for now but he had felt her shiver when their lips met, and he could see her dilated pupils even without direct eye contact.

"Okay, okay," he said, turning to Lindy and holding his hands up in surrender. "Let's get going."

As he drove away he looked in his mirror to see Millie still frozen on the pavement. Her hand lifted so that her fingers could touch her mouth.

"Yer a chancer, hey, laddie?" Lindy piped up from the passenger seat, and Pav smiled.

"That I am, Mrs McBride, that I am."

Pav eventually slowed to a stop in front of the small, terraced house. He got out of the car and pulled open the passenger door but Lindy remained firmly in her seat.

"I cannae get oot, laddie," she told him. "Millie always helps me." Pav nodded, extending his hand to take hold of hers.

"May I escort you inside, Mrs McBride?"

Lindy scowled at him but took his hand in a fierce grip to help lever herself out of the car.

Pav was taking nearly all her weight as he supported her onto the pavement. He couldn't imagine how Millie managed it at her size. As he walked her to her door his definition of slow pace took a hit. Lindy was practically going backwards. She stubbed her toe on the first step and some very colourful language was directed Pav's way (at least what he could understand was colourful, the rest was in Scottish).

"You dinnae tell me it were there!" she accused after her tirade was over.

"Sorry, I–"

"Millie always tells me where the step is. I dinnae have to tell the lass to do it either. She's a cannie as well a braw, that one." Once Pav had half-carried Lindy up the steps, the search for her keys in her cavernous handbag commenced. It was another five minutes before he had the door open, and once inside he realized that supporting Lindy up the steps was the least of Millie's duties. Lindy had him turning on her lights and *then* feeding her numerous cats.

"Lindy, I really must be getting–"

"Impatient lad, aren't you?" Lindy's low croaky voice interrupted him as she settled back into a large armchair in her sitting room. Pav suspected it was where she spent the night. "My Millie needs patience. Come over here." Lindy waved him over impatiently then when he was standing next to her chair she tugged on his hand so that he would crouch to her level.

"She needs kindness," Lindy said, her accent still strong but her words much clearer now. Pav suspected that when she wanted to Lindy could speak however she wanted. Her faded blue eyes caught his and it was like she was peering into his soul. "I've been around a long time, laddie. I know pain when I see it. You be kind to her, you ken me?"

"I understand," said Pav as the smile he'd been wearing faded from his face.

The truth was that he didn't. Not completely. But he wanted to. He wanted to understand a beautiful woman who shut herself off from others to such an extent that she had built a reputation as a notorious bitch. A woman whose anxiety didn't allow her to speak in public. A woman so brilliant that she would revolutionize a whole aspect of medicine, but had so little self-belief that she would not consider attending a single international conference. A woman who would go to bingo with her gran every week and make sure that an old lady she wasn't even related to was safely home, whilst showing little or no impatience or annoyance.

And he'd eaten one of those shortbreads tonight.

There was no going back after that.

Chapter 13

Lamb to the slaughter

"JUMPED-UP LITTLE KNOW-IT-ALL BITCH," LUCAS muttered under his breath, and Pav stiffened next to him. Millie was across the conference table, her face giving nothing away, but when his gaze flicked down to her hands he knew she'd heard the arrogant bastard: they were curled into tight fists and the whites of her knuckles were showing.

"Watch it," Pav growled low. Lucas flicked him a look of annoyed confusion before focusing back on the cause of his irritation.

"I've already consented the patient," Lucas told the room through gritted teeth, but his eyes were focused on Millie.

"You consented her for the wrong procedure," Millie told him, or to be more accurate she told his chest, before looking down at the notes in front of her. To everyone else at the meeting her words would sound cold, devoid of any emotion; only Pav could make out that fine tremor in her voice and the stress-induced tightening around her eyes.

"I consented her for an open procedure and that is what she is going to get."

"The evidence is clear that a percutaneous destruction of the stone would lead to enhanced recovery and lower post-op risk." Millie paused then, with visible effort, unclenched her fists so that she could pass a sheaf of papers across the table. Lucas levelled a furious glare at her before he snatched them out of her hands. Millie flinched and sat back in her chair.

She was scared.

Christ, Pav was going to lamp this moody bastard if he carried on like this. Lucas had settled back in his chair and was now glaring at the papers in front of him. Despite his annoyance, Pav had to bite back a smile. Millie was right: the evidence was clear.

"I'm not having this conversation," Lucas spat out. "I'm a consultant surgeon and this is *my* patient. You're not even a fully functioning junior doctor, if the rumours are true."

"Lucas," Pav said in a warning tone which Lucas, the dumb bastard, ignored.

"It's true," Lucas said, his voice rising along with the colour in his face. By contrast Millie's cheeks were almost deathly pale. "She's not a consultant. Why are we letting her dictate this stuff to us? Why is she even here? She's a junior bloody doctor but she can't even do *that* right. Pisses everyone off too much to be let out on her own."

The MDT was a weekly run-down of the complex urology patients and their treatment plans. The urologists, the pathologists, the oncologists and more recently the interventional radiologists were in attendance. Millie always came with another of the radiology consultants (until recently Pav had just thought this was because they travelled in packs, but he now realized that she was too junior to be radiology's official representative in the meeting. The fact that the useless blokes that generally accompanied her didn't seem to have any idea what they were on about didn't seem to matter). Usually Millie said very little in the meetings. Instead she whispered to the consultant she was with or passed them notes with the relevant information. It was unfortunate that Lucas had decided to be on his period the very same day that there was no consultant with Millie. Pav would be having words with the fucking radiology department, but not before he'd sorted this mess out.

"Sit down, Lucas," he said, managing to maintain his calm voice despite his growing anger.

"Pav, mate, I've already booked the patient onto my next list. This is complete—"

"Judging by this lot," Pav said, pointing at the now discarded papers in front of Lucas, "you booked her for the wrong procedure."

"Now just a—"

"Shut the fuck up," Pav snapped, and Lucas' mouth fell open. "Sit down." Still gaping at Pav, his mouth opening and closing in shock, Lucas sank down into his seat.

Pav was a "good lad". He was charming, sometimes outrageous, mostly easy-going; he did not issue sharp orders at meetings with an almost fierce expression on his face.

"Now you listen up, *mate*. I'm going to let it go this time that your knowledge of the subspecialty you have been specifically employed to deal with is woefully lacking. Open removal should only be used as a second- or even third-line option; even with a stone this large. I will be asking for an audit of your other cases to see if the management decisions were evidence-based or not. Millie might not be a consultant... yet. But that makes the fact she knows a hell of a lot more about this, frankly, quite scary."

Lucas narrowed his eyes and his mouth flattened into a disapproving line, but he sat back in his chair. Pav was the Surgical Director. Lucas had to accept his opinion, but from the way he glared at Millie through the rest of the meeting it was obvious he did not like it at all. Millie's hands stayed clenched so tightly it had to be cutting off the blood supply to her fingers, and when she wasn't doing that she kept straightening her files and lining up pens in front of her.

So when the meeting came to a close and Millie bolted for the conference-room doors Pav decided to let her go. She needed to calm down in her office. He would check on her later.

"So, she's *Millie* to you is she, Pavlos?" Lucas sneered as Pav pushed up from his seat. "Okay, I get it. First name terms and all that. Not a single other person I know calls her anything other than Dr Morrison – well, that is if you don't count Nuclear Winter as an actual name – but you, for *you* she's Millie."

"Careful, Luc," Pav muttered, feeling a muscle jump in his cheek.

"This proves once and for all that you will fuck anything that moves," Lucas said as the room started to empty out. "Christ, I already thought your standards were low after that locum last year, but I did at least think you went for actual live females rather than poorly reanimated corpses with as much personality as a badly programmed android. Jesus, didn't she freeze your dick off the first time?"

Pav's vision clouded with fury. It wasn't a totally alien feeling; with three beautiful sisters at the same school as him and a lot of arseholes wanting to trash-talk them when they couldn't get into their pants, Pav was no stranger to this type of anger. But it had been years since he'd been driven to it. Without thinking he spun around and stalked over to Lucas. His expression must have communicated just how angry he was, as Lucas took a quick step back, lost his balance and fell into one of the chairs behind him. Pav leaned over Lucas's shocked frame and pointed a finger into his chest.

"Don't you *ever* talk about her like that again or I swear to God it won't just be your career that's fucked up."

After Lucas gave him a sharp nod Pav released him and stepped back. Movement at the doorway of the conference room caught his eye and he turned to see Millie a few feet inside, her eyes wide and her mouth open as she regarded the two men in front of her. Lucas, still breathing heavily and bristling with fury, flew out of the chair and stormed around the table, before skirting Millie without giving her a second look.

"I... I came back for my bag," Millie's shaky voice came to Pav, and he watched her retrieve it from under the table. "I thought everyone would have left. I... um..." She started backing away towards the exit and Pav moved quickly to cut her off.

He took a deep breath to help calm himself down as she spun to face him. Not only had that stupid twat wound him up, but also he found himself unreasonably annoyed that he should always be trying to block Millie's escape from him in some way or another. Why couldn't she be like the vast majority of the other females Pav interacted with? None of those women ran the other way.

"Uh... hey, Mils," he said softly, watching with satisfaction as heat hit her cheeks and her lips parted on a sudden exhale, "how much did you hear?"

"I... um... you... you were very angry," Millie whispered.

"Yes, I was," Pav told her, narrowing his eyes as she took a small step back. "I'm sorry, Millie, but in my opinion he deserved a lot worse. But that's not what I want to talk about. I want to know how much of that shit you heard."

"I... you..." Millie spread her hands in front of her. "Do you do that a lot?"

"What?" Pav asked, frowning at her and cocking his head to the side.

"Get angry and... shout at people. Do you do that a lot?"

"He can take it, Millie," Pav told her. "If it makes you feel any better he likes to play Head or Gut when he's drunk: nearly broke my jaw last year. There's no way he's reporting me to HR for... *encouraging* him to sit in a chair."

"Head or Gut? What on earth is–?"

"So, now we've established that the little prick deserved it," Pav said, cutting her off, as he had no intention of explaining the dynamics of Head or Gut to Millie and giving her any more ammunition to keep backing away from him, "now, I'd like to know what you heard."

Millie looked beyond him to the door and sighed. "It's nothing I haven't heard before. Believe me. I don't even blame people for disliking me."

The matter-of-fact way Millie spoke about something Pav knew had to hurt her made his gut clench. He walked to her slowly, relieved that she wasn't backing away from him anymore, and reached up to put his hands on her shoulders.

"They don't know you."

Millie rolled her eyes. "If they knew me they would think I was even *more* weird than they already do."

She said it as if she was telling him the weather. To anybody else it would seem that it was all the same to her, like she was just stating a fact. But Pav could feel the tension in her shoulders under his hands. He was great at reading people, always had been. Millie might be the most complicated, guarded woman he'd ever met but he knew that, whatever she said, other people's opinions *mattered* to her. He knew that although her words sounded practiced, as if she'd accepted and become used to the situation, it still hurt her. But he also knew that he wasn't going to be able to change the way she viewed her life right now. He had to pick his battles.

"Tonight," he said, and she frowned in confusion at the rapid subject change. "I'm taking you out for dinner tonight. Okay?"

She bit her lip. "I can't tonight."

"Look, it's just dinner, I swear. I don–"

"No, really, I can't. It's book group again. They want to do it every week and... well... Kira's coming to pick me up this time." She lowered her voice to a whisper as if expecting Kira to leap out from under the table at any moment. "I'm a little scared of her to be honest. I didn't know how to say no."

Pav almost groaned. He'd been the one to coerce the girls into forming a bloody book group for the express purpose of coaxing Millie out of her shell. It seemed that his tactic was backfiring on him. Did they *have* to meet every goddamn week?

"I'll pick you up," he told her, and her eyes slid away from his to his shoulder.

"Uh... I don't even know where we're going."

"I'll find out, don't worry," he told her.

"Um... okay," she whispered, and then something beautiful happened. Her clear grey eyes met his and she smiled. It was the first spontaneous smile he'd managed to squeeze out of her. He felt like he'd won the Olympics. He started to lean in. She blinked as her smile dimmed and her eyes lost focus.

"There you are, Dr Morrison." An impatient voice sounded from the doorway and Pav's head jerked away from hers. Millie blinked again. They both turned towards the balding man who was pushing his way into the room. Pav recognised him as the head of the radiology department. The one who'd helped him bully Millie into presenting at the Grand Round. A wave of guilt swept through Pav, morphing rapidly into anger at the guy's next words. "I thought you'd got lost on the way back from the meeting. There's a whole stack of reporting to do, you know. We kind of need you down in the department." His eyes flicked from Millie to Pav's hands on her shoulders, and then to Pav himself. "Oh... er... hello, Pavlos, old chap. What are...?" He trailed off and rubbed his beard.

Much to Pav's annoyance Millie had lost that unfocused look in her eyes; it had been replaced with anxiety and her hands had coiled back up into tight balls. She pulled back from Pav and took two steps away.

"Barney," Pav said through gritted teeth.

"I was just getting back," Millie muttered, looking down at the carpet and pushing a rogue lock of hair, which had escaped the complicated hairstyle at the back of her head by sheer force of will, behind her ear. Pav caught her arm as she passed him.

"Sorry, Millie," he said as she shot him an adorable, wide-eyed, annoyed look. He bit back a smile. Millie's annoyance he could handle, in fact he was unreasonably heartened that she would show him that much emotion. He was getting somewhere. "But I need to talk to Barney for a sec. I'll catch you later, okay?" Millie nodded in vigorous agreement and pulled her arm away to leave.

"Right," Pav started as soon as the door closed behind her. "Barney, were you aware that Millie came to the meeting alone today?"

"Well..." Barney paused and scratched his head. "She seems to cope okay with this stuff and we're so stretched on the consultant rota at the moment that we may have just..." He trailed off and shrugged. "I'm sure Dr Morrison conveyed the relevant facts."

"Her name is Camilla, Millie for short. But *I'm* sure you already know that," Pav told him in a low voice.

"Uh... right, yes, of course, I–"

"You know as well as I do that a registrar issuing orders to a room full of consultants is not going to go down well, however many facts she manages to convey. And passing her off as a consultant is not going to work from now on. Not after Lucas's little outburst in the meeting."

"Look, we've all got to pull together at the moment," Barney told him. "If that means a perfectly capable junior like Dr Mor... I mean *Millie* has to go to a couple of meetings without her hand being held, then..."

"How many of your other registrars would you send unaccompanied to the MDT?"

"Uh..."

"How much of your reporting does Millie do?"

Barney's face went red and he looked away for a moment. Pav had his answer.

"I'm guessing it's *way* over the average consultant, right?"

Barney took a step back and started to rub the back of his neck. "Look, she's like a goddamn *machine*, okay? The amount of work she gets through... it's insane."

"You can't just keep using her for service provision and for the shitty meetings you lot are too bloody lazy to go to."

Barney let out a huff of breath. "She knows all the data, all right? She doesn't need us. Hell, when somebody does go with her they have to ask her how to wipe their own arse anyway."

"She was uncomfortable in that meeting, Barney. You know what a prick Lucas can be and how he's resisting this move towards the non-invasive stuff you lot deliver. It was like sending a lamb to the slaughter."

"A lamb?" Barney spluttered, his eyebrows shooting up into his hairline. "Have you met Dr Mor... I mean Millie? She's a bloody robot. My stapler has a bigger range of emotions."

Rage swept through Pav for the second time that morning. His hands clenched at his sides and he had an overwhelming desire to punch this joker in his smug, pudgy face. He took a step towards him, and at his murderous expression Barney's face paled. "She is *not* a robot. You know she isn't. You were there at that Grand Round and you saw what happened."

"Well... I... I... that was..."

"That was a sensitive, anxious-to-please, terrified woman being pushed beyond her limits."

Barney crossed his arms over his chest and narrowed his eyes at Pav.

"*You* were the one to push her there, you hypocrite."

"My mistake: I accept that. What I will not accept is more of the same. She has feelings. Christ, she's so frighteningly intelligent that she probably over-thinks, and worries more than any of us numbskulls." Pav sighed and some of the angry tension drained out of his body. "Look, she works hard for you and she enjoys it. I'm not asking for that to stop. All I want is for you to do what you're supposed to do: protect her, look after her. She's your trainee."

"She doesn't *need* any bloody training," Barney shot back. "She knows guidelines that haven't even been published yet."

"You still have to support her. She may know all the guidelines but she doesn't know how to implement them. How to put her case forward for them. It's your job to help her with that. You can start by calling her by her goddamn name."

Barney pushed his hand through his hair and shrugged. "Okay, okay. I'll try and... change things up a bit."

"Great," Pav said, forcing a smile and slapping Barney on the arm with a little too much force to be considered friendly. Barney gave him a nervous smile and started backing away. "Oh, and Barney?"

"Yes?" Barney turned back with his hand still on the door handle.

"I can make things difficult for you. Understand?"

Barney swallowed.

"Stop taking the piss with this, yeah?"

Chapter 14

Professor X

"Hello, Willy Fiddler," said Kira as she pulled open Millie's door with a huge smile on her face. Pav frowned. Millie had told him Kira was coming to pick her up at eight. It was now just before seven and Pav had been hoping to beat her to it and take Millie to the group instead.

"Kira, what are you wearing?" he asked as he pushed into the house.

Kira's partly blue hair was tangled up in a messy knot on the top of her head, complete with the couple of permanent small plaits with rainbow ribbons running through them. She had a loose man's wife-beater on, which displayed her black lacy bra at the sides and where it dipped down low in front, combined with a pair of totally indecent denim short shorts and cowboy boots. Who in their right mind wore cowboy boots in London after 1997? Her lipstick was the same blue shade as the streaks in her hair.

"Yo! Bitches! Get your arses down here pronto. We need to load up and roll out." Kira strutted down the corridor as she shouted, and went to the kitchen counter where there was a full shot glass waiting for her. She downed it and winced. "Badger me backwards, that stuff is rough as a hedgehog's arse."

"What the hell is going on? I thought this was book group night. Why are you downing shots?"

Kira slammed the glass back down on the granite and poked him in the chest. "Field trip, my man," she told him.

"Field trip?" Pav frowned. "Is that why you're dressed like a hippy prostitute on speed?"

Kira laughed. "How did you know that's the exact look I'm going for? Environmentally conscious, tofu-eating slut-whore."

"Kira?" a new voice sounded from across the room. Millie's friend Eleanor was standing in the entryway to the kitchen biting her lip. "I don't think she's going to wear it. Oh... hey there, Dr..."

"It's Pav," he corrected, smiling at El whose eyes went slightly unfocused for a moment. Extracting information from this one should be a lot easier than insane-bohemian-on-crack. "Would you mind telling me what exactly is going on?"

"Well–"

"Hey," Crazy Woman interrupted, punching Pav quite painfully in the arm. "Turn off the charm-beam, Romeo, and leave El alone. You'll find out soon enough. *Right.*" She moved towards a flustered Eleanor and took her by the arm to steer her out of the kitchen. "Show me the patient. I'll sort her out."

MILLIE PULLED AT THE HEM OF HER SKIRT AND WORRIED her bottom lip. Okay, so maybe she'd been feeling the sting of loneliness more over the last few years, maybe she wanted to break out of her self-imposed isolation a little bit. But going out in a tiny black dress with her hair totally out of control and her make-up in a style that could only be described as "skank" was a little extreme. When she'd told El she couldn't go out like that and started to search for another outfit, Kira had bowled into her room and snatched the far more conservative clothes right out of her hands, dumping them on the bed.

"I promise," Kira told Millie, shocking her by taking both her hands in hers and giving them a shake. "I promise you'll feel comfortable in this once we get where we're going."

"Kira," Millie forced out (she was still getting used to being on first name terms with this woman, leave alone handholding), "I can't wear this *anywhere*. I just can't. It's... it's beyond my limits. I'm sorry. I–"

"Do you trust me?"

"Er..." Millie trailed off. She didn't want to insult Kira, but she didn't know her. Not really. It took a long time for Millie to trust anybody. If she could have lied she would have, but she'd never been very good at that either.

Kira just smiled. "I don't blame you, Professor X." This nickname had been a new development over the last week; something to do with x-rays and Millie's "super-powered brain". Millie was not about to object; she vastly preferred it to Nuclear Winter. "I wouldn't trust me either, but I'm not a bitch. You only ever incurred the stick-up-her-arse Kira 'cause I thought you *were* a bitch."

"I'm sorry about that," Millie whispered, heat flooding her cheeks. "Sometimes I just don't know how to–"

"Hey," Kira said in a soft voice, one that Millie hadn't ever heard her use before, "I understand now, okay? You just be you, X. The rest of us need to get over ourselves. We find that mega-brain of yours intimidating sometimes, is all."

"Kira, stop embarrassing her. God, it's like a disease with you," a deep voice sounded from down the hallway.

Millie peeked around Kira's body and froze. She was kind of getting used to Pav now. In the two weeks since he'd first come to Gammy's home he had made lots of trips down to the department to hang out in her office with her and Don, bringing her coffees, asking unnecessary questions about that week's MDT, shooting weirdly hostile glances at the head of her department. He'd even come back to the residential home for bingo night again where they managed to convince him to give a talk on urology. The fact that most of the residents were women and didn't have the necessary equipment to make the in and outs of prostate disease relevant to them did not seem to put them off: it was a record turn-out for an outside speaker; Millie doubted that even Mary Berry would draw that much of a crowd.

Well, she may have been getting used to him, but that didn't mean his sheer physical beauty and charisma wasn't a shock for a few moments every time she saw him again. Tonight he had on a fitted shirt, which showed off his broad shoulders and well-defined chest. His jaw was covered in dark stubble, and his thick dark hair looked a good couple of weeks past needing a cut; the hint of a curl at the ends where it met his shirt collar gave Millie the inexplicable urge to throw herself into his arms and run her fingers through it. She was losing her mind.

Pav saw her as Kira moved to the side and, just like he had for the last two weeks whenever their eyes met, he smiled his wide, glamorous smile and she felt her stomach drop and heat hit her cheeks.

"Woah!" he said through his smile, covering the distance between them in just four long strides, then placing his hands on her hips and looking her up and down for a long moment, before his eyes came back to hers. His smile had dimmed and his expression was almost fierce; then he blinked and shook his head as if to clear it. "You look amazing," he whispered in her ear after he'd kissed her cheek. She felt him inhale at her neck for a long moment before he pulled back and took her hand in his. Once her dazed expression cleared and her mind started to function again, she regained the power of speech.

"Uh... hi," she breathed. His smile widened even more and he tugged her forward.

"Right, where's your coat?" he asked, glancing down at her legs and frowning. "You got any floor-length ones?"

"She has two floor-length coats," El chimed in. She was standing next to Kira in the hallway and for some reason they were both grinning at Millie like crazy people. "One black cashmere, one camel wool. I recommend the black cashmere." El slipped past them and rooted through the coats on the stand until she found what she was looking for.

"Wow, you guys sure know each other's wardrobes well."

"El is the best personal shopper in Selfridges," Millie explained. "She's picked out everything I own."

"Okay," Pav said with a little frown of confusion. "Er..." He trailed off: maybe it was better not to get into this zone. What did he know about women and fashion? Maybe they *all* had personal shoppers. He thought about Kira's general attire and then Libby's ratty trainers and jeans and rapidly dismissed that idea.

"I can't choose clothes for myself," Millie explained in a small voice. "I... I haven't got any taste and it's really important to me that everything is... I mean, that I look..." She looked down at her feet and pulled her hand out of Pav's to take the coat El was extending to her.

"You just want to look right," El said softly. "There's nothing wrong with that. And you *do* have taste."

Millie rolled her eyes. "El, I never make any comments on what you pick for me."

"I can tell when you don't like something," El told her as Pav took the coat from Millie's hands and held it out for her. It took a moment for Millie to actually put her arms through the relevant sleeves, she was so shocked by a gesture she'd only ever encountered with Don before. "You wrinkle your nose."

"I... what?" Millie had lost the thread of the conversation. She now had the coat on and Pav's hands were resting on her shoulders.

"When you don't like something. You wrinkle your nose. I always pick out the stuff that is nose-wrinkle free."

"I... really?"

"Millie. I've been working with you for the last five years. You know... I got promoted two years ago – I'm in management now. But I like working with you so much that I come down from the offices to the shop floor for your appointments. You have taste. What you're short on is confidence."

"Um... thanks," Millie said, giving El a weak smile, choosing to keep the fact she didn't agree with El to herself. Millie was a pragmatist: she knew what she was good at and what she wasn't. She was not good with people, and she did not have any taste. These were facts. They were not the product of low self-confidence.

"Okay, X and co.," Kira cut in, pulling her own lime-green fake fur coat on and ushering them all out of the door. "Time to roll out. I guess you can come with for the ride, Pretty Boy."

"I'm staying with Millie for more than just the ride, Kira."

Kira scanned his outfit and then smiled in a distinctly evil way.

"This'll be fun," she told them all as they left the house.

"THERE IS A MAN, WITH JUST A... A SCRAP OF LEATHER covering his genitalia, dancing in that cage," Millie said, her wide eyes fixed to the site above her and her mouth hanging open. "He's all shiny. Why is he so shiny?" She tilted her head to the side and squinted in order to get a better look, much to Pav's annoyance.

Libby burst out laughing. "Live it up, Mils, honey. There's more where that came from."

"This place is *full* of men," Millie whispered. "And they're all... I mean..."

"We're all bloody perfect, darling," a male voice drawled next to them. Pav instinctively pulled Millie to his other side and narrowed his eyes at the newcomer. "Oh," the man said, putting his hand on his well-defined chest over his heart, and throwing his blonde head back dramatically. "I *love* the caveman possessive thing, Gorgeous. Very Bruce Willis circa 1985. If only I were a five-foot-five beautiful submissive brunette. You'd have my ovaries rivalling Cirque du Soleil. Alas, apart from making me sport a slightly uncomfortable semi, your antics are all for nothing. My crumpet's buttered the other side."

Pav blinked, then relaxed his stance and a slow grin spread across his face. "Right," he said through a chuckle. "Of course."

"We don't get many real live vagina lovers in here, apart from the lesbians," the man said, cocking his head to the side. "You're obvs not gay. Bi-curious?" He gave Pav a cheeky wink. Pav held his hand up and shook his head.

"Nope," he said firmly. "Definitely in the vagina-loving camp here."

The new man sighed and fixed his gaze on Pav's chest for a moment. "Shame," he said. "Your grooming is *almost* up to our standards. You'd have to get rid of that lot though." He tapped Pav just above his shirt collar where some of his chest hair was showing.

"Mark!" Kira flounced into the middle of the group and threw her arms around the new man. He swung her from side to side and gave her a kiss on the cheek. "Ki-Ki, darling, you didn't tell me you were bringing real-life hetero men with you. I thought it was girls' night?"

"Yes, well. He decided to tag along," she said, then added: "Bi-curious," in a stage whisper that was louder than most people's speaking voices. Pav felt a few eyes near their group turn towards him and he sighed. He'd already had his arse pinched at least twice. Kira's little announcement would be like a red rag to a bull with some of these blokes. "Right, everyone. This is Mark. I met him in the sexual health clinic."

"Ki-Ki," sighed Libby. "You *worked* together in the sexual health clinic."

"Shut up, Lib!" Kira hissed. "We like peeps to think we have to go get checked regularly. Makes us more edgy – right, Marky Mark?"

"Definitely, darling," Mark drawled. "If people don't think I'm getting my end away enough to have to have monthly swabs taken my reputation will be in tatters." Mark peered round Pav to smile at Millie. Pav shifted to the side and ushered her into the group. Her face was pale and she had a death-grip on her handbag. He took his arm from her shoulder and prised one set of her fingers off the bag, transferring the death-grip to him.

"You must be this girl-genius I've heard so much about," Mark said, softening his tone from Obnoxious Gay to Warm-Hearted Auntie for her benefit. Pav glanced at Kira and she gave him a small nod. Mark had been briefed about Millie. "You look like a sexy Audrey Hepburn. I can't wait to show you around."

Millie's lips were pressed firmly together. She closed her eyes for just a moment, then managed to prise them apart and force out a "thanks". Mark smiled even wider.

"Okay, Screaming Orgasms all round, ladies!" he shouted.

Tara and Claire screamed in agreement. Millie shot Pav a panicked look as Mark took her arm.

"I don't think I–" she started to say as she resisted being pulled forward toward the bar and away from Pav.

"Don't worry, darling," Mark said, tugging her firmly along. "You don't need your bodyguard in here. He, on the other hand..." He trailed off as she glanced back at Pav. A couple of bystanders had sidled up to him in the space of the last thirty seconds, and by the feel of the large hand on his arse they were wanting to test just how bi-curious he was prepared to get. "Well, let's worry about that later."

Chapter 15

Fuck all the men

THE WORLD FELT AS IF IT WAS EVER SO SLIGHTLY TILTED TO the side. Millie hiccupped. She was drunk. For the first time in her twenty-six years she was actually inebriated. When she'd arrived at the bar with Mark and discovered that Screaming Orgasms were in fact alcoholic beverages in shot glasses, she'd informed him that she didn't drink.

He frowned. "Ex-alcoholic?" he'd asked.

She told him no but had explained about the interaction of alcohol with primary and secondary targets within the brain causing alterations in gene expression and synaptic plasticity, leading to long-lasting alteration in neuronal network activity.

After that speech he burst out laughing and slammed a shot down in front of her. "I think it's time to shake up your neuronal network, baby," he told her. "I'm sure there'll be enough brain cells up there to take the hit."

Millie had looked from him to the shot and frowned. Mark's reasoning was totally devoid of logic. Nobody could afford to "shake up" their neuronal network.

"Leave her alone, mate," Pav said, sliding the shot glass

down the bar away from her. He'd managed to extract himself from his male fan club in a surprisingly short space of time. "She doesn't drink. There's no *way* she could handle spirits."

Millie narrowed her eyes at Pav. His arms were crossed over his chest and his mouth was set in a stubborn line. As far as he was concerned that was the end of it: Millie was not going to be drinking. For some reason his arrogant assumption caused an unfamiliar surge of defiance to sweep its way through her.

Screw logic.

Where had logic gotten her anyway? Locked away in her house night after night. Living within her narrow limits. Almost universally disliked by the entire hospital. Slowly she reached forward, leaned across Pav and closed her fingers around the small glass.

"Millie?" Pav asked, but before he could react she slid the glass over to her, lifted it to her lips and drank it down in one gulp. Surprisingly it was creamy and sweet, with just the hint of a burn. The last alcohol she'd drunk had been at a wine tasting with her parents when she was sixteen. That had made her wince and turn a little green much to her parents' disgust (they told her it was a three-hundred-pound bottle and that it was just *typical* that she couldn't appreciate the quality).

"Woah, babe!" Tara said from Millie's side. "You could have waited for us." Millie watched as the rest of the group downed their own shots together, all except Pav who had ordered a beer and was rolling his eyes.

"Don't worry," Kira said, throwing her arm around Millie and giving her a squeeze. "We'll get another round."

"Look," Pav objected as another tray of shots appeared in front of them, "I really think this isn't a very–"

"Here's to the men we love," shouted Kira as everyone raised their glasses. "And here's to the men that love us. But the men we love aren't the men that love us, so *fuck* all the men and here's to us!"

As if on automatic pilot Millie gripped the small glass again and threw back another lot of the sweet-tasting liquid. She blinked when she was done, a warm feeling spreading out from her stomach. For some reason the environment didn't seem as intimidating. More of Mark's friends joined the group. They were all gorgeous, they were all loud and they were all very, very gay. None of them gave Millie the chance to be shy.

After her fourth Screaming Orgasm Kira and Tara dragged Millie onto the dance floor. She'd never danced in her life. Not once. For some reason Pav came with them, staying close to her the entire time (this did not seem to deter the majority of the men they passed from giving him the eye, occasionally winking, and more than occasionally squeezing his bottom, which seemed to amuse Kira to an extreme degree). Millie didn't understand why Pav was still there. She thought he would have left ages ago. Maybe he was enjoying the attention? Although, judging by the scowl on his face, that explanation was unlikely.

Even though Millie had never danced before (and she suspected that without the Screaming Orgasms she wouldn't have considered it now), it wasn't as scary as she'd always thought. The dance floor was crowded. They were all pushed together so much that most of her body's movement was being dictated by other dancers. Pav's body was right behind hers and his heat was soaking very pleasantly into her back. She felt dizzy a couple of times but there were strong hands on her hips when she started to waver. Kira's dancing was hilarious. In the restricted space they had available she pulled what she termed as some "serious shapes" including squatting to her knees and doing a kind of Cossack dance, star-jumps and poorly executed headstands; at one point she even managed a forward roll. With Kira's antics and the sheer number of people dancing around them, Millie was fairly sure nobody was watching her. She felt free to move, free to laugh, just... free.

Pᴀᴠ ᴘᴜʟʟᴇᴅ ʜᴇʀ sᴏꜰᴛ ʙᴏᴅʏ ɪɴᴛᴏ ʜɪs ᴡʜᴇɴ ʜᴇ sᴀᴡ ʜᴇʀ head start to bob about two minutes into the taxi ride. Within seconds she was fast asleep tucked into his side. Her chest was rising and falling in deep, even breaths and her body was totally relaxed against him. It was weird seeing her that way. She was so tense the entire time when she was fully conscious. Her face looked completely different without that tension. Despite the make-up she looked about twelve years old.

But you could still see the shadows under her eyes, and her cheekbones were still way more hollowed-out than they should be. Just like the usual no-alcohol rule, Pav had only ever seen Millie eat the most disgustingly healthy stuff. No, scratch that: he'd never actually *seen* her eat. He was guessing she was too nervous for that when he was hanging around her office. But he did see the various salads and green juices she had on her desk at lunchtime. A girl her size should not, in Pav's opinion, be firing down terrifyingly healthy food like *quinoa* (he wasn't entirely sure what that was but it was on the label of most of her sad-looking offerings).

She shifted and slung a slim arm over his stomach. A sober Millie would be horrified by the position they were in, but at the moment she was far from sober. If it had just been the shots she did before the dancing, maybe Pav wouldn't have had to half-carry her out of the club. It was after the dancing and when they settled into one of the booths that things really got hairy.

Kira (who was pretty hyper when sober – drunk, she was bouncing off the walls) declared loudly that they were going to play "I Have Never". As it turned out Millie had never done *anything*. Between them and the rest of the table, most sexual acts, some of which even Pav hadn't heard of, were covered, and all manner of other things besides. If you hadn't done what was described, you drank. If nobody had done it, the speaker drank. Millie drank every time. Pav suspected that if someone had said "I have never eaten without cutlery" she would have drunk. So from being a complete teetotaller, Millie had become the biggest pisshead at the table.

Some of this Pav liked very much. It meant he had the opportunity to see her giggle. She was smiling and giggling most of the evening: Mark and Kira were funny fuckers, Tara and Claire were just plain outrageous and El and Libby were live wires in their own slightly less obvious ways. Millie didn't say much but when she did speak it was quite often hilarious – whether she intended it to be or not:

"It was his fault!" shouted a drunken Tara, referring to the fact she had conceived a boy four years ago. A lovely boy whom Tara adored, although he was a little wild and difficult to contain in her small flat. "*His* balls were full of boy sperm. That's the problem."

"Actually," Millie interrupted, slurring a little and with her tiny grin on her face. "Your vagina was probably hostile. It's all to do with the viscosity of your mucus and how easy the male or female sperm can penetrate through it."

The whole table erupted at that. Eventually Tara managed to ask, through her tears of laughter: "Are you really calling my vagina hostile? I'm not sure whether she's insulted or pleased. Not every day you hear that your fanny's a badass."

So yes, hearing Millie laugh and seeing her relax her guard a little was definitely a plus. But Pav was not so keen on the nearly-passing-out-in-the-club section of the evening, or the bouncers looking at him like he was a rapist as he carried her out to a taxi (Kira, El and Libby had managed to convince them that this was not the case, but not before they'd attracted a fair amount of attention on the street outside). And now Millie wasn't just semi-conscious, she was completely out for the count.

The cab pulled up outside her house and Pav gave her a gentle shake.

"Hey," he said. "Millie, we're here, love." He thought back to the last time he was at her house and remembered the sizable alarm system he saw her programme before they left earlier. He was going to need that code from her. She gave a small groan and then burrowed herself further into his side, her body relaxing deeper into sleep.

Pav sighed and told the driver his address instead.

Chapter 16

Pathetic

"WHERE AM I?"

Pav opened his eyes to see Millie standing by the bed. He'd wrestled her unconscious body out of the car and carried her up to his flat earlier, having to grapple with his keys whilst still supporting her next to the door. After a few attempts at waking her up on the sofa in the living room in order to get some fluids down her, he'd carried her to his bed, taken her shoes off, put her in the recovery position, and pulled the duvet over her small curled-up body. Now she was up and out of the bed, looking confused and swaying slightly on her feet.

"I don't feel very well," she whispered, and Pav sat up to turn the bedside light on. He felt bad that he'd slept in the bed with her now, but he'd been too worried that she would vomit in her sleep to leave her.

"Right," he said, sliding out of the covers and walking around to her side slowly. Her face was a little green and her wide eyes were fixed on his chest.

"Woah," she breathed, her pupils dilating as she swayed on the spot again. Pav glanced at his bedside clock; it was two in the morning and he was willing to bet Millie was still as drunk as a skunk.

After a moment she slapped a hand over her mouth and her eyes went even wider. Pav covered the distance between them in two long strides, picked her up by her hips and lifted her quickly into the bathroom to bend her over the toilet. She heaved and then was violently ill. Pav remembered every detail of *his* first encounter with alcohol and he felt her pain. She continued retching a few more times as he held her hair at the back of her neck with one hand and then wetted a cloth with the other, which he passed to her when she was finished. She sat back onto the cold tiles, blinking rapidly and looking in danger of passing out again. Pav sat down next to her and pulled her onto his lap, handing her the cloth. She allowed this, a testament to her less than sober state, as she wiped her face and neck.

"Pathetic," Millie mumbled as she let the cloth fall to the floor, seeming to lose even the strength in her arm to hold it.

"What, love?"

"I'm pathetic," she said. "Can't even drink like a normal person."

"You're not pathetic. All of us have gone through this."

"Pathetic, weak, over-emotional," she continued, as if she hadn't heard him.

"Er..." Pav frowned down at her face. *Over-emotional?* She was way off base with that one. Her head was resting on his chest and she was staring off into the distance with unfocused eyes. "Millie, that is a load of bollocks. What makes you–"

"Weakness, that's the trouble with me. Weak, weak, weak, all the time. No backbone." Her words were trailing off as she relaxed against his body. All this was stated with absolute conviction; she believed every word and she had done for a long, *long* time. It was all so far from the truth that Pav struggled to think how she could have come up with it, unless...

"Millie, baby, who told you that? You know that none of what you're saying makes any sense."

Millie let out a small humourless laugh, so hollow that it sent a weird shiver up Pav's spine.

"If you knew me better, you'd agree with them, I promise," she told him, again with absolute conviction.

"But who are *'they'*, honey?"

"You're so beautiful," she told him, ignoring his question and her voice fading as her body became heavier with sleep. "Everything about you is so bright, so... magnetic." She gave another of those little humourless laughs. "Your charisma and mine are off the scale, just in different directions."

"Baby—"

"I like it when you call me that," she whispered.

"I know," he said pulling her closer.

"I could go my whole life with just that. Just that word. One word from a man like you..." She trailed off and he watched her eyelids flutter closed. He sat there for a moment, oblivious to the cold tiles, with her small, warm body curled up in his lap. His chest tightened as he replayed her words. One thing he knew for sure as he sat there was that *he* would be the one who found out who had made Millie believe those things as absolutes. And he would be the one who made her see them for the lies they were. Her guard would be up again tomorrow. Those shields would be firmly back in place. But Pav had experienced that small window of insight now and there was no going back as far as he was concerned.

MILLIE WAS LYING ON SOMETHING WARM AND FIRM. HER head was banging and her mouth was so dry her tongue felt like sandpaper. With great effort she opened one eye and then the other. What she saw wrenched her straight out of her drowsy state and into immediate panic mode. She was lying on a chest and staring at a tanned column of throat. To her horror her arm was slung over the six-pack of a man's abdomen in an almost territorial way and her leg was hitched over his muscled thigh. She jerked back, making a noise halfway between a grunt and a squeak from her dry throat and sat up. Looking down, she was horrified to see that she still had on the dress from last night and that it was a crumpled mess. Her eyes felt scratchy and when she rubbed them her hands came away with telltale black smudges on them. She reached up to her head, and the bird's nest of hair she could feel sitting there caused another involuntary squeak.

"Hey there," a low, rumbly voice said from her side, and she jumped in reaction. When she turned and looked down she saw his beautiful dark brown eyes staring up at her; his stubble was thicker than she'd ever seen it before and the sleepy smile on his face made him even sexier than normal.

Millie's face paled and she flew off the bed, running for the bathroom, and slamming the door in her wake. Once there she stared at her reflection in horror. Her eyes were ringed with black and her hair was matted on one side of her head. She sat down heavily on the edge of the bath and screwed her face up; embarrassment, acute and painful, washed over her. The feel of her nails digging into her fingers helped keep a check on the anxiety, and she tried to slow her breathing down. A knock sounded at the door and her eyes flew wide, one hand going to her chest and the other going up to ward off any intrusion.

"Millie?" Pav's voice sounded from behind the door, no longer edged with sleep. "Babe? You okay in there?"

Millie's throat worked as she tried to get some form of word out, but the anxiety was too much.

"Okay, I'm gonna come in now. I just–"

"No!" she screamed, then covered her mouth with her hand. She closed her eyes again. If he didn't already, after this Pav would know that she was truly nuts. He had pushed the handle down but released it at her scream. Millie dug her nails into her forearm, pinching as hard as she could this time, and forced herself to speak. "I mean. No, sorry. I'm... I'm going to have a shower."

"Okay," said Pav, sounding uncharacteristically unsure. "I'll be right outside though, yeah?"

Millie managed to shower. She scrubbed away all the make-up and she washed her hair with Pav's shampoo. That in itself was not easy. She'd used the same shampoo and conditioner for years. She never varied her routine. It took her an hour and a half to get ready in the morning and she always had all of her products around her to achieve it. She needed her *things*. Pav didn't even have conditioner. When she was done she found a huge dressing gown and put it on, rolling up the sleeves so that her hands could grab toothpaste and search for a spare toothbrush. She stood in front of the door for a full minute after she had finished, working up the courage to push the handle down.

"Hey," Pav said softly when she finally emerged. He was sitting on the bed, facing the door, and she had the feeling he'd been there for a while. Thankfully he was wearing jeans and his chest was now covered in a worn T-shirt – but he still looked unfairly perfect. His lips twitched as Millie tried to walk in the dressing gown and nearly tripped over the long towelling material, but his smile died as he focused on her face. "How are you feeling?"

Flashes of last night had been flicking through Millie's

mind since she'd woken up. She remembered feeling so comfortable on the car journey from the club. God, some of the snippets of what she'd said whilst curled up on a bed of Pav were making her cringe. She had vomited! She, Camilla Morrison, had actually experienced an ethanol-induced emesis.

"Hey." She flinched when she realised Pav was now standing right in front of her. He reached up and enclosed both her hands in his warm ones, then slowly prised them apart. "What the hell?" he said, concern adding an edge to his voice. "What's this?" Millie blinked, then looked down at her inner forearm. Some of the bruises had come out from last night and there were fresh marks that she'd given herself just now.

"It's fine," she muttered, trying to pull them away, but he kept hold gently but firmly.

"It's *not* fine," he told her. He moved her back to sit on the bed and forced her arms to stretch out in front of her for him to inspect. "What on earth–?"

Millie felt her face flush and she jerked her hands away again before getting up in a sudden movement and backing away from him.

"You... you don't understand," she said, her voice annoyingly shaky. "I get s-stressed and then..." She trailed off, acutely embarrassed. It was weakness. She knew that. She had been told that since she was a child. But the bruises always faded, they never left any scars so her parents had tried to ignore it.

"Okay, okay. I'm sorry," Pav said, his voice back to soft as he walked towards her slowly with his hands held up in front of him like he was approaching a wild animal. "But... what's got you so stressed *now*?"

"What do you mean?" Millie asked, her voice rising with disbelief. "Of course I'm stressed. I don't have my clothes. I washed my hair with your shampoo. I don't have any make-up with me. I'm wearing your dressing gown. I... I... of *course I'm stressed.*"

Pav looked confused and honestly Millie understood his pain. To a man like him, who actually looked *more* attractive tousled after sleep, her concerns over her appearance must seem bonkers.

"Look," she said. "It's really important to me to look... to look..."

"Perfect?"

Millie shook her head. "No, not perfect but... just not... me. I need my make-up. I need the stuff El picked out for me to... to..."

"To hide," Pav told her, and she blinked. "You need it to hide. You need a mask."

Millie had never really thought about it that way, but it made a lot of sense. She nodded slowly. "And... to be in control," she added in. "I... when I was a child I didn't... I didn't prioritise the way I looked. In school I was a few years ahead of myself. The children in my classes largely ignored me as I was so much younger. The kids my age... well, they didn't always ignore me. Which was..." She looked away for a moment, imagining Pav at school: good-looking, outgoing, intelligent in an approachable way. "I wish they had ignored me," she whispered after a long moment, and his hands gave hers a squeeze.

"You were bullied."

Millie shrugged. "By the time I left school I *knew* appearance mattered. I tried during my first degree, but the results were disastrous. I met Eleanor when I was eighteen."

"You had enough money for a personal shopper when you were eighteen?"

Millie nodded. "I had enough money to buy my *house* when I was eighteen. I have... a lot of money."

Pav smiled. "Clearly."

"It's not my money. I mean, it's Gammy's money. My Grandpa owned a lot of property, most of it in London. When he died most went to my father but Gammy was left a hotel. A very nice hotel in central London. She sold it and put it in trust for me, one I could access from eighteen. She wanted me to be able to... she wanted me to be financially independent... from my parents."

"From your parents? But why–"

"Look," Millie cut him off. She was in no fit state for a discussion about her parents. Her head was still banging and she had to find her clothes. How was she going to get home? "I really need to get going and..."

"Right," Pav said briskly. "Breakfast for you I think. And painkillers. But first." He reached for her and before she knew what was happening she was being held in his strong arms against his warm body. He was hugging her. It was one of the few spontaneous hugs Millie had ever had and she could feel her nose stinging in response.

"It's only me here, okay?" he muttered into her hair. "You don't have to worry about looking a certain way."

Millie breathed in his scent mixed with the washing-powder smell of his T-shirt, and sighed. Usually physical contact like this made her anxiety worse. But with Pav it was like his warmth was seeping though her skin and into her bones. The sound of his strong, steady heartbeat sent a wave of calm over her and she began to feel the stress lift away.

"And I think you look beautiful in my dressing gown," he said.

"Liar," Millie whispered, but she was smiling despite herself. She even found her arms coming up to hug him back.

Chapter 17

This is me

PAV MADE HER PANCAKES.

Millie hadn't eaten pancakes since Gammy made them for her on a Shrove Tuesday ten years ago (luckily Millie had managed to fire one down before her mother threw away the mix, muttering about carbs and "religious nonsense"). The Martakis Pancake-Making Process seemed to involve every bowl, whisk, and pan Pav owned and covering most of the surfaces in his kitchen with flour, egg and milk. Millie tried several times to help clean up, but was ordered to sit back on the breakfast-bar stool, where she continued to watch the destruction in abject horror. When Pav triumphantly placed a pile of pancakes covered in bits of banana and hastily-applied Nutella, he laughed at the look on her face.

"This is killing you, isn't it?" he asked, sweeping his arm out to the kitchen war zone and then kissing her on the nose. She looked at her pancakes and then back and up at him. For some reason she found it was becoming easier to meet his eyes.

"Please, *please* let me clean this up now," she begged. "It is genuinely causing me physical pain."

"Nope," Pav told her through his cheeky grin, which together with his dishevelled, flour-sprinkled hair and sparkling eyes made him almost unbearably attractive. "You are going to get some calories down you along with some ibuprofen. Only way to cure a hangover. I'll tackle this lot later."

Looking around the flat Millie could see that there was a fair amount of mess that Pav had no doubt been meaning to "tackle later" for a while. Urology journals were scattered over a good amount of the available surfaces, empty mugs sat on side tables, a pile of what looked like clean washing was sitting on one of the chairs. She bit her lip and he laughed again. "Think of it as therapy."

"Therapy?" Her eyebrows went up and he laughed even harder.

"Hey, look," he said, his voice softening as his laughter faded to an understanding smile. "I know you like order, and that's okay. It's just that maybe you could start feeling like that's a choice and not a..." he paused and searched her face, reaching up to tuck a curl of her rapidly drying hair behind her ear, "not a compulsion." Millie felt her face heat and she looked away from him. There was no way she could attempt to deny that order and control were a compulsion for her.

"I'm sorry," Pav said, dipping his head in an attempt to maintain eye contact, "lots of people have trouble with that type of shit. You know that, right?"

She nodded and her hands started twisting in her lap until his larger ones came up to cover them. "Er... that psychologist guy. Do you just work with him for the project or...?" he was talking cautiously now, obviously sensing that this was a subject he needed to tread carefully with.

She raised her head and met his eyes, taking a deep breath in and releasing it slowly. "I have mild obsessive compulsive disorder and more severe social anxiety," she told him. "I have had cognitive behavioural therapy with Anwar and it... it helped me. I can function... but it didn't fix me, not completely."

"Right, sorry, I didn't–"

"This is me, Pav," Millie said softly. "It's not something I can change. I have limits and I've had to accept that–"

"But that's not true," Pav cut in, moving right into her personal space as she sat on the stool. "You've been going beyond what you thought were your limits for weeks now." He dipped down to give her a brief kiss on the lips as if to make his point.

"Pav, I..."

"How many people did you have supporting you the last time you had CBT?"

"I..." She trailed off again and bit her lip. The truth sounded too sad even for her.

"I mean... did your family know that you... ?" Every time Pav had tried to wheedle out any information about Millie's family other than Gammy, she'd shut him down. She even avoided asking him too much about his own, in case the subject of hers came up.

"No."

"Did anyone–"

"Look, I'll eat one of these things," Millie said, poking at the stack of pancakes dubiously. "But I can't eat all five."

"All right, love," Pav said softly, tucking that rogue curl back behind her ear again and kissing her on the side of her head. She knew this discussion wasn't over. Pav was stubborn and he got his way. But for the moment she was willing to do anything, even make an extremely unhealthy breakfast choice, if it meant he would drop this subject.

By the end of that Sunday morning her hair had dried into its natural waves. She still had no make-up on, and she was wearing a combination of Pav's shirt and his tracksuit bottoms with the waist rolled down and the legs rolled up several times. She looked ridiculous. Pav told her she looked "totally gorgeous". Which was another one of his charming little lies.

Her hair had not been allowed to be in its natural state for years. She always ironed it with straighteners and then pinned it back with an army's worth of hairgrips. Hardly anyone saw her without make-up on. She'd been taught how to apply it by experts, bought whatever they recommended, then painstakingly applied her mask every day. It was ridiculous to believe that she could look anything other than a complete state without all that.

But after the first hour in Pav's small flat the strangest thing started happening. It was the way he looked at her, his casual affection, his obvious and pushy reluctance for her to leave (he went as far as to hide her shoes in this endeavour): it all started to have a slow effect on Millie. She started to actually believe that maybe, maybe she didn't need the mask. Maybe she could be acceptable without two hours of prep work. Maybe even beautiful. It was another one of her limits that she had thought was set in stone, and another one that Pav was smashing through with his usual impatience.

He insisted on driving her back to her house that afternoon, before letting himself in and announcing that he was taking her out again that night, declaring: "I need to catch you whilst you're free and still in a defenceless hangover zone of numb acceptance."

The idea that Millie's social calendar was so full that Pav had to seize his opportunity was laughable. She told him so. He just smiled, grabbed the tea she made him and settled in to watch the rugby on her television whilst she went off to get dressed in some normal clothes. After staring at her wardrobe for a full minute Millie realised that she did not have an outfit prepared. This was the first spontaneous thing Millie had done in... well, ever. So she had to phone El, who had gone from nice-and-friendly-but-kind-of-because-she-had-to-be,   to extreme-friendliness-and-nosiness-to-the-point-of-being-rude, in the space of a couple of weeks.

As expected she gave Millie the third degree about Date With Pavlos Outfit, and at one point she squealed, actually *squealed*. It was clear that Eleanor no longer considered herself just Millie's personal shopper, she considered herself a friend. Once she'd finally managed to pin El down on what she should wear and thanked her (normally Millie's thanks would be in the form of large tips – something that El had always tried to refuse, saying she got commission on what Millie bought, but something Millie had been adamant about), she felt a stab of anxiety. Millie liked Eleanor. She had been comfortable with the client/personal-shopper relationship. It didn't rely on Millie's less than sparkling personality: it was a business. It was well defined. This, being friends with El: this was more unstable. What would happen when El realised that Millie was more work than she was worth? At least before it was less... messy. She sighed and moved to put on her perfect outfit before applying her perfect make-up. Whilst waiting for her hair straighteners to heat up, Millie looked at herself in the full-length bedroom mirror. Maybe it *was* time for a bit more mess in her life. She shook out her waves and frowned at her reflection before moving to the hair straighteners and turning them off.

Then they went to the pub.

Millie had never been to her local pub before. It wasn't something that would ever occur to her to do. But with Pav she did it. And she did it with her hair loose around her shoulders. She didn't once have a panic attack. Not once did her throat close over and her voice seize up. They talked about the paper

Pav was writing; she tried to explain a statistical method to him, but when he grimaced, she offered to simply do the stats herself.

"But, I *love* statistics," she told him when he objected. "It's like... it's like drugs to me," which made him laugh. Millie loved making Pav laugh. She told him about Rosie: how gifted she was, all the crazy things she used to make Millie do in that hour before she dropped her at nursery (woodlouse-hunting round the back of the hospital had been the weirdest little excursion).

Millie didn't drink anything (after last night she wasn't sure she would ever drink again) but she did eat carbs after five o'clock, something she had not allowed herself to do in five years. And not just any carbs: *chips*. Even as a child she'd rarely ever eaten chips.

And they were bloody fantastic.

MILLIE SMILED AS SHE HEARD THE NOW FAMILIAR kerfuffle that always heralded Pav's arrival at her office. Anywhere he went he was like a celebrity walking into an awards ceremony. He called out greetings, teased people, high-fived porters; his confidence was like a force of nature.

"Hi, Pav," she said, not taking her eyes off the screen until he came up behind her and spun her chair to face him.

"How did you know it was me?" he asked, and then, in typical Pav style, gave her a brief hard kiss before she could answer.

"You make a bloody entrance like you're the rooster in a hen house," muttered Don. He tried to look annoyed but Millie couldn't miss his lips twitching. Don liked Pav, and for some reason he liked Pav for Millie.

"You're just as much of an attention whore, you sly old

dog," Pav teased as he plucked Millie out of her seat, sat in it himself and settled her back down on his lap. "I've seen you working the radiographers like a potter at his wheel. They're all over you up there."

"Bugger off," Don muttered, his cheeks pink as he went back to his one-finger typing.

"Don, I don't mind doing that for you. If you just–"

"You keep your fancy-man entertained and out of my business," Don said, determinedly stabbing at the keys one at a time.

"I shouldn't be sitting on you," Millie whispered, and tried to get up but Pav's arms around her waist kept her firmly in place.

"He told you to keep me entertained," Pav said. "Maybe you should do a dance or something?"

Millie rolled her eyes and stopped struggling to get up. Pav tended to get his way. "What are you doing here?" she asked as one of his arms released her waist and his hand started stroking through her hair.

This was the thing about Pav. Casual affection seemed to be hard-wired into his DNA. And he was slowly but surely getting Millie accustomed to it. After years – in fact if truth be known practically her whole life – of little or no physical affection, it took some getting used to. What scared Millie the most was that she was not only growing accustomed to it, she had almost begun to crave it. The buzz she felt being this close to him, how secure she felt in the circle of his arms, the way his warmth and charm calmed her anxiety. It was all incredibly addictive, and when it was taken away she wasn't sure how she was going to handle it.

Millie would love to be the type of person who just shrugged and decided to "cross that bridge when I come to it", but she was a natural worrier, a planner, much more an "analyse the data, predict all the possible outcomes and obsess over them in a futile fashion"-type person.

"We've got to talk about the conference," he told her, and the warmth that had seeped through her in his presence was chased away by fear. She knew Pav was treading carefully with this. She knew he didn't want to push her too far again, not after witnessing how bad she could get that day in the lecture theatre; but she also knew he was determined that she consider it. Having had no luck in convincing Millie to speak, the conference organisers were now going to anyone they thought could make her go. She'd had the CEO of the hospital down here twice to discuss it with her. The head of the radiology department cornered her at every available opportunity to see if she would change her mind. And Pav, being the Surgical Director, was being contacted as well.

"I can't," she whispered, pulling away firmly this time to stand next to her desk and cross her arms over her chest.

"It's groundbreaking stuff, Millie," Pav told her, his voice betraying some of the understandable frustration he must be feeling with her. "You have to at least *go* to the conference. I know it's hard but—"

"No," she said, taking a step back from him and feeling her nails dig into her forearm. Of course Pav didn't miss a thing. He frowned and his eyes dropped to her folded arms; then he stood, walked forward into her personal space and gently prised her arms apart. He gave the red marks on her forearms a dark stare before looking back up at her and searching her face.

"Okay," he said, his voice now soft and the frustration from a moment ago gone. "We'll talk about it another time. But you know I can go with you. I wouldn't let you do it on your own."

Millie nodded and let out a slow breath she hadn't realised she'd been holding. She knew Pav was convinced he could change her mind. He understood her, to a certain extent – but the reality of her limits wasn't something he could fully comprehend. Going to a conference with hundreds of strange people and actually speaking in front of them: that was so far beyond her limits he may as well be asking her to fly to the moon.

She knew the frustration in his voice from earlier was just the beginning. He wouldn't put up with her neuroses forever. Eventually they would annoy him too much. But until then she had decided to simply enjoy being with him.

"Right, so Saturday," he said, and she blinked up at him.

"Uh... what about Saturday?"

"My sister is engaged."

Millie cocked her head to the side and frowned.

"Oh... um, congratulations?"

"You're coming to the engagement party."

Millie's eyes went wide and she tried to pull her hands together but they were being held firmly by Pav's much stronger ones.

"I... I can't meet your family," she whispered.

"Why not?" Pav was frowning. He was genuinely confused, as if meeting his family was not a massive deal and as if she would not be a complete embarrassment to him.

"I just... I..."

"They'll love you. My mama loves everybody."

Chapter 18

Unique

"MAMA, WHAT IS YOUR PROBLEM?" PAV HISSED ONCE THEY were out of Millie's earshot. He'd left her with two of his sisters (the actual bride to be had disappeared half an hour ago) and some of his cousins so he could try and talk some sense into Mama. Glancing over there as he pulled Mama away he could see Millie's mouth was set in a thin line and her knuckles were white from her grip on the champagne glass she was holding. To be fair to them his sisters and cousins were trying, but the short cold responses they got in return were not showing any signs of improving. He sighed and turned back to Mama; he had to make this quick.

"My problem? *My* problem? That woman is the one with the problem. My God, your Great Aunt Agathias was more pleasant, and she only opened her mouth to spit at people near the end. At least that was entertaining. Pavlakis *mou*, please; she is a walking corpse."

"Mama!"

"Ugh! Look at her. Designer clothes, looking down her nose at everyone. Does she ever smile?"

"She's shy. She has... anxiety."

Mama's eyebrows shot up and she blinked once. "That woman is not worried, she is cool as a bowl of tzatziki."

"You don't know her, Mama," Pav said through gritted teeth. "Give her a chance."

Mama rolled her eyes. "What was wrong with the last one? Now she knew how to have fun."

"Yes, Mama, she did know how to have fun. She had a lot of fun; some of it, I might add, was not with me."

"Okay, okay. So nobody's perfect. At least she spoke. This one, all she does is stand there with a sour face."

At that moment Pav felt a small hand touch his arm. To his horror Millie was standing right next to him, her face pale and the hand that was holding the champagne shaking very slightly.

He should have known when he picked Millie up that this was not going to end well. She'd opened her door to reveal an elegant outfit, totally at odds with his family's vibe: her mask of make-up was secure and her hair was back in that bloody roll again. He didn't say anything, thinking that she needed her armour to face a situation she found intimidating.

He should have said something.

As soon as his mama and sisters saw her when they arrived at the Greek restaurant hosting the engagement party, Pav knew they saw the wrong Millie. Then she had recoiled from his mama's hug, her body held stiff with shock. And Pav couldn't explain that Millie just wasn't used to random hugs; that you had to work up to it with her. That when she was tense and worried about making a good impression she froze up. His sisters had just looked at each other in bewilderment, and his mama looked hurt. Millie had managed a stiff little hello to everyone, avoiding all eye contact, but since then she'd been more or less silent.

His uncle had welcomed her to his restaurant, doing the

standard boast of how it was the best Greek food in London. Telling her that "Even the Greeks, they come here from Greece to eat my food." Millie had managed a non-committal hum, taken a sip of her drink and tried to smile. But the smile-attempt was by far the worst fake smile Pav had ever seen from her, and that was saying something. It was more of a grimace really.

"I think I'm going to go home now," Millie whispered to his shirt collar. "I... I have a headache." Pav glared at his mother, who pressed her lips together before biting one of them and looking guilty.

"No, don't go yet," Mama said, moving forward and into Millie's space. Millie drew back until Pav's arm halted her retreat and he felt her stiffen. "I have cure for headache, passed from my mother's mother to my mother, to me. I will get it. Wait, wait."

"Mama, I don't think..."

"Ah! Here it is." Mama withdrew a small pot of tiger balm from her handbag and unscrewed the lid. There was nothing his mama did not think Tiger Balm could treat. "I just need to..."

"No," Millie said as Mama's fingertip came up toward her temple. Then she twisted away from Pav and took a step back. Mama frowned and her hand slowly lowered back to her bag.

MILLIE TRIED TO GET MORE WORDS OUT, BUT THE HURT look on Pav's mama's face froze her vocal cords. *Why couldn't I just be normal? For once: just this one time, why couldn't I just fit in?* she thought. But there were so many people packed into that small restaurant, and they all talked at her at the same time. They were all so colourful and warm and *loud*, just like Pav. The difference between them and her was jarring.

"Talia, let the girl be." Millie turned to the soft voice of Leon Martakis, Pav's father, the only person in the room who did not seem to have taken an instant dislike to her. After hug-gate with Talia Martakis at the start of the evening, Leon hadn't attempted physical contact other than to touch her arm for a moment as he told her softly that she was welcome. Unlike his family, he seemed to be a quiet, watchful man. "Not everyone uses Tiger Balm as a cure-all – in fact you may be the only one."

Talia sniffed and gave a jerky nod. "Of course," she said as she shoved the little pot back in her bag.

"I... I'm sorry... I..." Millie couldn't think of a single expla-nation that wouldn't make her look even more weird or rude.

Talia waved dismissively and plastered a fake smile on her face. "Don't worry. Eat, eat. I... I have to sort the cake." She turned and bustled away. Leon gave an apologetic smile before he followed after her.

"I've got to go," Millie said once they were out of earshot.

"Look, calm down a minute," Pav told her, his large hands coming up to steady her upper arms. "You just need to relax and–"

"I'm sorry. I can't do this. All these people... you have so much family."

"You were okay in the bar the other night and then the pub with me," he said, a hint of impatience creeping into his voice. "Why can't you think of it like that?"

Millie closed her eyes and took a deep breath. "That was different. I didn't *have* to make a good impression on anyone at the bar, and I was with just you at the pub. You don't under-stand how this works... how *I* work."

Pav sighed and lifted one of his hands off her arm to run it through his thick hair.

"Maybe this was a bad idea," he muttered. Millie felt the strange combination of bitter disappointment that she'd let him down and relief that he knew this was a step too far for her. "Okay, look, I've just got to tell Mama I'm leaving, then–"

"No," Millie shot out, "please, *no*. You stay."

"Millie, I'm not leaving without you. I brought you here. I'm taking you home."

The irritation and impatience was clear in his voice now, and she felt her heart sink into her stupid designer shoes. But she knew him well enough after these last few weeks to see the stubborn set of his jaw as a sign that he wasn't backing down. So she sighed and gave a quick nod.

"Wait here," he said. "I'll just be a minute."

Once Pav was pushing back through the crowd and Millie was on her own, she noticed the people around her staring. There was nowhere she could look without catching someone's eye. The worst thing was that they all gave her encouraging smiles, which she did a poor job of returning. She edged along the bar until she was at the back wall, and then slipped through the exit into the deserted corridor.

Finally alone, she leaned back against the wall and let out a long breath, her head falling back onto the plasterboard with a soft thump. After a few seconds she heard a loud sniff and her eyes flew open. She scanned the empty corridor for a long minute before movement in the coat rack caught her eye. There were two large racks of coats pushed up against the wall. And some of the coats on one of them were shaking slightly. Millie's head tilted to the side as she approached them. Another muffled sniff came from their direction and she narrowed her eyes. Before she knew what she was doing, she'd pushed her hands into the coats to part them, and was confronted by a tear-stained woman sitting on the floor behind.

"Uh... hi," Millie muttered, too shocked for her vocal cords to seize up. She recognised the woman as the bride to be: Pav's sister, Allegra.

"Hi," Allegra muttered miserably, and Millie wondered what she should do. If it were her sitting there she would want the coats drawn back and to be left in peace. But should a tearful nearly-newlywed be left alone to cry it out? As a compromise Millie pushed through the coats herself, sat next to Allegra and pulled them back into place behind her. They sat in silence for a few seconds. Millie thought about asking Allegra if she was okay, but as the answer to that was obvious she decided against it.

"You're Pav's girlfriend," Allegra said in a shaky voice.

"Uh... not really," Millie admitted. It wasn't as though she and Pav had formalised their relationship. And, having never had a boyfriend, Millie didn't really feel qualified to answer. In any case Allegra seemed to be grappling with bigger problems than the official status of Millie and Pav's relationship.

"I... I..." she gasped, her chest rising and falling rapidly, "I can't... breathe. I feel sick." Millie turned to face her and watched the colour drain out her face as panic washed over her features. Her breathing was getting faster and faster, her eyes looking a little wild.

"You're having a panic attack," she told her.

"But... I feel like I'm... like I'm dying."

"You're hyperventilating. Your alveolar ventilation is excessive and too much carbon dioxide is being removed from your blood. This causes hypocapnia, and a respiratory alkalosis, which produces certain symptoms: dizziness, tingling in the hands and feet, sometimes even loss of consciousness."

"You... you're a bit weird," Allegra managed to get out.

"Yes," Millie told her. "But... I'm also right. So, slow your breathing down. Not deep breaths, just slower. And use this." Millie dug into her purse and pulled out the paper bag she kept in there for emergencies. "Create a seal around your mouth and breath into it, slowly."

After a minute with the paper bag Allegra's breathing steadied to a normal pace and the panic left her eyes. Millie slowly reached up and took the bag away.

"Woah," Allegra said in a hoarse voice. "That was insane. I've never felt like that before."

"Panic attacks are not fun," Millie told her, stashing the bag away.

"How'd you know so much about them? Are you a doc like Pav?"

"Yes, but I knew how to deal with a panic attack way before I studied medicine. I have them all the time."

"You do? Well that... sucks."

"Yes." Millie sat back against the wall alongside her new companion. They sat together for another minute.

"Aren't you going to ask me what I'm panicking about?" Allegra eventually asked. "Actually, don't worry. You'll think I'm being silly."

"I once had a full-blown panic attack over a Pot Noodle. I can't think of a sillier reason than that. Didn't make it any more fun though."

"Uh..." Allegra let out a snort of laughter. "Sorry, sorry," she rushed to say after, "it's just I've always thought Pot Noodles were fairly unthreatening foodstuffs."

Millie smiled, the relief of being shielded from the party making her facial muscles loosen up again. "I read the ingredients. It contains monosodium glutamate, which can poison the nervous system. I was convinced my nerves were de-myelinating. They weren't."

"Christ, that's the last time I eat one of those buggers."

"Oh no, my reaction was out of proportion. There are studies that..." Millie blew out a breath of air. "Sorry, you don't want a rundown of all the studies. I find it hard to stop myself sometimes."

"You're pretty unique, aren't you?" said Allegra through a smile.

"If by unique you mean strange, then yes, you'd be right."

"I like it."

"Uh... thanks?"

"You're not my brother's normal type."

Millie's smile died and she focused on her hands in her lap. "I know," she whispered.

"That's not a bad thing," Allegra rushed to say. "If you'd met some of the other birds he's brought home..." She trailed off and sucked in a breath through her teeth. "Let's just say, it's good you're a bit... different."

"I don't think your mother thinks that," Millie said, swallowing the sudden lump in her throat.

"Oh!" Allegra said, clearly surprised that the unfailingly friendly Talia could have taken a dislike to anyone. "I mean... sorry. She's usually–"

Millie waved her hand as if to dismiss it. "Don't worry. Pav already told me she loves everyone. I'm a special case. I... I'm not good with people. My panic attacks can be like yours just was, or they can be more of a sustained anxiety reaction which makes it really tricky for me to speak or smile or... well, it makes me seem... cold."

"What a pain in the arse for you."

Millie sighed. "Yes, it is."

They sat in silence for another minute. Millie began to wonder if she should climb out of the coats in case Pav was looking for her.

"I'm pregnant," Allegra said out of the blue.

"Uh... okay," replied Millie, not quite knowing what to say in this circumstance.

Allegra let out a stuttering breath.

"I found out yesterday and..." She sighed and looked up at the ceiling. "My sisters' weddings were perfect. Everything just how Mama wanted, and now I'm–" she sniffed as a lone tear tracked down her cheek "– I'm going to be a huge blimp on my wedding day. And we won't be able to afford all the John Lewis nursery furniture I've had on Pinterest since I got engaged, not with all the money we're ploughing into the wedding.

"But Mama's excited. She's over the bloody moon. Already picking out baby stuff, taking over. She doesn't understand why I'm upset." Allegra huffed and leaned back against the wall. "My family can be suffocating. All this fuss. We're not even at the wedding yet and still everything is so... so much."

Millie shrugged. "They love you. Your happiness will be important to them. Tell them what you want *your* wedding to be like."

"Is your family like this?"

"No."

"Must be nice."

Millie forced herself to look up into Allegra's eyes; she needed to maintain eye contact when she imparted this next piece of information. "My... parents are about as far from your family as you can get, and I promise you it is not nice. Not even close."

"Right," Allegra whispered, her eyes going soft as she scanned Millie's face. Millie looked away quickly and started pushing to her feet. She'd given away far too much, but nobody who was surrounded by as much love as Allegra should ever resent it or the family giving it. That was a waste. Allegra stood with Millie and caught her hand.

"My mascara okay?"

Millie took in the racoon eyes and shook her head. "Wait a minute." Within seconds she'd extracted cleansing wipes with which she took away the black marks; powder foundation, which she swept over Allegra's face; liquid eye shadow that she blended over her lids in seconds; and mascara that she applied with even strokes. Allegra looked at herself in Millie's hand-held mirror.

"Bloody hell! You're like some sort of make-up ninja. This is insane. I look better than when I arrived. Thanks so much."

"Um…" Millie trailed off as she bit her lip, stuffing the rescue kit she never left the house without into her clutch.

"Hey." Allegra took her by the shoulders and turned her so they were face to face. "Don't worry about the fam, okay? They'll come around."

Millie nodded, but whilst Allegra seemed to like her she doubted there would be any coat-hiding, talking-them-down-from-a-panic-attack opportunities with the rest of Pav's family members in the near future. She heard Pav's irritated tone in her head again and suppressed a grimace. There were unlikely to be any more opportunities for his family to "come around" anyway. Who wanted to be dragging a killjoy like her to parties like this?

"But *why* do you have to go now? You're always the last to leave. Your sister is getting married. Why would you break her heart this way?"

Allegra rolled her eyes at her mother's voice, which had now filled the corridor.

"Mama," Pav's voice cut through the air, loaded with exasperation, "I have *three* sisters. This is Allegra's second engagement party. She's having a rehearsal dinner in a month. I haven't seen her most of the night. I don't think I'll break her heart by leaving."

"If it wasn't for *that woman* you wouldn't even–"

Much to Millie's horror Allegra chose that moment to plunge through the coats, dragging Millie behind her.

"Mama. Shut up," Allegra hissed as she emerged on the other side. She brushed off her skirt and put one hand on her hip, as if springing out at people from behind coat racks was perfectly normal behaviour. Millie's wide eyes flew to Pav, who was frowning first at his sister and then at her.

"What the hell?" he muttered, taking a step towards her. "Hey, you okay?"

Millie was stressed, a little shocked, embarrassed, and her hair was mussed by the coats. And that was why she jerked away so violently that she stumbled back a step when Pav went to take her hand. He froze for a moment before his face went from a soft to a hurt expression. Talia's eyebrows had shot up and her lips were pursed. Millie was guessing that outright flinching away from her son's touch had not endeared her to his mother any more than before.

"I've got to go," she whispered before spinning on her heel and practically running out of the door.

She heard Allegra say, "Mama, listen," just before the door slammed behind her at the same time as she heard Talia mutter something in Greek which was not very nice at all. Millie wished she hadn't been bored enough whilst she was doing her Chemistry degree to learn the classics. She wished she didn't understand. (But when you were fourteen, at university and had no friends, boredom was pretty much guaranteed)

As she jogged down the street in her heels it occurred to her that maybe this was better. This way Pav could see her limits in a real way. He could see how integrating someone like her into his life would have an impact on everything, not least his family.

Chapter 19

At least try to be normal

"Yes, of course," Millie muttered as she closed her eyes and sank back into the sofa. Her hand, clamped around her phone, was starting to ache and she realised she'd been gripping it hard enough to cut off the circulation to her fingers. Beauty lumbered over to her and watched her tense face for a moment before heaving her great body up on the sofa and laying her huge head on her stomach. She started and let out a small bark of laughter.

"Camilla?" her mother's shrill voice sounded into her ear. "What on earth is going on there? Are you listening to me?"

"Yes, mother," Millie said, sinking her free hand into Beauty's thick fur and letting out a breath she hadn't realised she'd been holding. Seriously, this dog was like magic. She should be used as a therapy animal. The smell was something she needed to work on (Jamie had told Beauty earlier, quite accurately, that she "smelt of arse"), but anything that could make Millie feel even marginally better when she was speaking to her parents was a miracle.

"Are you... are you with someone?" Her mother's tone was

incredulous. Millie couldn't exactly blame her: her whole life had been almost entirely devoid of social interactions. Her mother knew how bizarre it would be for her to be with a friend.

"No," Millie sighed. "It's just a dog."

"A dog?" Her mother's voice rose in horror. "Please don't tell me you have gone and got yourself a bloody dog? What a ridicul–"

"It's not my dog, Mum. I'm... I'm at some else's house."

"But... why?"

The assumption that Millie was not there in a social capacity, despite the fact that it was actually her birthday that day, for some reason made her chest tighten. She was surprised. Millie had become adept at letting her mother's words wash over her for quite some time. They no longer had quite the power to inflict pain that they had when she was a child. She'd built up a tolerance to them. And anyway, compared to the poison her mother was capable of spouting, this was nothing. It *was* fair to assume Millie would be on her own on her birthday; she'd never spent any of her birthdays any other way.

"I'm babysitting."

"You're what? For Christ's sake, Camilla. What is wrong with you? Why are you wasting your time *babysitting*? Is this purely to annoy me?"

Millie sighed again. Throughout her life her mother had constantly asked that question.

"Have you made this purely to annoy me, Camilla?" – in response to a card she made at school when she was six, which was covered in glitter and shed on her mother's jumper.

"Are these dolls on the floor purely to annoy me, darling?" she'd said a year later, before scooping up the Barbies and dumping them in the rubbish whilst she muttered about gender stereotyping and pointless plastic crap (Gammy had given them to Millie and they were her favourite toys).

"There's dirt on the carpet, Camilla," she'd said once when Millie was eight, pointing to a tiny streak of black on the carpet. "Do you traipse through the house in your outdoor shoes purely to annoy me?"

Millie sometimes thought that perhaps she *had* been born purely to annoy her mother, because that was all she seemed to do. During her cognitive behavioural therapy the subject of her parents had come up as a source of stress. Various different methods of processing their comments were discussed, but after Millie had recounted a few examples Anwar's mouth had got tight and he'd told Millie to just stay away from her mother as much as possible. When Millie asked if that was avoidance, knowing that she was supposed to be facing her problems head on, Anwar broke from his usual casual, serene persona.

"You stay away from those fucking people at all costs," he'd said, his voice firm and dictatorial instead of soft and non-confrontational. "You hear me Millie? Stay away."

So over the last five years she had managed to stay away. She saw her parents once a year at Christmas (last year she hadn't even had to see them then as her father had a conference in America), and for some reason her mother rang her every year on her birthday. This was ostensibly to wish her many happy returns, but normally the phone call had more to do with her mother wanting something.

Her parents never asked why Millie rarely took their calls; Millie suspected that their pride wouldn't let them, but she also doubted that she was sorely missed. Her father barely knew her anyway, and her mother had repeatedly told her throughout her life how annoying she was. Her limits were not really tolerated by her parents, despite the fact that in recent years Millie had started to suspect that her mother had quite a bit to do with them being there in the first place. She had been a painfully shy child, which her parents had found intensely frustrating and embarrassing.

"The bloody girl's not right in the head," her father had moaned on the way back from a family political function he'd taken Millie and her mother to. Millie had been seven and had not spoken a word the entire afternoon. Her vocal cords had simply frozen up on her. "They thought she was backward or something. What an embarrassment."

Yet another thing Millie had done "purely to annoy" her parents. Not that it ever crossed their minds that a shy child would find hordes of adults intimidating, or even that it was bizarre to expect your child to hold a conversation when all the attention they received at home was a series of barked orders. Or to expect your child to play seamlessly with the other children there, when at school Millie had very little social interaction with her peers, due to her already working with children four years older (something her mother had pushed for so that Millie wasn't "held back" by being with children her own age).

Millie heard the key in the front door and frowned. Jamie and Libby had only left an hour ago and she had told them to stay out as long as they wanted. To be honest she'd been hoping Rosie would stay up later with her, but halfway through the game of Junior Monopoly Millie had bought for her, Rosie's yawns had become almost continuous. And she'd only lasted a minute into the story Millie read to her whilst they cuddled in bed before she'd been sound asleep.

Heavy footsteps echoed through the hallway and Millie turned to look over the back of the sofa.

"I've got to go. I–"

"Now you listen to me, young lady." Millie barely registered the sharp note in her mother's voice; she was too busy staring at a scowling Pav, who was filling the doorway from the hall into the lounge. "I don't care what excuse you think you can come up with. You *will* come to this function. We need to support your father in his campaign."

"Wh-what?" Millie muttered. "I can't..."

"Camilla, you've been testing my patience for five bloody years and it's about to run out. You know what, I've been thinking that it would be nice to see more of my mother-in-law. We've been discussing getting her moved to another, more convenient home out here in Hertfordshire. I don't think it's healthy for her to be stuck in the city; pollution and all that." Millie slowly turned away from Pav as all the colour drained from her face.

"What?" she whispered. "You can't–"

"Seeing as your father has power of attorney for her medical and financial needs, I think you'll find that I can do exactly that. Moving out of all that smog is an eminently reasonable idea. And it's not as though she has the capacity to make her own decisions anymore, is it?"

Millie squeezed her eyes shut and clenched her jaw, an uncharacteristic rage sweeping through her body, so strong it made her voice shake.

"You can't do that. She's happy there. Disrupting her routine, the people she's with, her carers. It would be... it would be cruel. Even you–"

"Don't be so melodramatic, darling, for goodness' sake. She's totally away with the fairies. She wouldn't know if we stuck her on a rocket to the moon."

"She had a stroke, Mum," Millie said through gritted teeth. "She can't walk very well. Her mind is–"

"Spare me the sentimentality, Millie," her mother spat out. "What a load of tosh. Your grandmother is demented and getting worse all the time. She didn't speak a word to us last time we went to that godforsaken place."

Millie took an unsteady breath and let it out slowly. Her parents hadn't visited the home for over two years. It wasn't godforsaken, in fact it was one of the best residential homes in the country. Gammy was happy there. She didn't cope well with change. And the reason she wouldn't have spoken to them is because she hated them both. It had nothing to do with dementia.

"You don't even pay for the home," Millie said; to her annoyance her voice broke at the end. She took another steadying breath to try and strengthen it: if there was one thing Valerie Morrison detested it was weakness. "Please." Another wave of bitterness attacked her at being reduced to begging this poisonous woman. "Please, don't do this."

"Well, *maybe* if you come and talk to me and your father *in person* at the party conference I'll reconsider. Maybe."

Millie lowered the phone slowly into her lap and sat back on the sofa, staring forward into the middle distance and not even registering the sofa dip as a big body took up the space next to her.

"Millie?" her mother's shout floated up from her lap. "I need an answer. Why can't you just be normal for a change? Why are you always such a basket case?" Pav stiffened by her side and with a jolt she realised how close he was and what he must have overheard. At lightning speed she snatched the phone to her ear again.

"Okay, you win," she said, her voice devoid of emotion now. "I'll come to the dinner."

"Good," her mother said, her tone back to cool and collected now that she had got her way. "And darling?"

"Yes?"

"At least try to be normal could you? For once."

"Right... normal." Millie ended the call before her mother could respond. She doubted Valerie wanted to stay on the line any longer anyway, and it was highly unlikely that she'd planned to wish her a happy birthday.

"Who was *that*?"

She turned to look at Pav. His scowl from earlier had been replaced by concern. The last thing Millie needed now was Pav's pity.

Over the week since the engagement party, Millie had done a very effective job of avoiding him. After she'd run away that night, luck had been on her side and she'd managed to jump straight into a black cab. By the time Pav had arrived at her house, she'd double-locked all the doors, turned off all the lights, and texted him to let him know she was home okay. She heard him knocking and calling her through her letterbox, saw the texts and missed calls on her phone, but decided that it was better if she ignored him. It was a coward's way out, she was well aware of that. But Millie *was* a coward. She was weak and spineless and she did not fit into Pav's world. Better he found that out now. If she was honest she'd thought that would be the end of it. That he would move straight on to pastures new. But over the weekend he'd texted her and rung her so many times she lost count. At first the tone of the messages he sent was concerned and slightly apologetic for his family, for putting her in that position. But after a day of them being ignored they'd become less concerned and more annoyed.

I'M SORRY XXX

MILLIE. COME ON. STOP BEING STUBBORN XX

TALK TO ME. YOU'RE BEING RIDICULOUS X

. . .

I DON'T DESERVE THIS

THAT LAST TEXT HAD BEEN FIVE DAYS AGO AND WAS THE final one she'd received. He'd tried to approach her twice at work, but luckily she'd had an excuse each time to get away. In the urology MDT, he'd glowered at her throughout the whole meeting and tried to block her exit at the end, but Barney, the head of her department, had come with her (since the disastrous MDT a couple of weeks ago they'd tightened up on her going to meetings alone) and when Pav tried to get in their way as they were leaving, Barney had propelled Millie out of the room in a rare show of protectiveness. And then she thought she'd caught him giving Pav a decidedly smug look as they passed him, which was... weird.

For the last two days Pav had given up trying to talk to her. When she snuck down to the cafeteria for a coffee to take back to her office yesterday, it was just her luck that he was there having a late lunch with the theatre team; his list must have overrun. She thought he was going to try and approach her again but he just spared her a quick scowl, rolled his eyes and went back to joking around with the rest of the table. Although she'd breathed a sigh of relief, her chest ached for the rest of the day. So much so that when she'd finished all the reporting for the whole department late that night, she'd found herself picking up her phone, pulling up his messages, and her fingers hovering over the screen to reply.

She'd just typed in *I'm sor* when an image of his mama's face, complete with disgusted expression, flew into her brain, followed swiftly by that of Pav's hurt face after she'd flinched away from him. It was no use – and if she was suffering this much heartache after such a short time with him she dreaded to think what she'd be like if she stayed with him any longer. She had limits; better she learn to live within them and stay sane with her heart intact.

"I... What are you doing here?" Millie said, staring down at her phone again. She heard him huff out a frustrated breath as he angled his body towards hers.

"Millie," he said in a warning tone, "I want to know who that was you were talking to."

"Uh... "

"Millie, I'm not leaving until you–"

"My mother."

Chapter 20

"When... when do we do that again?"

"What?" She chanced a look at Pav. His eyes were wide with surprise and his mouth had fallen open. "Why–?"

Millie jumped up from the sofa in a sudden movement and rounded the coffee table to the other side. He was too close. The smell of the washing powder from his clothes, mixed with his own more woodsy but clean scent, was too much at that close range. The couple of glances she'd allowed herself of him were enough to add to the brain scramble: his dark hair, slightly ruffled and just a week or so past needing a haircut; one of those T-shirts that pulled tight across his chest; dark stubble, a testament to his "no shaving unless I have to go to the private hospital" rule – he looked like a scruffy *GQ* model. He was almost too beautiful to be real.

"What are you doing here?" she asked again, forcing herself to make eye contact because, *seriously*, she needed to know why. Why was he doing this? What possible interest could she hold for him?

The concerned expression was replaced again by one of annoyance as he gritted his teeth.

"Jamie told me you'd be here, okay? I have a key anyway so I can take this beast out on my days off, and I thought, seeing as you have to be here if you're looking after Rosie, that you might talk to me." His hard voice, softened. "I deserve some sort of explanation, Millie. You can't just shut me out of your life and expect me to accept it. That's not how relationships work."

Millie bit her lip and looked away. Her distinct lack of even friendships was a testament to the fact that she had no idea how relationships worked, but the fact that Pav felt the need to explain that to her felt humiliating. She owed him something.

"I'm sorry," she said finally after a full minute of silence. "I just don't think we suit each other and... I..." She shrugged helplessly. "Look, Pav, your family were nothing but nice to me and I snubbed them. I clammed up and I hurt their feelings. You should be with someone like you, someone that lights up a room, who can cope with meeting a perfectly nice family for the first time without becoming a mute freak."

When she glanced back up at him the annoyance in his expression had morphed into a soft, slightly frustrated look.

He sighed. "You're not a freak."

A huff of air left Millie as she rolled her eyes to the ceiling and then back at the big man sitting on the sofa. "I go silent when I'm stressed. I can't cope with people I don't know touching me. I pass out from panic attacks. I..." She paused and then rolled back her sleeves. Her forearms were scattered with bruises from the stress she'd taken out on them over the last week. "I hurt myself to distract from my anxiety. That is weird, Pav. It's freakish. I don't know what you see in me and I–" She broke off when she realised Pav was no longer sitting on the sofa; he was right in front of her and he'd taken her hands in his.

"Jesus," he muttered as he pushed her sleeves up further and lifted her arms up, tilting them to one side, then the other.

182

"Baby, this is way worse than before. What have you been doing to yourself?"

Millie frowned. They were getting off topic and she wanted to go back to the point. "I–"

"I knew I should have *made* you see me earlier. Bloody hell. I'm such a thin-skinned selfish arsehole."

"For goodness' sake," Millie said, tugging on her arms, but Pav held onto them in a gentle but firm grip. "What are you on about?"

"I took you to that party. I pushed you too fast and then I let you deal with it on your own for a week because of my own poxy ego and pride. That's what I'm talking about. You wouldn't have hurt yourself like this if I'd have come to you sooner."

"It's not your responsibility, Pav. *I'm* not your responsibility. And I'd like to remind you that *I* was avoiding *you*. Not the other way around. You tried to talk to me."

"Clearly I didn't try hard enough."

She shook her head and he let her pull her arms away. This conversation was confusing her. As always after a phone call with her mother, Millie felt like a small piece of her soul had been chipped away; she felt drained. She couldn't deal with a randomly-angry-with-himself Pav who was taking her mental health problems on as his own.

"Look, I don't think I'm up to arguing with you at the moment, okay?" she said, her voice sounding weak, even to her own ears.

"Right, yes. I totally agree," Pav told her, and she breathed out a sigh of relief, ignoring the empty feeling of loss at the knowledge he was going to leave. But instead of walking out, Pav stepped into her personal space, forcing her to shuffle backwards to the sofa, then he sat himself down, pulled her next to him and tucked her under his arm so her head was resting on his chest.

"Agreed: no more arguing. Now, what are we watching?"

Beauty took the opportunity to move back to her position with her head in Millie's lap. Both man and dog were pinning her in place. For some reason the trapped feeling she might have expected didn't come. She closed her eyes and let her body relax. The firm muscles of Pav's chest moved under her cheek as he pulled her even closer, much to Beauty's annoyance, and then settled.

"Right then, Jamie, me ol' mucker," Pav muttered as he reached forward for the remote, taking Millie and a disgruntled Beauty with him. "What channels have you got on your telly other than the Beeb, you big tight-arse." He turned on Sky and starting working his way through all the channels. "Do you like Game of Thrones?"

Millie gave a non-committal shrug. She *loved* Game of Thrones, but Pav didn't have to know that. She felt his chest under her cheek shake with what she suspected was suppressed laughter. He turned his body towards hers and shifted her to face him, Beauty still keeping her legs pinned down. Her face was so close to his that she could feel his breath on her cheek.

"Okay, this is not a state secret, gorgeous. I swear I will not use this information for nefarious purposes. All I want to know is if you like Game of Thrones – it's kind of a Marmite thing and I don't want to make you sit through something you hate." Millie blinked, and then her eyes locked with Pav's dark brown ones. What had he asked her? All she could think was how beautiful he was. She shifted just that bit closer, almost as if her body wasn't under her full control, and his pupils dilated as his smile slowly faded.

Before she could really process what was happening he was sliding his nose along hers and his hand was pushing up into her hair. He pulled back for a second to scan her face before he moved his mouth to hers and pressed their lips together in a feather-light kiss. She melted against him. Up until then Millie wouldn't have said that was possible, but her bones literally drained of all calcium as she sank into him, her own hand leaving Beauty's head and moving into Pav's thick hair.

His pupils were now so dilated that his eyes were almost black. Feather-light kisses were a thing of the past. His hand tightened in her hair and he moved her head to the exact angle he wanted, before pressing his mouth more firmly against hers.

After a moment he pulled back, gently bit her lip and then murmured against her mouth, "Open for me baby, please." She gasped and when his tongue slid in, white-hot heat flashed through her body and a small moan escaped. She heard and felt a rumbling in Pav's large chest as he deepened the kiss, pushing her back onto the arm of the sofa and forcing Beauty's head off her lap. The hand that was not sunk into the thick softness of his hair now slipped under his jumper to feel the smooth, hot skin over the corded muscles of his back, eliciting another low sound from his chest.

He shifted and somehow managed to manoeuvre their bodies so he was lying fully on top of her. His weight, pressing her into the sofa, felt unbelievable. His hand had slipped up to her back and unhooked her bra, and then he started to move. She could feel him against her, his hips having fallen between her legs, and the pressure on her core was perfect. She gasped when his hand moved from her back to cup her breast before he started moving against her. Their kiss deepened until Pav drew away and started breathing into her neck and lightly biting her ear as he continued to move, all the while whispering encouragement to her, telling her she was beautiful. Millie couldn't have said how long they stayed like that, locked together, but she soon started to feel it building and building until stars exploded behind her eyes and wave upon wave of pleasure swept through her body.

For a moment an almost fierce expression crossed Pav's face as he looked down at her. His hands tightened on her breast and her back and she could feel his body tense. His eyes were full of such stark need that Millie felt a shiver of apprehension. Something must have shown on her face because after scanning it once Pav clenched his jaw so tight that Millie could see a muscle tick at the side of his face, let out a low groan, and then collapsed on top of her. He let her take all his weight for a moment before he lifted himself up onto his elbows. He grinned down at her, the fire still in his eyes but somehow restrained. A tender expression crossed his face as he brushed back the stray curls that had escaped from her ponytail behind her ear. Millie stared up at him with wide eyes; she could still feel the hectic flush on her face. A low growl next to them made them both turn their heads to be confronted by a large, angry dogface inches from theirs.

"That dog is a pervert," Pav said, reaching behind a still-stunned Millie to do up her bra and pulling her soft jumper back down into place. Millie was not sure what post-orgasm protocol was. Did she say thank you? That seemed odd. Before she could say anything, Pav had kissed the tip of her nose and then his weight was lifted from her body. He pulled her up and tucked her back under his arm with her head on his chest.

"Uh..." Millie started as Beauty's head settled back into her lap. "What–?

His chest had started shaking under her cheek and then she realised he was laughing. Had she done something wrong? For her it was mind-blowing, but of course he hadn't... well, he hadn't *finished*. Was she supposed to do something about that? Was she being rude even? Had it merely been... *amusing* for Pav?

"Christ," he said through his laughter. "I haven't done something like that since I was fifteen."

"I... I don't understand," Millie admitted. Her voice was tight, and as always Pav picked up on it. He made an effort to quell his laughter but his voice was still shaking with it when he managed to reply.

"Bloody dry-humping on a sofa. I'm sorry, Millie, you must think I'm a joke. And to top it all off we're actually babysitting right now." He started laughing again. "We're horny teenagers using babysitting as an excuse to get jiggy in the grown-ups' living room. Jamie would kill me and probably burn all his furniture if he knew."

"I do not think you're a joke," Millie said, her voice confused and a little fierce. "That was... that was..." His body had stilled next to hers and her voice dropped to a whisper as she lost some of her confidence. "That was incredible. I've never... I mean..."

"You've never fooled around whilst you were babysitting?"

Millie bit her lip and sank her free hand further into Beauty's fur. "Pav, I've never fooled around before... um... ever... with anyone."

"What do you mean exactly?" Pav asked; his tone was cautious now.

"I mean that you were..." She trailed off and squeezed her eyes shut tight, a wave of embarrassment sweeping over her. "You were my first kiss. I can't compare embarrassing teenage stories with you because... well... I don't have any."

"First kiss? But what... ?" There was silence for a good few moments as Millie let Pav digest this latest piece of her craziness. "I don't understand. Millie, you're beautiful. How is it that you... ?"

The absurdity of Pav being shocked by this information

overwhelmed Millie and she did something that she rarely ever did: she giggled.

"Pav, I barely engage with other people at all. I don't usually let anyone touch me. I have severe social anxiety. When exactly am I going to be kissing people? Leave alone... fooling around."

"Right, okay," Pav said. He sounded shell-shocked, but instead of pushing her away like a freaky twenty-six-year-old virgin would deserve, he pulled her in tighter to his side, grabbed the hand that was in Beauty's fur and entwined his fingers with hers before settling them both on his hard stomach. When Beauty objected he told her to bugger off. The dog responded by shifting her massive head onto Pav's lap and drooling on his arm.

A few long moments passed before Pav managed to speak again, and when he did, his voice was slightly strangled for some reason.

"So, going back to the original question: do you like Game of Thrones?"

"Yes."

"Okay then. Libby has them all on her planner, the little nerd, if you want to watch it from the—"

"I've seen all the episodes apart from—"

"Last night's," Pav supplied, a smile back in his voice. "See, you're perfect for me." He clicked through with the remote and selected the episode. Millie settled more deeply into him and let herself breathe in his gorgeous washing-powder-with-undercurrent-of-man smell for a few minutes. That time was spent ignoring the television (something unheard of for her whilst Game of Thrones was on) and building up her courage to ask Pav a question. She would have left it, but that experience was just too incredible to allow her to.

"Um... Pav?"

"Yeah?"

"When... when do we do that again?"

"Millie, I think we've done enough for now," he told her, his voice back to being strangled and hoarse.

"Er... have we?" she asked. "I mean... you...?"

Pav let out a choked noise, then cleared his throat.

"We're going to go slow," he said, his voice firm – he sounded like he was making a vow to himself.

"Oh." Millie's mouth twisted to the side. "Okay. Well. Let me know when we've waited long enough for it to count as 'going slow'."

Pav groaned as his chest started shaking with laughter. "Bloody hell, you're going to kill me; I've created a monster."

Chapter 21

You just wait until next year, right?

An hour later and a Game of Thrones episode down, Millie's phone buzzed. She knew it would be a text from her mother and she knew she didn't want to look at it, not whilst she was so comfortable next to Pav and underneath a giant dog's head. (Pav had tried to push Beauty off after saying, quite rightly, that she smelled of decaying flesh, but she was just too large to move with brute force.) So Millie ignored her phone, despite the barrage of texts that followed. Unfortunately Pav's hand was resting over her back pocket and he felt the vibration.

"You must be a fan if you won't even check your phone whilst a Lannister's head is being chopped off," he'd probed, and Millie just shrugged.

A minute passed before he spoke again. "Millie, what was all that with your mum on the phone earlier? It sounded... uh... well. Does she always upset you that much?"

Millie stiffened.

"You can tell me, you know," he said softly. "I promise you can trust me."

"I..." Millie trailed off, the right answer was yes; yes her mother did always upset her that much, if not more. That's why she had as limited contact as possible. "She didn't upset me," Millie lied, thinking that it might be easier than the complicated, unpleasant truth.

"Oh really?" Pav said. She glanced up at his face and saw that his eyebrows were raised. "So why were you as close to tears as I've ever seen you earlier, and why were you hurting yourself again? Didn't seem like a friendly chat to me."

"My mother is..." Hmm, thought Millie, how best to describe her mother? Surprisingly she heard Kira's voice in her head saying "raging bitch", and stifled a giggle. An actual giggle... whilst thinking about her mother. What was happening to her? "My mother is... complicated."

"Well, if she's going to be that unpleasant then maybe you should have it out with her. I could always–"

"No, no," Millie jumped in, panic cutting through her relaxed brain at the thought of Pav getting involved in the mess that was her family. "I mean, I don't speak to them anyway unless it's Christmas or my bir..." She stopped mid-word and clamped her mouth shut.

"Your what?"

"Nothing, forget I said any–"

"Camilla Morrison, is it your birthday today?"

"I..."

"Why didn't you say anything?"

"Um..."

"And why are you babysitting on your birthday? I'm going to kill Jamie when he gets back. Swanning off and leaving you holding the baby when it's your birthday. Tosser."

"Rosie's hardly a baby, Pav, and they don't even know that it's–"

Susie Tate

"Hello? Millie? Are you... Oh." Libby froze at the entrance to the living room and stared at a cuddled-up Pav, Millie and Beauty pile on the sofa. A slow smile spread over her face. Millie didn't think that Libby would appreciate sofa-cuddling when Millie was supposed to be in charge of a minor. She was pretty sure that was a big no-no in the childcare courses she'd sat through to prove to Libby that she was safe to look after Rosie. So she tried to sit up and away from Pav, who tightened his arm around her in response.

"Well, if it isn't the selfish duo back from their night of debauchery," Pav said, and Millie elbowed him in the ribs.

"For Christ's sake, what are *you* doing here?" asked Jamie, slinging his arm around his wife's shoulders. "Millie, is he bothering you? We should have taken away his key. Listen, Pav, I love you, man, but that does not mean that I want you in my house when I come home from a romantic evening with my wife."

"Lucky I was here," Pav slammed back. "Or Millie would have spent her birthday alone, thanks to you."

"Ugh," Millie grunted, having had enough of Pav's rant on her behalf. She managed to wriggle out of his arms and nearly did the splits stepping over the dog to stand next to the coffee table. Once she got her balance and brushed off the dog detritus, she felt her hair settle around her shoulders. She put a tentative hand up to ascertain that, yes: it was all over the shop and probably looked exactly like she'd been fooling around on the sofa. She sighed.

"It's your birthday, hun?" asked Libby softly as she stepped around Beauty to stand next to her. "Why didn't you say?"

"Shit, I'm sorry, Mils," said Jamie, his face falling. "We shouldn't have asked you to sit – it's just Rosie scared off most of our other regulars."

192

"Well, it's a bit late now to–" Pav started.

"For fu... goodness' sake, Pav," Millie said through gritted teeth, and everyone's wide eyes swung to her. She realised this was probably the first time they'd heard her come even close to swearing. Come to think of it, it was the first time *she* could remember coming close to swearing. Probably another little piece of Pav/Kira influence. She liked it. "I *wanted* to babysit. What do you think I normally do on my birthday?"

"Well, I..." Pav frowned and Millie rolled her eyes.

"I haven't celebrated my birthday in... well, to be honest, I can't remember *ever* really celebrating."

"Not even as a child?" Libby asked, her beautiful face showing surprise and a little concern. Millie shuddered when she remembered some of the parties her parents had made her endure (the type designed for adults and not kids, stuffed with people she didn't know but was expected to talk to – not that she ever could, which of course her mother assumed was "purely to annoy" her). "Don't you even see your family on your birthday?"

"Um... well, no. We're not really big on birthdays. I usually... well, I usually try to work late, and then..." She trailed off, hating that they could all see how pathetic her life really was. She felt a stinging at the back of her eyes and, like always, successfully fought it back. "Right, well, it's late so I need to get out of your way and..." There was a loud pop and she whipped round to see a champagne cork fly through the air from the kitchen.

"You're not going anywhere, young lady, until you've had some goddamn champagne." Jamie's voice was firm and even a little fierce. "Libby, have we got any cake?" He asked the question so forcefully it was almost as if the future of the human race relied on the answer.

"Uh..." Libby swept off into the kitchen and dug around in the drawers until she found a box of Jaffa Cakes.

"They're biscuits," Jamie said as Pav moved off the sofa and came up behind Millie, guiding her towards the kitchen with a hand to her back.

"It says 'cakes' on the packet and it's all we have."

"Fine," Jamie snapped, grabbing the packet, ripping it open and then shoving a small candle into one of the Jaffa Cakes that were now strewn all over the kitchen counter.

"Jamie, please, don't be silly," Millie said in a small voice as she tried to edge towards the front door. Pav was ready, though, to block her way. "It doesn't mat–"

"It bloody well does matter," Jamie told her, pinning her with a stare which put paid to any ideas she had about leaving. She bit her lip and Jamie's expression softened. "Come on, honey. Blow out a candle and we'll have some champagne. Five minutes."

Five minutes became forty-five. Millie dutifully blew out the candle and sipped the champagne. She felt awkward and uncomfortable with the attention. Ten minutes in she tried to leave again. But then after listening to the flow of conversation around her, realising that they didn't expect anything from her except to be with them, she started to relax. She even told them about her Knock System: a way she had of knowing who was knocking on her office door when she was on call to be prepared and less stressed when they confronted her. There was Alpha Male Knock (Jamie and Pav both fitted into this category), Funny but Not Funny Knock, Too Much Testosterone Knock, Lunatic Knock (Kira was the main culprit here and to some extent Jamie also fell into this category).

"What if they knock like a normal human being?" asked Libby through her laughter.

"Ah, yes, the Normal Knock; only radiographers seem able to pull that one off."

Before she left, Millie, much to her confusion and not a small amount of alarm, was hauled into a big bear hug from Jamie. To be honest Millie hadn't had the impression that Jamie was a big fan of hers in the past. He'd always seemed wary about her looking after Rosie. She'd been worried for a while that he knew that she was the secret source for the money Libby received as a "grant" from the Deanery. But when he didn't confront her about it, she realised that it was just her that he found lacking in some way. She hadn't thought much of it. People not taking to her had been a regular theme in her life. But she hadn't realised until she was engulfed in his arms how much it meant to her to have him accept her. She suspected there was a small dose of pity prompting that acceptance, but Millie wasn't going to argue.

"I'm sorry you had a crap birthday," Pav told her on the journey home. She'd walked as she didn't like driving in the dark (one of her limitations), so he gave her a ride back in his car.

"What do you mean?" Millie asked, genuinely bewildered.

"Oh, babysitting, a bloody Jaffa Cake, cheap Prosecco – not exactly the most fun evening in history."

"That was..." Millie paused and swallowed down the emotion that was threatening to bubble over into her voice, "that was the *best* birthday I've ever had. The best."

She looked over at him and saw his jaw tighten and his knuckles turn white on the steering wheel. That piece of news didn't seem to have made him any happier.

"You just wait until next year, right?" he told her, the same fierce undertone in his voice that had been in Jamie's earlier. "You just wait."

Millie sat back in the seat and stared out at the road ahead.

Next year.

Pav thought he would still be involved in her birthday plans in a year's time. Her chest felt so tight she thought it might burst. As she closed her eyes and let a small smile tip up her lips, she did what she hadn't allowed herself to do for a very long time: she let herself hope.

Chapter 22

What did she have to lose?

"AHA! THE NAUGHTY LITTLE BIRTHDAY GIRL," SHOUTED Kira, jumping up from the table in the cafeteria and running over to Millie, who was shocked into immobility by the coffee stand. "Come with me, Professor X., I have something to show you."

Millie took a step back, glancing around at the attention they were drawing, but Kira was too quick for her. She grabbed her hand and started dragging her across the crowded hall. Dr Metta, a pathologist in his mid fifties known for his foul temper, thinning hair and pot belly, got in Kira's way at one stage and she accidently knocked his coffee all down his front. For a moment he looked like he was going to explode with rage. But before he could fully detonate, Kira had grabbed some tissues from the table next to her and dropped to her knees in front of the man, only to start rubbing his crotch. He was so shocked by the manoeuvre that he didn't manage to get a word of protest out. By the time she was done and had risen to kiss him on the cheek, it was clear that he didn't know whether to scream bloody murder at her or thank her profusely. He opted for a sharp exit.

Kira winked at Millie and continued to drag her to the table. Pav, Jamie, and Libby were all grinning as they approached, and Millie was too busy taking all their welcoming faces in to see what was on the table in front of her. When she did look down she was so surprised she did a double take. It was a huge, slightly misshapen black cake with a haphazardly iced white skeleton on the top, and there were a few candles stuck at varying angles in the centre. Millie tilted her head to the side in confusion, and then her eyes widened.

"It's an x-ray cake for Professor X.," Kira said, proudly sweeping her arm out towards the box. "I know it looks professionally made–" Pav snorted and Kira glared at him "– but it was *actually* made by me." Millie stood frozen to the spot and just stared at the cake. "Er... we should sing!" shouted Kira. "Ha–" Pav jumped out of his chair and clamped his hand over Kira's mouth.

"No singing," he told her, and Kira rolled her eyes and made a grab for his hand.

"Ki-Ki," Libby said, and all eyes turned to her. "No, honey. Too many people."

Pav let his hand fall away and Kira came up to stand next to Millie, giving her a gentle shoulder bump. "Sorry, Prof, you know I can get a tad bit overexcited. Sometimes it's difficult for me to understand shyness. I'm getting there, okay?"

Millie had yet to speak or even move. She could feel the atmosphere around the table shift slightly from upbeat to concerned. Even Kira's expression was a little unsure, and that girl was never unsure about anything, ever.

"Uh... maybe I should take the cake away until later," Kira said slowly, her hands reaching out to pick up the tray. Millie moved on instinct to intercept her and enclosed her wrist with one of her hands.

"No," she bit out, and Kira blinked, her expression wary. Millie cleared her throat and shook her head. "I mean, don't take it away. I..." She paused for a long moment. Kira had turned towards her and was waiting for her to continue with her head cocked to the side. Millie still had her wrist enclosed in her hand. The words she needed to find refused to come to her. She couldn't get anything past her throat, which had completely closed over. Kira was starting to frown, and Millie knew she had to do something, so she used the hand at Kira's wrist to pull her forward. And then she did something she hadn't done in over twenty years. She initiated a hug.

"Thank you," she whispered in Kira's ear, once her arms were wrapped around her. It took Kira a shocked moment to register Millie's intent, but once she had, Millie was squeezed so hard she couldn't breathe for a good few seconds.

"You're super-welcome, Prof," Kira whispered back into Millie's ear, and then started swaying their bodies from side to side. "By the way, my hugs go on forever and ever and ever–"

"Ki-Ki, let her breathe now, okay?" Pav was standing, and managed to prise Kira away from Millie so that she was able to inhale some much needed oxygen. Once free, Pav kissed the side of Millie's head, tucked her under his arm, and then steered her to sit next to him at the other end of the table.

Kira went about cutting up the cake and offering it round to anyone who would accept a slice. Seeing as the icing was black and the cake itself was blood-red, most people politely declined, other than everyone at their table, to whom Kira made it very clear that that was not an option.

Nobody had ever made a cake for Millie. Her mother had ordered in large, tiered cakes for the birthday parties she threw (before she'd realised that her daughter was too shy to impress any of the adults she'd invited and therefore did not warrant any sort of birthday celebration – that happened when Millie was six). She didn't think Kira would ever be able to understand how much it meant to her, and she knew she didn't have the words to explain. But she vowed that she'd pay Kira back in some way.

Millie was good at working out what people needed, and she was good at getting it for them. Last year she'd had a pair of Louboutin boots anonymously delivered to Eleanor's office at work after seeing the longing on El's face when she'd been trying them on as Millie arrived for one of her fittings. El had been embarrassed to be caught checking out the merchandise for herself in work hours, and had shoved the boots to the side, but not before Millie had noted the size. Eleanor had asked her about it but Millie feigned ignorance.

Don had been talking about how Irene had been bugging him to get her a new oven for months. The second time Millie was invited to dinner there, she took a small tape-measure and mapped out the space for said oven whilst Don and Irene were in the dining room. She had a new one delivered and installed the next week. Irene had thought it was Don; Don hadn't known what to think, and when he asked Millie she kept her mouth shut.

Then of course there was Libby's "bursary": nobody other than Pav knew about that, and that was the way Millie wanted to keep it.

So somehow she knew she'd pay Kira back. And for now she was going to eat blood-red sponge with a terrifying amount of food dye involved, and she was going to love every minute.

"Hey, Prof," Kira said through a mouthful of cake before she swallowed it down (not any easy feat without a fair amount of water – Millie suspected that a few essential ingredients like, say, butter had been forgotten in the cake-making process), "whatcha gonna do about that big deal of a conference thingy? Isn't it in a couple of months?"

Millie's gaze flew up to Kira and then over to Pav, who shrugged and gave her a sheepish smile.

"Sorry, Mils. I might have let slip about the conference. But it is a big deal, you know. You should at least consider it."

For some reason, the fact that Pav had discussed the conference with Kira didn't sit well with Millie. She felt herself stiffen and took a deep breath to force her body to relax. *This is what having friends is like*, she told herself. They talk to each other about you. They care about what you do. There was nothing there to make her feel uneasy. She just wasn't used to this kind of attention. She forced a smile.

"I can't speak at a conference," she said. "I mean, you saw what happened when I..." Pav's arm slipped around her back and gave her a squeeze, and Libby gave her a soft look from across the table.

"But we can get round that," Kira said, bouncing on her seat in excitement. "I mean, we could do some coaching and some practice. Work on some techniques to handle the stress of it and calm that big brain of yours down."

"Kira, I don't think that–"

"Just try it?" Kira wheedled. "You know that everyone needs to hear about the results, and you know it needs to come from the person that's developed it. Come on, the practice'll be fun. We can do that instead of book group for the next three weeks. What about your psychologist mate? You think he might be able to help?"

"I... Anwar's not–" She was cut off before she could explain that Anwar wasn't her friend, he was her therapist.

"Why not try it, Mils?" Pav asked, giving her another squeeze. "You might regret letting the opportunity slip through your fingers. Plus, don't you want to rock up to that conference and show all those smug bastards what real change looks like? Shake things up a bit."

"I know it needs to be presented," Millie muttered. "Anwar's agreed to go and I was actually going to ask Dr Carver if he would mind–"

"Ugh! Millie you can't let that pompous arse take all the credit for your work."

"He wouldn't be, he'd just be presenting the–"

"Millie, you *know* he'd take the credit."

Millie looked away from Pav's furious eyes. Yes, she did know that, but she didn't actually care. It was never about the acknowledgment. The last thing Millie could ever be accused of was being a glory hunter. She glanced around the table. Everyone was watching her. After the cake and the fuss they'd made she felt a little bad disappointing them, reminding them of her limits.

"I... I've *had* therapy with Anwar," she told them as she stared down into her lap and shrugged her shoulders. "I have *a lot* of cognitive behavioural therapy. That's the reason I set up the study: because I know how powerful it can be. In some ways it's been indispensable, but it only goes so far. It's really helped me but it can't work miracles..."

"But you didn't have *us* then," said Kira, her voice strong and confident.

"Kira's right, Millie," Libby said, her voice quieter but no less firm. "You might find you make more progress with extra support behind you."

Millie bit her lip. Could she change more than she had? The idea of living more normally was tempting. What did she have to lose?

"Okay," she said eventually.

"Yeah, baby!" Kira shouted, punching the air and drawing a fair few curious glances from beyond their table. "This is gonna be fun. We're going to public-speak the crap out of you by the end of the month."

Millie let out a small giggle at Kira's theatrics, earning her another shoulder squeeze and kiss to her temple from Pav. A shiver went down her spine as she looked up at him, and she smiled. The worry about why he'd discussed the conference with the others was forgotten.

For now.

Chapter 23

Nothing you can't do

KIRA WORKED FAST. IN FACT, SHE WAS LIKE A WHIRLWIND.
Anwar had called Millie that night.

"A woman called Kira cornered me on the orthopaedic
ward today," he explained. "She's very... er... outgoing. Isn't
she?"

"That's one way to describe her," Millie muttered.

"Seems like there's been a fair bit of change recently,"
Anwar probed. Millie knew he'd seen her and Pav around the
hospital together. He'd probably heard about the cake in the
canteen as well.

"You... er... could say that."

"Do you think we should fit in another session, Millie?"
Anwar was one of the first people to call her by her Christian
name. He'd asked her before they even sat down for her session
with him six years ago what she was comfortable with him
calling her. At the time it had been a real novelty to have
someone address her with informality, even if she was paying
them to do so.

Millie thought about all the changes over the last three

months and how overwhelming they sometimes felt, and agreed to meet Anwar that night.

"So," HE GRINNED ACROSS AT HER NOW. "THIS IS different."

For some reason Millie had wanted to meet Anwar at the pub. It was quiet enough that they would be able to talk, and she knew in the back of her mind that she wanted to show him how far she'd come. Anwar had always told her that her limits were not set in stone; that she could do anything if she would let herself.

Millie managed a small smile and watched as he blinked in surprise. She'd always been concentrating so hard at their previous sessions that she rarely, if ever, relaxed her mouth from a grim line.

Anwar's grin widened, his white teeth stark against his dark skin. He was attractive, objectively, Millie had always been able to see that, but he didn't affect her like Pav. Nobody ever had.

"I like him for you, Millie," Anwar said through his smile, and Millie looked away, feeling her cheeks heat. "When you collapsed in the lecture theatre his face was... well, the best way to describe it would be 'fierce'. We had to pry him away from you. Did you know that?"

The memories of that awful day were hazy for Millie. She did vaguely recall Pav's loud objections to her not going to the emergency department.

"He's... kind," Millie whispered, and a strange expression crossed Anwar's face before he cleared his throat.

"Millie, I'm sure he is kind," Anwar said slowly. "But you know that's not why–"

"They want me to present at the conference," Millie

blurted out, cutting him off. She did not want to go over Pav's motivations for being with her, be that kindness, pity... it was too stress-inducing to consider.

"Okay," Anwar said, his eyebrows going up in surprise. "How do you feel about presenting?"

"I... I think it's beyond my–"

"Millie, if you say 'limits' I will scream," he told her, deadpan.

She shrugged and almost smiled again imagining the big man in front of her letting out a girly shriek. "Well, it is. You saw what happened before."

"You had a panic attack, Millie," he said slowly. "It doesn't mean you can never speak publicly again. You know that, right?"

She looked away and took a deep breath. Anwar sighed. "Millie, I–"

"He kissed me," she blurted out, and he blinked at her in surprise.

"Er... right... so..."

"I wanted him to... I mean it was... I just..." She trailed off and stared at her hands on the table, waiting for Anwar to fill the silence.

"This is a huge step forward, Millie," Anwar said eventually. "This shows that you can push past some of the boundaries in your mind."

He broke off as his hand shot forward to grasp onto Millie's, and pull it out from her other sleeve. She hadn't even realised she was pinching the skin until the pressure was removed. Anwar let go of her hands once they were separated and Millie slipped them under the table and out of sight.

"Why does this make you anxious?" he asked. "Describe exactly the negative thoughts, then we can deal with them."

"I love him," Millie whispered.

"Mils, that's not a negative—"

"When he was actually kissing me, I wasn't thinking anything, except..." Her cheeks heated again and she bit her lip. It seemed that kissing Pav, doing anything physical with him, was a temporary cure for her anxiety. Her mind was blessedly and totally blank when they were together like that. It was afterwards that the doubts crept back in.

"Okay, so not whilst he was kissing you, but you felt worried after. What were you thinking? Can you put exact words to the worries."

"Okay, so first I was thinking that... that I loved him – Pav, I mean."

"Right."

"And then... and then I started to think about when he would get tired of me, of how much I'd miss him. Then I worried that would set me back, that I might have even more... limits." Millie took a deep breath before going on. "Then I thought, what if after he leaves me and meets someone without limits, someone easy, what if he regrets ever being with me? What if he resents me for wasting his time? What if he ends up hating me?"

There was a few moments of silence as Millie stared down at the table.

"Oh, Mils," Anwar's soft voice eventually whispered. Millie looked up to see that he was staring at her with a tender look on his face. She shrugged and Anwar leaned forward to put his warm hand over her cold one.

"Right, let's break them down, all right? You know the CBT drill. We have to look at each thought and confront it head-on with logic. As always I'll remind you that I know how clever you are, so I know you have an awful lot of logic at your disposal – let's tackle this stuff with that. Because this is a big step forward, Millie. Allowing yourself to trust somebody to that extent... it's a massive leap for you. And you know what, if you can make that kind of progress, there's nothing you can't do."

"Wooh! Wooh!" Kira cheered as they watched Libby and Claire flip down the two aisles onto the stage and swing around the poles. It was Saturday afternoon and the club that Tara and Claire danced in was deserted. For some reason Kira had declared that book group, or rather the Let's Try and Sort Millie Out Group, as it seemed to have become, would be conducted here this week.

Eleanor, Kira and Millie had just arrived and were standing at the back of the club. Libby had already been there for a couple of hours going over the new routines she was teaching the girls. Although she no longer performed (her "bursary" allowing her to give up that extra money), the owner kept her on retainer as a choreographer. Millie suspected that it was a very large retainer given the affection the owner had for the woman who had made his club a real success. Since Libby had joined the dancers a few years ago and taken over the routines it had become the most famous strip club in London.

Kira jumped up on the aisle in front of them and ran down it with her hands milling in excitement. Halfway along she fell into an ill-advised forward roll before jumping back up to her feet, swinging up onto a pole and falling on her arse. Millie had never seen anything so funny in her life. She felt it bubbling up through her chest and her mouth trembled, and then she started laughing. Once she'd started she couldn't stop. She could hear El giggling next to her and took a deep breath in to try and control it, but then it started up again.

Turns out, Millie's laugh was loud. It was so long since

she'd laughed properly that it came as a bit of a shock. When she finally managed to get a hold of herself she had tears running down her cheeks, and she was pressing her lips together to stop herself being set off again. The image of Kira's inelegant forward roll after the girls' professional flips kept replaying in her mind.

Instead of looking annoyed, Kira was beaming at her from the stage.

"Hurrah!" she shouted, her arms going straight up into the air. "See, I *knew* this was a good idea." She gave Libby a pointed look and Libby rolled her eyes in response.

"What are we doing here, Kira?" asked Millie through a few giggles that were still trying to escape as she and Eleanor walked up to the stage.

"You, my gorgeous girl, are going to work the pole," Claire told her, and Millie's smile abruptly fell away.

"Wh–"

"Come on, lady," Kira said, jumping down from the stage and grabbing Millie's arms so that she could move them both in a swaying motion from side to side. "It'll loosen you up. Get that stage-ready mindset on the go."

"Kira," Millie said, attempting to halt the swaying but somehow finding herself in a dancer's hold with Kira's hand around her waist and her other hand holding Millie's out in front of them. "There are not going to be any..." Millie paused as Kira spun her out and then pulled her back in again "... poles to work on the stage at the conference. I'm not sure the same skills are needed."

"Of course they are," Kira told her as she continued to sway them both in a little circle. "Confidence, control, not being afraid of the audience: it's all the same whether you're stripping or public speaking."

"Have you ever stripped, Kira?" Eleanor asked, her voice just as sceptical as Millie's.

"Um... actually she has," Libby put in from the stage through a huge smile. "It was kind of an amateur night. Kira brought the house down."

"Oh God!" cried Claire. "Was that the time she crawled on her belly like a snake, then did that air-cycling on her back? I thought I'd die laughing."

"My moves may be unconventional, but they said what they needed to say, get me?"

"They said that you are mentally ill, Kira," Libby told her. "Steve still hasn't let any amateurs back up on stage and it's been two years."

Kira sighed. "I can't help it if that man has no eye for talent. Right, now let's get this pony in the bridle; let the waffle see the Nutella." Everyone stared at Kira blankly and she sighed. "*Let's go, people.*" She clapped twice and Claire rolled her eyes.

"Okay," she said, sitting down on the edge of the stage. "Have you ever danced before Millie?"

"Uh..." Millie shifted on her feet and her lips twisted to the side. "Ballet. I used to do ballet. But the teacher said I..." she paused for a moment, then straightened her shoulders "... she said that I was too robotic. I don't think she'd wanted to put it that way but my mother was pushy and wanted me to take the main parts in the performances, to be the star, and eventually my teacher had to let her know it wasn't possible. That I could learn it all perfectly, but I would never be able to *dance*. Mother pulled me out after that. I was nine."

"Did you enjoy it?" El asked, and Millie shrugged. She had loved the costumes. She loved being with girls the same age. It had been fun.

"Yes," she whispered, remembering how devastated she'd been when her mother had ordered her to collect her stuff. The regret and sadness on her teacher's face as she was dragged away. "Yes, I loved it." She felt El's hand squeeze hers for a moment and then release.

"Great," said Kira into the silence, jumping off the stage and landing in front of Millie. "Stripping is just like dirty ballet. You'll be all over it in no time."

Millie smiled and shook her head. "I don't think that..."

"Come up here," Claire said, offering Millie a hand and staring at her expectantly. "We'll start slow." Millie hesitated for a moment. Claire gave her an encouraging smile and Kira a small shove from behind. She drew in a breath and reached up to Claire. Tara grabbed her other hand and she was pulled up on stage.

"First things first," Tara said. "You all need to chuck a pair of these babies on. Nobody can work a pole without some friction, and leggings are not going to cut it." Millie caught the black scrap of material that was chucked at her chest and held it up to inspect it. It was a pair of gold satin hot pants with Main Attraction written across the back in sequins.

"It's the waitress uniform," Claire explained. You've got to be able to grip the pole with your legs." Millie looked at the girls and then at the hot pants in her hands. Kira was already pulling off ripped jeans to reveal a pair of red pants, then pulling on the shorts over them. She pinged the waistband and jumped once on the spot.

"Ready!"

Millie looked from the shorts to Eleanor, who shook her head and smiled.

"Come on, hun, we'll find the changing room."

Chapter 24

The stupidity of the Y chromosome

"I TOLD YOU IT WOULD BE FUN," KIRA SAID AS LIBBY turned down the music.

Millie pushed back the hair from her face and smiled. Really smiled. For the first time since she could remember, her face actually ached from laughter. They'd been "dancing" for the last hour and every minute had been absolutely hilarious. When Millie had eventually been dragged out of the changing room by a tenacious Eleanor, she hadn't thought she could go through with it. Yes, it was a Saturday afternoon and yes, the bar was shut so the only people watching would be the girls – but still: she was in hot pants, *with* sequins on her arse. She looked ridiculous. But they'd set all this up for her; she didn't want to disappoint them. So she'd taken a deep breath and stepped out onto the stage.

Claire and Tara had taken the lead, seeing as Libby's speciality was the "floor work" (all the flips and balance acts) and the others were into working the pole. The three of them showed some simple spins and then Eleanor, Millie and Kira were up. All Millie had to do at first was hop up, grasp the pole between her legs, and spin. Once they'd all managed that, things became more complicated and a little more embarrassing: strutting round the pole, "throwing attitude" at the crowd, higher spins, faster spins, "slut drops" – Millie had been too self-conscious at first to really try any of it; but when the music was cranked up, and with Kira going nuts on her pole (following a bizarre routine that could have only been made up in her crazy mind), Millie surprised herself and actually started dancing. By the end she could get higher up the pole than either El or Kira. After her last spin she realised the others were all watching her with big smiles; they started clapping when she reached the floor.

"Jesus Christ." Millie heard a low male voice from below the stage and her head whipped round to see Pav standing beside one of the tables looking up at her with his mouth open. She felt the blood rush to her face and scrambled to stand up.

"Oi, pervert!" shouted Kira. "No blokes allowed. Millie, tell him to bugger off. Wait a minute, how did you even know we were here?"

Pav didn't respond. He didn't even look at Kira; his eyes were glued to Millie and she started to feel self-conscious in her tiny hot pants. "Hello? Looky Lookerson? Have you had a stroke or something?" Kira had jumped down from the stage and was waving a hand in front of Pav's face.

"Ugh!" Pav finally acknowledged Kira's presence and batted her hand away. "You're *so* annoying: like a little mosquito. How do you manage it?"

"Practice and persistence, my perverted friend," Kira told him, poking him in the chest and earning herself a fierce scowl before he went back to watching Millie. "Now, let's start again as you seem a little slow. Why. Are. You. Here?"

"Well..." Pav shrugged and shifted uncomfortably on his

feet. "Jamie *might* have let slip where you guys were going and I..."

"You thought you'd come and get yourself an eyeful," chipped in Tara, her hands going to her hips.

"No, no," Pav protested, raising his hands in surrender. "Honestly, I just wanted to check that... I mean, I wasn't sure Millie would be happy with..."

"You thought we'd upset her, didn't you?" Libby asked as she crossed her arms over her chest and narrowed her eyes at Pav. "Jamie told on us because he was worried and now you've come to swoop in and save Millie from the evil oversexed bitches pushing her out of her comfort zone."

"Er... well..."

"Give us some credit, Willy Fiddler," Kira told him, giving him another poke, then leaping back up onto the stage to stand next to Millie. "She's had a blast, haven't you, X?" Kira slung an arm over Millie's shoulder and shook her from side to side. "Sorry, hun, I'm sweating like an avocado in Shoreditch."

Pav sighed and ignored Kira. "Er... are you guys done then or...?"

"We'll be done when we're done," Kira told him. "You can wait outside. Go on, shoo!"

"Millie," Pav said, turning to her and his face softening, "you okay with... all this, love?"

He wanted to know if the girls were pushing her too far. He wanted to know she was comfortable with what was happening, that she wasn't being bullied into anything. A feeling of warmth spread from her chest out to her fingertips. She was starting to believe that he cared about her. Really cared.

"I'm okay," she said and managed a small smile, which smoothed his frown of concern. "It was... it was fun." Kira turned her around and gave her a full hug. Millie couldn't even move her arms to return the gesture as they were pinned to her sides with the force of it.

"Five minutes, Big Man," Kira told Pav when she was done and Millie could breathe again. "Wait out in the lobby."

FIVE MINUTES, PAV THOUGHT BITTERLY AS HE PACED THE corridor outside the entrance to the club. More like twenty-five. He groaned and took a seat on the bench against the wall, willing his body to come back under his control. When Jamie told him earlier what the girls had planned for Millie, Pav had decided to rush down here and put a stop to it. *Jamie* might let his woman perform at that club (okay, well, if Libby ever heard anyone say that Jamie *let* her do anything she'd probably kick them in the nuts with her crazy gymnast moves) but Pav wasn't about to have Millie made uncomfortable in that place. The last time he'd seen her there had been the night Jamie had hired out the whole bar and transformed it from strip club to theatre for Libby to perform. Millie had been visibly stressed just watching the stage then; Pav didn't want her put in a situation that made her feel unsafe.

And yes, Jamie said it was "just girls", but who the fuck knew what bastards could be lurking about a place like that? Nobody was watching his woman prance about a pole... *Ugh,* he thought, *when did I become such a bloody caveman?* He'd never been over-possessive with a woman in the past. With hindsight he suspected that he might have overreacted a tiny, tiny amount. There were only six of them in there, and definitely no blokes allowed. He felt like a bit of a dick now, truth be known. In fact, he would have slunk away unnoticed, but he... couldn't; not after he'd seen her up there in that outfit. Not after he'd seen her spinning round that pole, laughing. No way his body was letting him leave without her. It was his small head in control at the moment, and the bastard needed to get a hold of himself, or all those women were going to know what a state he was in. Twenty minutes (okay, more like ten, but time seemed to be moving inordinately slowly) of thinking about his yiayia's fungal toenails hadn't seemed to alter his Neanderthal reaction to a scantily clad Millie. He was just glad he was in jeans and not his chinos.

"Hey," Millie's soft voice drifted from the exit and he took his head out of his hands to smile up at her. Once he swept her body with his eyes, however, his smile dropped from his face.

"Where are your trousers?" he asked. His voice was a little choked but honestly there was only so much a man could take.

"They're called leggings, Willy Fiddler," Kira told him in disgust. "Please, get with the twenty-first century."

Pav swallowed and forced himself to look away from Millie's legs, which were in what he thought looked like a pair of black tights with neon pink fireworks exploding all over them.

"I thought we'd be dancing, and El... El sorts all my active-wear out. I... um... she said these were what everyone wore to... be active," Millie said, frowning down at her non-trousers.

"They are not trousers," Pav said, and Kira rolled her eyes.

"Pav, you've seen me wear leggings hundreds of times, you weirdo," Kira said.

"Have I?" He thought he'd remember if women were all randomly walking around without trousers on. Then again, maybe it *was* just because it was Millie.

"Thanks, girls," Millie mumbled, her face a bright shade of red. Pav began to regret his questioning of her trousers' where-abouts. "I'll just be off now."

"Great, yes, me too," Pav said, grabbing her hand as she went past and then opening the heavy oak door for her to exit the building. He was aware that he'd made a bit of an arse out of himself, and decided to brazen it out by striding confidently past the others.

"Bye Millie, bye Weirdo," Kira called after them, and Pav shook his head as he let the heavy door shut behind them.

"Uh, where are we going?" Millie asked after Pav had tugged her along the pavement about fifty yards. "And... and why are we running there?"

"I'm not..." Pav slowed his steps when he realized that *he* might not be running but Millie, with significantly shorter legs, definitely was. "Shit, sorry," he mumbled, drawing to a halt and turning to face her.

"Listen, Millie, I really, really want to take you home," he told her. "In fact I think I'm trying to drag you home. In all honesty I'm pretty much on automatic pilot since seeing you up on that stage." He sighed. "Maybe I should take you home... to your home. Let myself calm down a bit."

Millie cocked her head to the side and her hair fell over one of her shoulders, an adorable little frown of confusion marring her forehead.

"Calm down? I don't understand. Why do you need to calm down?"

A group of noisy lads passed by them at that point and Pav pulled Millie to the side of the pavement next to the entrance to Barclays. He took her face in his hands and pressed his lips against hers. She jerked in shock for a moment, and her gasp meant that when he pressed his lips back on hers he could slip his tongue inside. One of his hands went into her hair and the other down to where her non-trousers started. After a moment she seemed to forget where they were and kissed him back, both her arms going up around his neck. When he finally broke away he rested his forehead on hers, their breath mingling between them. Her pupils were so wide that only a rim of light grey iris remained. She looked shell-shocked.

"Right," he muttered, his mouth inches from hers. "So that's what I mean by calm down."

"But why–"

"Millie, I just watched you *pole dance* in *hot pants*. And now, *now* you don't have any trousers on. A man has got his limits, okay?"

"Oh." She flushed red again and then a small smile formed on her lips.

"That's why I should take you home... to your home... and leave you there."

Her smile dropped and she pulled her forehead from his. "I..." She broke eye contact to stare at his throat and he felt the familiar bite of irritation at the loss. But then after squaring her shoulders she looked back up at him and drew in a deep breath. "Well, I want to go home to *your* home with you, and... and I don't want you to... to... I don't want you to calm down."

He stared down at her for a moment and she lifted her chin and squared her jaw, making him smile. Before she could change her mind he grabbed her hand again and started back off down the road to his car.

Chapter 25

Yes, I trust you

MILLIE SAT ON THE BAR STOOL AND FLICKED THE hairband she had around her wrist. Anwar thought it might be helpful as an alternative to the pinching she normally did as a reflex to cope with stress. The bite of the band against her wrist worked nearly as well, with less bruising. Soon Millie hoped she would stop even that. But sitting here watching Pav drag the contents of his fridge out onto the kitchen island and stare at it all with his hands on his hips, she was feeling the nerves again.

Since they'd arrived at his house he'd been acting strangely. When they arrived he dragged her inside at a rate of knots and turned her to face him. She was sure he was going to kiss her – then he swore, took a step back, and ran both his hands through his hair until they were linked behind his head and he was looking up at the ceiling. That was when he started his frantic fridge evisceration. On the counter between them sat a sad-looking packet of ham, which was a week out of date, half a cucumber that had seen better days, and a bottle of Lucozade.

"Bloody hell," he muttered.

"Uh... Pav, are you okay?" Millie asked, flicking her band once.

"I should feed you," he told her.

"Why... ?"

"Because I've just dragged you back here. You haven't eaten supper and I can't..."

Millie frowned again and gave the band another flick. The movement caught Pav's eye and he zeroed in on her wrist.

"What are you... ?" He moved around the island to where Millie was sitting and stood in front of her to take her wrist in one of his hands. He used the other to smooth a finger over the rubber band. A wrinkle formed between his brows as he leaned forward to inspect the skin around the band more closely. She looked down and realised there were a series of faint red marks where it had snapped back onto her wrist. She pulled it away and shifted off the stool to step back, embarrassed.

"It's... um... to help relieve stress without..." She shrugged and pulled her sleeves down lower on her arms, an instinctive reaction, even though her bruises had faded.

"But... why are you stressed now?" Pav asked.

Millie looked down and bit her lip. "You're acting weird," she muttered. "You're usually so relaxed and it's like I've made you angry or something and I..."

"I'm not angry with you, Millie," Pav said, his voice back to the gentle tone she was used to with him. Her fingers went back to the band but he moved forward to wrap his hands around her wrists, preventing her from flicking it. "I'm not... it's just I..." He paused and took a deep breath in through his nose. "Seeing you up there. Jesus. It was like an out-of-body experience. You're always so... controlled, so..."

"Cold, uptight," Millie supplied, knowing that was how people saw her.

"No, baby, no," said Pav, his voice now even more gentle.

"Never cold. Just a bit closed, maybe... remote. Then I walk into that bloody place, all ready as your knight in shining armour to rescue you from being scarred for life by Kira's idea of a good time, and I see... I mean, bugger me: you on that pole, your hair flying out as you spun, your legs. I may never recover."

Millie frowned at him, slowly shaking her head, and he made a low sound in the back of his throat, almost like a growl.

"Do you have any idea just how beautiful you are?" he murmured, both his hands going up either side of her head to still the shaking, and then into her hair as he pressed his mouth to hers. Her mind blanked as she kissed him back, barely noticing as he backed her out of the kitchen and towards his bedroom door.

It was only when her calves hit his bed and she nearly toppled backwards that she realised where she was and pulled her mouth from his. She watched as awareness slowly came back to his somewhat drugged expression, and he blinked before dropping his hands to his sides. His bedroom was small but the bed was huge, taking up most of the space. The walls were a surprising dusky orange colour and she noticed multiple certificates covering a large area above the bed. "Shit," Pav muttered, pacing away from her and pushing his hands into his hair again. Millie felt her hand go to her mouth and her fingers trace her lips. "Okay, okay. Let's calm things down. Take a breath. We can order some food in and..."

"Why?" Millie asked, her hand dropping back down and her head cocking to the side as she felt her brow wrinkle with confusion.

"Because..." Pav cleared his throat and she noticed him visibly swallow as he looked over at her. "Millie, I don't think it's a good idea to do anything in my bedroom when I'm worked up like this. Maybe we could choose a day when I haven't watched you pole dance in hot pants. We could go on a day trip to a sewage factory, or to visit my yia-yia; you could actually wear some trousers. Then we could think about..."

"You won't hurt me," Millie told him, her brow clearing as comprehension dawned.

"Millie, I wouldn't mean to, but–"

"Shh." Millie surprised herself. She wasn't normally the type of person to shush somebody. But Pav was wrong. It didn't matter how "worked up" he was, he would never hurt her. And the fact that it was *her* that had actually worked him up was giving her some rare and much-needed confidence. He wanted her. She could see it in every move he'd made since he'd picked her up from the club. She could feel it in the air between them. "I don't want to go to a sewage factory. I want you."

"Millie–"

"I... I want you," she said as she walked across the room to where he was standing. She put her hands on his biceps and could feel the tension in the muscles under her fingertips as he strained to hold himself back. He was actually shaking. "Please," she whispered.

It was as soon as that word left her lips that she could see him snap. She watched his eyes flash as his arms shot forward to her body, pulling her into him and lifting her up so that her legs were around his hips. And then he was carrying her back to the bed. This time when they went down it was Millie pulling him by the neck of his shirt. He hovered over her for a moment as his dark eyes stared into hers. She reached up, one of her hands going into his hair, the other to the back of his neck, then she raised her head off the bed to bring her mouth to his. About halfway she lost her nerve and stopped, her lips hovering a fraction of an inch from his, feeling his hot breath on her face. His whole body was tense, a muscle frantically ticking in his jaw. A few seconds passed before he made a low, tortured noise in the back of his throat and his lips moved to hers.

Whatever plans he'd had to put this off, make her supper, do what he considered was the right thing, were quite obviously obliterated, and his kisses pushed her head back into the bed. She let out a small moan as her body took more of his weight, and he used the opportunity for his tongue to sweep into her mouth. A thrill shot through her. Nobody had ever kissed her like this, like they wanted to consume her, like they were desperate for her. She'd always thought that intimacy would be frightening. Having never been on the receiving end of much physical affection in her life, she thought she would find it intimidating and invasive, but instead she felt powerful and on some sort of high. His smell, the feel of his hard body, the way he moved over her that made her instinctively rock against him: it was so all consuming that the embarrassment, the fear, never had a chance to rise to the surface. He pulled away slightly, breathing hard, his eyes glittering and black.

"I have to..." His voice came out hoarse and he broke off to swallow before continuing, "I have to see you, baby. Please?"

Both his hands went to the hem of her T-shirt. She took a deep breath, then nodded once. That was all the encouragement he needed to pull it up and over her head, leaving her lying on the bed in just her bra. Before she could lose her nerve, or look at his face, her hands went to the waistband of her leggings and she pulled them down and off, then lay back again, holding her breath.

El had chosen all of this stuff for her. The set she had on now was ultra-feminine, light blue with lace edging. All Millie's underwear was pretty frivolous in contrast to her conservative dress code. She let El go as nuts as she wanted as she never thought anyone would be seeing it.

Pav had levered away from her slightly to allow for her

leggings to come off. When she risked a look at him to gauge his reaction, she saw that his eyes had gone wide as he swept them along the length of her body.

"Bloody hell," he whispered, almost reverently, which made Millie feel powerful again even as she felt her cheeks heat with embarrassment. She reached out to him and tried to undo one of his shirt buttons, but her fingers failed her and her cheeks heated even more as she fumbled.

Pav smiled and closed his hands over hers before pulling them away so he could grab the back of his shirt and yank it over his head. He then wasted no time undoing his belt and pushing off his trousers, leaving him in just boxer shorts. Millie had time to take in acres of olive skin over the defined musculature of his broad chest and shoulders before he landed back on top of her with his warmth pressed against her body. He took off her bra with an efficiency that was kind of intimidating, and for a moment she felt a flood of apprehension.

"I... I've never... uh..." She bit her lip and looked away, apprehension now turning to all-out fear. Not fear of Pav, but fear of failure; fear of exposure; fear of anything less than perfection. Pav must have had tonnes of sex. He'd certainly managed to work his way around the hospital with some efficiency, if the rumours were true. And here she was, maybe the only twenty-seven-year-old virgin in London, lying underneath him.

"Hey," his soft voice drew her eyes back to his. "I can hear that big brain of yours whirring away in there." He smiled and his hand came up to her face to cup her jaw. "We don't have to do anything you don't want to do. Seeing you in your bra and knickers could keep me going for months. If it's too much we'll stop and do something totally unsexy like eating beans on toast and watching The One Show. You don't have to..."

"I want to... I..."

Bugger, she could feel her throat closing up again. Of all the times for her stupid hang-ups to kick in. At this rate she would die a virgin. If she didn't do something they would lose the moment. She could already see the concern filling his eyes and feel his weight easing off her body. Okay, so verbal communication was out. She would just have to approach this another way.

One of her arms went up around his back and her hand felt the skin over the muscles there, while the other went to his neck and pulled him down. He hesitated for a moment, and in desperation she gave his hair a tug, willing him to move. It worked. His face fell into her neck and he started kissing around to her ear and then down to her chest. A large hand worked its way under her back and lifted her to him. The look on his face as he took in her bare chest was almost wild. His mouth fell to her breasts and from then on Millie didn't have time for her insecurities. All thoughts other than what he was doing to her were driven out of her head, maybe forever.

By the time they were both naked she had forgotten any apprehension. Her need for him eclipsed everything else. His smell, his skin, the way he held her, the way he moved against her: he enveloped all her senses at once. When he finally sank into her she barely felt the twinge of pain. He froze for a moment until she shifted against him and then he moved. He moved in the most amazing way: at first slow and tentative as if he didn't want to hurt her, but as her hips rocked against his, he tensed and started moving faster, harder, just like she needed him too, until she was climbing for something. As she fell off the edge of the cliff face she experienced the most intense pleasure she had ever felt in her life. It was like some sort of out-of-body experience. Then she watched his face contort and every muscle in his body pull tight as he fell off the cliff straight after her.

"BLOODY HELL," WHEEZED OUT PAV. HIS VOCABULARY FOR the last few minutes had consisted entirely of those two words with the occasional "Jesus Christ" and "bugger me" thrown in for good measure. As soon as the life-changing sex had reached its conclusion and Millie's eyes had started refocusing, he'd hauled her up the bed and settled her under the duvet, tight against him. Pav was beginning to understand that any time to regroup was bad for Millie. She needed to be kept in the moment with him, not allowed to retreat back into her thoughts. Constant barrages of physical affection seemed to work for him with her, so he was going to employ that tactic with ruthless efficiency, especially now.

For some reason he hadn't expected Millie to be a virgin. Looking back, though, that was ridiculous, since she'd already told him she'd never "fooled around" with a boy before. Did he think she had just had some sort of odd, only-genitals-touching sex with someone? When he thought about how closed she was before he got to know her and how she shied away from touch in general, especially with strangers, he realised that it really wasn't that much of a surprise. He kissed her forehead and gave her a squeeze with both arms wrapped around her. His heart still felt like it was beating outside his chest, and he could feel hers hammering against his skin.

"Are you okay?" he asked, realising she had yet to speak or in fact make any noise whatsoever. Maybe she was traumatised. "Millie? Baby, did I hurt you?"

She moved then, her head shaking violently from side to side. Then, after taking a deep, shuddering breath, she spoke.

"Why... why would you think that? No. I..." she cleared her throat "... I mean, I think I..." She took another deep breath and swallowed, before lifting her head from his chest so she could meet his eyes. "Thank you."

Pav took in her earnest expression with bewilderment. She meant it. She was thanking him for the most incredible sexual experience he'd ever had in his life. He pressed his lips together but eventually his shoulder started shaking and the laughter broke through. Millie frowned and started to pull away from him but he hauled her back.

"I'm sorry..." he said, forcing his rogue chuckles under control. "I'm not laughing at you, I promise. It's just you've got to understand why it's so funny to be thanked for what we just did; for what you just gave me." He felt her stiffen with embarrassment, and held back a sigh. "I know that was your fir–"

Her fingers shot up over his mouth to stop him mid-sentence. "Don't say it," she squeaked. "Don't..." He reached up and gently prised her hand away from his face, holding it on his chest.

"It's nothing to be embarrassed about, Millie. I'm honoured, totally blown away."

"I... I didn't really know what I was doing," mumbled Millie, her body still stiff against him. "You're probably used to... I don't know... sexperts or something, not..."

Another chuckle rose up in his chest but Pav fought it back. "Millie, gorgeous, that was the best sex I've ever had in my life. It was practically a religious experience. I don't think I'll ever recover. You might have broken me."

"Oh," she breathed, as she blinked and then scanned his face, no doubt looking for the lie in his expression. "Really?"

"Really."

A tiny smile tilted the corners of her mouth and her body relaxed into his.

"So if you're done thanking me for the most incredible

night of my life, I think we should get up and I should feed you."

"Um..." She paused for a moment and then shocked Pav by burying further into his side and kissing his jaw. "If you... I mean, maybe we could... do it again?"

Pav was not successful in fighting back his laugh this time. "I'm sorry but that's not going to be possible."

"Can't you... ? I mean, it *feels* like you could..." Millie's eyes dropped to her thigh which was resting against his excited-again-already groin.

Pav groaned. "Millie, you're killing me. *I* might be so turned on that I'd be able to defeat basic biology and go another round, but *you* need to wait a few days."

"I don't think that's true. I–"

"We can do other... *stuff*."

Millie gave a tiny huff of annoyance and Pav smiled, kissing her temple and then lifting her face so he could slide his nose against hers and whisper in her ear. "I promise you'll like the other stuff. Do you trust me?"

He had asked her that with a smile still in his voice. She lifted her face again to look into his eyes, her face now serious.

"Yes, I trust you."

There was a weight behind her words. Pav felt like she was giving him another gift. His smile dropped and he nodded once, trying to convey that he didn't take her trust lightly. As he pulled her lips to his he decided that supper could wait, at least for a little while.

Chapter 26

You're not trying hard enough

MILLIE SMILED DOWN AT HER NOTES AS SHE LISTENED TO what could only be Pav's arrival at the meeting. She knew it was him without having to look up. He was without exception the loudest, most extrovert person in any room. Even his footsteps seemed louder than the average person. She could usually hear him approaching her office a good five minutes before he actually reached her door.

When he burst through the double doors of the meeting room greetings were called, jokes exchanged, backs slapped; he lit up the space with his smile, his laughter, his energy. As a lifelong, confirmed introvert with a history of slipping into rooms unnoticed and doing the least possible to draw attention to herself, Millie still found Pav's ability to sail through life without any awkwardness slightly intimidating, but also incredibly magnetic. He was five minutes late but that didn't faze him, and he certainly didn't let it inhibit him.

In the month since they'd finally slept together he'd been like a tornado sweeping through her life. It was both exhilarating and terrifying. They spent the majority of nights together now and he was steadily working his way under her defences with a lethal combination of affection, charm and sex... lots and lots of sex. Millie had not realised what she'd been missing out on all these years but she was certainly making up for lost time now.

"Right, team," he said, pulling a chair from the wall and squeezing it between Millie and Jamie once he'd given Jamie a shove to the side (nearly knocking him off his chair) and Jamie had punched him in the arm. "I'm pumped for the morbid stuff – let's get it on."

"Glad you decided to join us, Dr Martakis," said Mr Crawley, the head of the urology department. "Your excitement for the quarterly morbidity and mortality meeting is commendable. Let's hope your figures hold up to scrutiny shall we?"

Pav grinned. "You betcha, Bossman." Mr Crawley sighed the sigh of a man who had tolerated Pavlos for the last ten years.

He had not been Pav's "Bossman" for at least two of those years, but before Pav had been appointed as a consultant at St George's he had trained under him. Mr Crawley liked to act as though Pav was the bane of his existence, but was, like most people Pav interacted with, quite obviously charmed by him. This was evidenced by the fact he had appointed Pav as a consultant after his training had finished, and that the corners of his mouth were twitching even as he rolled his eyes at Pav's antics.

"Let's start with the interventional radiology and the ureteric stenting. Do we have someone to present?"

Millie looked down at her hands and breathed out a slow sigh of relief. She had written up the figures and pulled the presentation together, then given it all to one of the other registrars. There was no way she was presenting anything to the meeting. As the registrar started going through the slides Pav touched her forearm and leaned down to whisper in her ear.

"Hey, I watched you write that up. Why are you letting Dullard up there take all the credit?"

She breathed in deeply and shivered, happy to be surrounded by his scent and to feel his breath on her cheek. Just being close to him eased the anxiety she always felt at meetings like this, but there was no way she was going to speak, even in a whisper. Instead she wrote on her paper in front of her: *You know why*.

Pav frowned and his mouth tightened but he gave a short nod.

It had been a while since he'd brought up the conference. She knew he still wanted her to go and speak, but even after all the confidence-building stuff she'd done with the girls and the extra CBT she was having with Anwar, after seeing her at the Grand Round and the palaver it caused, Pav had to understand that was impossible.

Another hour later, after going through all the complications from any urology procedure over the last three months, the meeting was over. Millie attempted to make her standard rapid, low-profile exit but Marcus, the radiology registrar who had given her presentation, blocked her way to the door.

"Thanks, Millie," he said, a wide smile lighting his face. "A couple of us are off down the pub after work. I could buy you a drink tonight if you were keen? It's the least I could do in the circumstances."

Ever since Millie's collapse and subsequent rehabilitation this had been happening with alarming frequency. Men had been approaching her, talking to her, asking her out. After years of zero male interest it was more than a little confusing. She wasn't sure if it was the humanising effect of the collapse that did it, or the fact she was maybe starting to act a *little* more normal. To her horror Pav caught hold of her hand.

"Sorry, mate, we've got plans tonight," he said, his naturally louder-than-average voice carrying over the sounds of people leaving. "I could bring Millie along to the pub on the way though, if it's a radiology social?"

The challenge in Pav's voice was hard to miss and his chest had visibly puffed up as he faced the other man.

"Well, it's not exactly a social... just, like, a couple of us. You know." Marcus trailed off and shifted uncomfortably in front of them.

"Oh yeah?" Pav asked, his eyebrows rising and his tone full of fake curiousity. "I know a good few peeps down in x-ray. Who's up for it?"

"Well... uh..." Marcus scowled at Pav and took a small step back before he looked at Millie again. "Maybe another time then," he mumbled.

"Yeah, yeah, *maybe*," Pav said. "So, Mils, what time shall I pick you up tonight?"

Millie saw multiple heads had turned in their direction and felt heat burn in her cheeks. There was no way her voice was going to function with this many eyes on her. Pav frowned and cocked his head to the side in obvious confusion, moving right into her personal space, which drew even more attention from the room.

Jamie came to her rescue. He drew up next to them and shielded her from the majority of the curious eyes watching her.

"Pav, you're embarrassing Millie," he whispered. "Let's go."

"What?" Pav looked around as if noticing the other people in the room for the first time. Then he grinned and proceeded to practically drag Millie from the room. He held her hand all the way back to her office and, once there, gave her a kiss on the cheek, right in front of Don.

"You're going to have to get used to public displays of affection I'm afraid," he told her, still grinning. "I'm a PDA type of guy."

He was like a whirlwind. His energy seemed too big to be contained within the walls of her small workspace. His grin died a little as he realised she had yet to speak. "Hey," he said, more softly now. "Mils? You okay?"

"Maybe you should slow down a little, young man," Don said, his kind eyes taking in Millie's flushed face. "Let her get used to all this."

"I..." Millie took a deep breath in and then let it out slowly, resisting the urge to pinch her forearm. "It's fine." She straightened her spine. If she was going to be with someone like Pav she was going to have to be a little braver. And she wanted to be with him so desperately. If there was any motivation to help her change it was this man and the prospect of losing him. She would just have to toughen up. She forced a smile. "I'm fine."

Pav's grin died a little more at the sight of her forced smile.

"I know I'm a pushy bastard sometimes," he said, his voice now soft. "I'll tone it down, all right?"

Millie shook her head. He shouldn't have to tone anything down – not for her. "I'm fine." She widened her eyes at Don, giving a quick shake of her head, and he frowned across at her.

"Okay," Pav said into the silence. "So shall I come to yours or pick you up to come over to mine tonight?"

He didn't ask if she was free. Pav knew that if it wasn't Friday night bingo or a book group Millie was always free. She bit her lip.

"Er... I... I can't see you tonight."

"*What?*"

Millie knew she was boring and predictable but the surprise on Pav's face was still slightly galling.

"Are you working?"

Millie hesitated. She hadn't exactly been avoiding telling Pav about tonight, just hoping he might have had something on himself. Unlike hers, Pav's free time was stuffed full of all sorts of other things: football and then the pub with the boys (he'd dragged her to watch a tournament last weekend – she'd thought she'd hate it but Libby came with Rosie to keep her company and cheer on Jamie, which meant Kira had been there too; between Kira's inappropriate cheerleader routine on the sidelines and Rosie's nonstop five-year-old chatter, it had actually been kind of fun), family meals (he'd tried to drag her along to these but so far she'd refused – the humiliation of the bad impression she must have made on his mother was still too fresh), squash, tennis, urology department nights down the pub... the list went on. But with her luck, of *course* he would have to be free tonight. And of course he would want an explanation why she wasn't. Not for the first time Millie wished she could lie convincingly.

"I've got to meet my parents tonight," she told him, her eyes dropping to his shirt collar.

"Oh..." He paused and then ducked down to catch her eye again. Pav hated being denied eye contact, and over the last month she'd become much better at maintaining it – only breaking into old habits when she felt under pressure or uncomfortable. "Well... I could come with you."

Millie shook her head back and forth rapidly and started stepping away from him, but he caught her hand in his.

"No, no, no. I mean..." she said quickly. He was frowning at her with a hurt expression. She bit her lip thinking of all the times he'd wanted her to get to know his family compared to how she was shutting him out of hers. But he didn't understand. How could he, with his large, loving family – all expressed emotion and unchecked affection; how could he possibly *ever* understand?

"Trust me. I'm doing you a favour. My parents are..."

His other hand reached up and closed over hers, pulling it out from under her sleeve. She'd started pinching the skin of her wrist without even registering what she was doing. Pav had attacked her wristband with his kitchen scissors last week after she'd nearly drawn blood from snapping it during an appraisal at work.

"Hey, hey, hey," he said gently, both of his hands now holding hers. "Don't get yourself worked up, okay? If you don't want me to meet your parents yet, that's fine. I'll see you tomorrow."

Millie looked up at him. His eyes were earnest but there was still a hint of hurt in their depths. In relief she let out a breath she hadn't realised she'd been holding. At least she thought it was relief. For some reason there was some disappointment mingled in there too. She instinctively knew that Pav meeting her mother and father would be a disaster, but the urge to have him there was surprisingly strong. When she was with him she didn't feel like the little girl who was a perpetual disappointment. She didn't feel like she wasn't enough. She felt... well, not exactly brave but brav*er*.

But she'd dealt with her parents alone her entire life. One more night wasn't going to make any difference.

PAV PUSHED OPEN THE OFFICE DOOR AND WAS SURPRISED to see just Don sitting in front of his computer, frowning down at the keyboard. He'd decided to try and talk Millie into letting

Susie Tate

him come tonight after all, and she never usually left before five.

"Well, don't just stand there," Don snapped once he registered Pav's presence. "Come and sort this damn machine out for me. Bloody thing won't let me in."

"Er..." Pav's eyes flicked over to Millie's empty chair. "Well, you kind of need your passwords."

Don grunted in annoyance.

"Millie deals with all of this nonsense," he mumbled. "Bugger, I'll have to leave the rest till Monday." Pav had long since realised that without Millie, Don would not have been able to carry on working. The two of them had a perfect symbiotic relationship – Don's affability and charm with Millie's know-how and work ethic. "Blast. Thought I could be useful for once."

"Where *is* Millie?"

"Oh, she had to go home on time tonight. On pins and needles all afternoon about "getting ready". She headed off at four to the hairdresser's."

"I thought she was just meeting her parents?" Pav asked, frowning in confusion. His mama was lucky if he shaved before he came home to see them. Don turned around in his chair to face Pav and gave him a shrewd look.

"She hasn't talked to you about her parents much, has she?"

"Er... what makes you say that?" Pav said, sending his own shrewd look Don's way.

"Because if you knew anything about that girl's parents you would never say she was *just* going to meet them. Do you know who her father is?"

Pav crossed his arms over his chest and he frowned. "How about you stop speaking in riddles, Don?"

Don huffed and rolled his eyes. "You're not *trying* hard enough."

236

"What does that mean?"

"It means that you, my boy, need to ask more questions. Do you know how long it is since Millie's seen her parents?"

"I... well, she doesn't really talk about her folks. I know Gammy. She's quite the character. But..."

"Her grandmother's a different story altogether. You must have been aware that Millie *has* parents. Why haven't you asked her, for God's sake?"

"Well, I overheard her on the phone to her mum once. I guess the convo did seem a bit off to me but... I..." Pav scratched the back of his neck and then glared down at Don. "Here's an idea: why don't you tell me?" he asked through gritted teeth.

Don's criticism was hitting home in an uncomfortable way. Pav shifted on his feet as he thought about how much the conversation tended to revolve around him when he was with Millie. She always asked him about *his* day, *his* work, *his* sport, *his* family. The problem was that everything he said seemed to absolutely fascinate her; it was hard with that level of ego-stroking not to bang on about yourself.

"She hasn't seen her mother or father for at least two years."

"What? But... but why? Did they fall out?"

"No."

"I don't understand."

Don put his hands behind his head and leaned back in his chair to look up at the ceiling. "Well," he said after a ridiculously long pause. "Why don't you take the initiative and *find out*?"

"I guess I'll ask her tomorrow but–"

"No," Don said, his normally soft voice now firm. "You find out tonight. Go with her and meet them."

"She doesn't want me to, Don."

"Millie may not want you to, but what Millie wants and what she needs are two different things. I can't believe you're going to take that lying down either. You're such a pushy bastard about everything else."

"I'm not sure I–"

"Just go," Don snapped. "She's not leaving till eight. You can catch her at home."

Pav ran his hands through his hair and then put them on his hips. "Right, okay, but if she's furious I'm going to heap the blame on you, old man."

As Pav turned to leave Don shouted out after him: "Put on a suit and shave. You'll thank me. I promise."

Chapter 27

Huge asset

"WHAT ARE YOU DOING HERE?" MILLIE ASKED AFTER she'd wrenched open her front door. Pav's mouth fell open and he took a step back.

"Bloody hell," he whispered, his eyes sweeping her figure in the long, deep-blue evening gown she was wearing. Her hair had been artfully styled into an up-do of waves at the side of her head. Her make-up seemed even more flawless than her usual perfect, and her heels were a few inches higher than normal. "You look... incredible."

Millie wasn't listening to him. Her eyes were darting up and down the street. "You have to leave," she whispered.

Maybe he'd misjudged this situation. Her face had drained of colour and there was actual panic in her grey eyes. But Don had implied that she needed him to be here. For the hundredth time since that conversation earlier, Pav cursed himself for being such a self-absorbed arsehole and not bloody knowing why Millie's parents were such an issue.

"Okay, look, can I just stay to meet them? What's the worst that could happen?"

Millie bit her lip and looked away from him for a moment.

"You're not ashamed of me are you?"

Her eyes snapped back to his. "Of *course* not," she said, her voice and expression fierce. "I would never... I mean... nobody would ever be ashamed of you."

She looked horrified that he would even suggest such a thing. A split second later and she had grabbed his hand and dragged him into the house. Once the door was closed behind them he grinned down at her still fierce-looking face, slid one hand around her tiny waist and the other up to her neck to touch the sapphire earrings she had on.

"Have I told you how stunning you look?"

"Pav, I–" He cut her off with a brief kiss, or at least it was intended to be brief. Once he was engulfed in her expensive perfume and had her chest pressed up against his, it turned into something a little less PG than anticipated. She blinked up at him as he pulled away, her lipstick smudged, her pupils dilated and her breathing shallow.

"Okay," he said, keeping his hands on her but allowing them both some space for sanity to return. "Before they arrive I think we should talk about wh–"

A loud burst of staccato knocks interrupted his speech and Millie jumped in his arms.

"My father–" she started, only to be cut off by another burst of knocking. She sighed, her shoulders drooping and her gaze dropping to the floor. After closing her eyes briefly she straightened and turned to the door, opening it wide. Pav started to smile, ready to launch an all-out charm offensive on these people and prove to Millie that his gate-crashing was not the end of the world. But in the shock of recognition his smile died and his mouth fell open. The current Secretary of State for Energy and Climate Change, and bookie's favourite for the next Prime Minister, was standing on the doorstep next to his wife: David and Valerie Morrison. David wasn't as tall as he looked on the telly but he had the same greying hair, the same three-piece suit, the same smug expression and a pair of all-too-familiar grey eyes. Valerie looked exactly the same in real life: thin, perfectly tailored – the only difference being the black evening gown that now replaced her normal suits.

Pav was standing slightly behind Millie and to the side, so they didn't notice him at first. Valerie stared at her daughter, her eyes sweeping from the top of Millie's head to her shoes before they narrowed.

"Mother," Millie said, her voice devoid of any emotion.

"Your lipstick is smudged," Valerie told her, her lip curling in disgust. "And your heels don't tone with your dress."

Pav cleared his throat. Millie's mother's gaze snapped over to him and her eyes narrowed even more before she cleared her expression. She did another sweep, this time of Pav's appearance; he was glad he'd worn his best suit, and exceedingly grateful to Don for the warning.

"Mother, Father, this is Pavlos Martakis." Millie's quiet voice cut through the silence. "He's a consultant surgeon at St George's hospital. Pav, these are my parents: Valerie and David Morrison."

Valerie's posture visibly relaxed at the mention of consultant surgeon and her eyebrows lowered. Pav shook himself out of his shock after witnessing possibly the coldest family reunion in the history of the planet, and moved forward to the couple with his hand out to shake.

"Pleasure to meet you," Pav lied as he shook first Valerie's (he didn't dare go in for a kiss) and then David's hand. David Morrison was known for his global-warming-sceptic views and his politics were the polar opposite to Pav's.

"Right, yes... well, this is a surprise," David said, his politician's facade slipping into place to mask his obvious shock.

Valerie was frowning as her gaze flicked between Millie and Pav.

"Are you here for work, Dr Martakis?" she asked, with a fake smile. "Is there a project you and Millie are doing together? I'm terribly sorry but we are going to have to steal her away for the evening."

"No," Pav said slowly. He moved next to Millie and felt her stiffen as he put his arm around her shoulders. "No, Millie's my girlfriend. We're together. I asked if I could meet you both."

Valerie's carefully controlled expression dropped for a moment and her mouth fell open as her eyes went wide. Her father simply burst out laughing; it wasn't a kind, encouraging laugh either, it had a cruel, mocking edge to it.

"Sorry, sorry," he said, after he'd controlled his hilarity. "It's just... girlfriend? Young man, I've known Millie all her life and that seems... unlikely."

Pav's expression closed and he pulled Millie even closer into his side.

"I'm not sure what it is that you see as unlikely, Mr Morrison."

Valerie flicked her husband an irritated look, then stared at Pav again, having managed to school her expression. Her head tilted to the side as if she didn't quite know what to make of him. "You're coming *with* us tonight?"

"Yes," Pav said.

"No," Millie put in at the same time. Pav gave her shoulder a light squeeze, remembering Don's words from earlier and just instinctively knowing that he wasn't going to leave Millie alone with these people.

"Yes," Pav repeated. "I'm coming too."

"Right, well..." There was a brief pause as Valerie looked between them again. "We'll wait in the car whilst you fix your make-up and change your shoes, Camilla. We need to leave in ten minutes."

"You understand what's expected of you?" Valerie asked as Millie stared out of the window of the Mercedes. She was sitting in the back with her parents; Pav was in the front with her parents' driver of the last fifteen years, Michael.

"Yes," Millie said.

"I don't want a repeat of last time," her father put in. "You've got to actually speak, Camilla. None of this mumbling like a mental deficient."

"And you can't hide in the loos like you did at your graduation party," her mother said. "I'll never understand you. We put on a huge dinner for you to celebrate, and you barely spoke a word and cowered away for most of the night."

Her parents were trying to keep their voices down so that they couldn't be overheard from the front, but if Pav's back stiffening was anything to go by, that was not working. Normally Millie wouldn't have responded. She'd learned long ago that fighting back against the relentless criticism didn't get her anywhere. It was in general better to just shut herself off from it. But whilst it was okay for just her to hear all her faults listed, knowing Pav was listening too was humiliating.

"I didn't want a party," she said, her voice brittle and tightly controlled. "You knew that."

There was a pause as her mother took a shocked breath. "How dare you, you ungrateful brat," she whisper-hissed, grabbing Millie's elbow in a death grip. "Lots of normal young people would have killed for a big party in their honour."

Millie snorted; actually *snorted*. It was the most disrespectful she thought she had ever been to her parents.

"It was not a party for me. It was a party for you... to show off to your friends. No, that's not right... to your acquaintances. You wanted to use me to show off the fact that your clever daughter graduated medical school before she was even twenty-one. Just like you're using me tonight. It was nothing to do with *me*. None of my friends were even there."

Valerie turned her cold glare on Millie and a shiver went up her spine at the hatred in her mother's eyes. "You didn't *have* any friends to invite, Camilla." Millie swallowed hard. She hadn't allowed this woman to see her cry since she was five years old, and she was not about to start now.

"Get your fucking hand off her, now."

Millie started as Pav's angry voice filled the Mercedes. He was turned fully round in his seat, his eyes locked onto Valerie's grip on Millie's elbow.

"How dare you sp–"

"I don't know what the bloody hell is going on here," Pav cut her off, his voice now low and dangerous. "But I do know that if you don't remove your hand from your daughter's elbow right fucking now I'm going to do it for you."

"Well..." Valerie huffed, but she did release Millie's arm. "I don't think that–"

"Millie may not have had friends back then," Pav told her. "But you'd do well to remember she does have them now."

"Now, now, old boy," said David, his fake smile having little effect on Pav's furious expression. "You know what families are like. Things can get a bit heated and all that. No need to go off the deep end."

"I know what *my* family is like, *sir*," Pav replied through gritted teeth. "And I can assure you it's a world away from this."

The car pulled up to the entrance of the Savoy just as Pav finished his speech. Millie was in a state of shock and sat frozen in place as Michael (who had been studiously avoiding the drama unfolding in the enclosed space, just as he had pretended to ignore so many ugly exchanges in the past, other than giving Millie small encouraging smiles or taking snatched opportunities to squeeze her hand) pushed open his door and stepped out. Instead of moving to the back passenger door where her father was sitting, Michael moved to Pav's door and yanked it open. As Pav emerged, Michael gave him a slap on the back and shook his hand.

"Well... I... what a ridiculous, vulgar display," Valerie muttered as she was forced, likely for the first time in a long time, to open her own door. Millie's stomach clenched as she followed her mother out of the car.

A nanny had tried to intervene when Millie was nine during a particularly spiteful tirade from her mother. She was replaced the next day. A teacher at school had even gone as far as reporting her concerns of emotional abuse to social services after an ugly parents' evening. That had resulted in a couple of visits to their house from a harassed-looking, over-worked social worker, during which her mother put up a good front.

The fact that Millie lived in a huge house in Hampstead (the social worker had joked during her visit that she was more used to visiting drug dens in far less salubrious parts of North London) also contributed to the case being dropped. The teacher had left the school shortly after. So Millie had been conditioned to think that any help from outside was pointless. Indeed, it often resulted in a person Millie had cared about being removed from her life. Her parents were a force to be reckoned with, and they had power. Millie had never been in a situation before where they didn't have the upper hand. And if she lost Pav...

"You okay?" his low voice sounded close to her ear as he slipped his hand into hers and pulled her away from the car to stand next to him on the pavement. His tone was gentle but his words were still tight with anger.

She nodded. "Look, maybe it's better if you don't come in... I mean..." She trailed off and Pav turned her towards him, taking her other hand.

"Maybe we should both go home," he said, and she rested her forehead against his chest, just for a moment.

"You don't understand," she whispered. "I have to go with them tonight. It's... it's complicated, but I *have* to. What they say to me... it doesn't affect me, not anymore."

"Maybe not," he said, his tone laced with doubt. "But I am not leaving you here by yourself. I don't care how complicated it is."

She sighed and then looked up from his chest to his face. His mouth was set in a stubborn line; he was so beautiful.

"Okay, but don't engage with them. Don't argue with them. Speaking to them like I did in the car was a mistake. They're... easier to handle if you don't respond. Trust me."

"Okay, baby," he whispered back a little too easily; then he stole a brief, hard kiss and dropped one of her hands but kept the other as he walked her towards the entrance.

"Ah, the prodigal daughter!" Mr Tinsdale, the party whip, cried as Millie was steered towards a group of Tory ministers and supporters inside the entrance to the ballroom. "We were beginning to think you were a figment of your dad's imagination."

The group all laughed and Millie managed to force a small smile. There must have been about ten of them, mainly older men but with some women and two younger ministers. The youngest she recognised as the Minister of State for Energy and

Climate Change, Barclay Lucas, who'd been in the news relent-
lessly for the last few months as an avid supporter of cold
fusion and the energy revolution – which was in direct opposi-
tion to her father, who unfortunately held the higher office and
had succeeded so far in stalling the process. A green Tory was a
rare thing indeed and Mr Lucas had been very vocal about
making the UK carbon neutral over the next five years. The
press loved him. It didn't hurt that his looks were catwalk-
worthy and his relationship status was single. Instead of chuck-
ling like the rest of them, Mr Lucas was staring at Millie's
father like he was something he'd scraped off the bottom of his
shoe. Millie liked him instantly.

Her mother gave her a sharp elbow in the ribs and her body
jolted slightly into Pav, who still had her hand in his. He glared
over her head at her mother and opened his mouth to say something. Desperate to head him off, Millie forced a smile and
made her mouth form words.

"Yes... um... I exist," she told the group, drawing more faint
chuckles. "I'm Camilla."

Silence. She bit her lip. Her conversational reserves were
totally depleted. She felt her throat close over.

"And you're a doctor, Camilla?" Mr Tinsdale pushed,
staring at her in a strangely assessing way.

"I'm a radiologist," she managed to get out through her tight
throat. Pav squeezed her hand.

"Oh, so you're one of the chaps... er, sorry... chapesses who
sit in the hospital basement and look at x-rays all day?" Millie
was about to nod but she stopped herself at the sound of Pav's
irritated voice.

"Well," he said, drawing out the word as he unleashed the
most charming smile in his arsenal on the assembled group. "I
guess she *does* do that, when she's not extracting actual blood
clots from the arteries of the brain to restore blood flow for the

stroke team, or inserting nephrostomy tubes into my patients to drain their obstructed, infected kidneys and save their lives, among many, many other things. Then, yes, I guess she does sit in the basement a fair bit, making sense of complex scans and images whose interpretation is beyond the capabilities of every other speciality."

There was a long pause, during which a few throats were cleared and Millie noticed Barclay Lucas's small smile.

"Pavlos Martakis," Pav added, extending his hand to Mr Tinsdale, who gave him a tight smile and shook it with obvious reluctance. "I'm Millie's partner."

"You're a urologist?" Barclay Lucas put in.

"Yes, I met Millie at the hospital. Never been to one of these political shin-digs before and... between you and me," he mock-whispered, "I'm not actually a Tory, but even a die-hard Jeremy Corbyn fan does what needs to be done for his missus."

Barclay Lucas stared at Pav for a moment before he let out a bark of laughter. For a man who was rarely photographed even smiling, it was quite a sight.

"You're married?" Mr Tinsdale asked.

"Not yet," said Pav, giving Millie's hand another squeeze as she turned wide eyes to his profile.

"Yes, well," her father cut in quickly, "as you can all see my daughter *does* in fact exist, and being a professional working in the NHS she'll be a huge asset to the campaign next summer."

"Aren't you getting a little ahead of yourself, David?" Barclay asked, his smile dropping and the more familiar icy expression replacing it. "We haven't even had the first-round ballot yet. The Prime Minister only announced she was stepping down last week."

"Of course, of course, old boy," David blustered. "But I think we can all agree that..."

The ringing in Millie's ears cut off her ability to hear any more and she took an involuntary step back. She felt her vision narrow as the sweat started forming on her back. Her father really was going to go for the leadership of the Conservative party. He was going to run for Prime Minster. Everything made sense to her now: the insistence that she attend this fundraising dinner tonight; the threats her mother had made to get her here. They needed her to be the dutiful daughter during the campaign. They needed her for his image.

But Millie couldn't be photographed; she couldn't be on camera beside her father on a stage for the whole country, the whole world, to see. Her head started shaking from side to side in a reflex action of denial. "Excuse me," she whispered as she yanked her hand from Pav's and turned to run to the nearest toilet.

Chapter 28

You'd be surprised what people will believe

"Camilla, you get out of there this instant."

Millie pressed her head against the cool wall of the cubicle and tried to block out her mother's voice. The very little she had managed to eat that day had made a dramatic reappearance a moment ago, and she was still shaking from the effort of all the retching. She concentrated on slowing her breathing and employing her Cognitive Behavioural Ts herapy techniques.

"Stop," she whispered into the small space. Thought-stopping was something that was normally fairly effective when she was with Anwar or alone in her house and able to shout it out loud without fear of being overheard. The idea was that when you went into a negative thought spiral that was out of your control, actually vocalising a command for it to stop would work. In the past she'd pinched her forearm at the same time to help, and more recently flicked the elastic band on her wrist; but she'd had to forgo that tonight with her outfit. So just whispering "stop" whilst you were on your knees of a posh toilet cubicle with your hostile mother only feet away was not the best circumstance for maximal efficacy.

"I told you what the consequences would be if you were stubborn about this," Valerie hissed.

"You..." Millie's voice was unsteady and she hated that show of weakness; she took a deep breath in through her mouth and let it out through her nose. "You said one night. One. Not a whole campaign."

She forced herself to her feet and pushed open the door. Valerie moved back to let her through, her face flushed red with anger.

"We don't ask much of you, young lady," she said, her voice trembling with rage. Millie moved to the sink and turned on the tap before bracing both hands either side of it and letting her head drop down for a moment. The hotel they were in was fairly lavish and the bathrooms were huge: there was an actual sofa in one corner. She absently noticed that one of the cubicles was occupied – a pair of stilettos were visible under the stall door. "We let you do your own thing, go your own way, demanding nothing. But if you refuse to stand by your father's side in this, you will regret it."

Millie held one of her hands under the cool water and then brought it up to the back of her neck before splashing her cheeks and rinsing her mouth out. She would deal with her mother in a moment. In the background she heard the main door to the ladies open; her mother was too far-gone in her rant to notice.

"I'll have your precious grandmother out of that home and living with your father and me before you can say "dementia'."

"You'd have to prove that that was in her best interests," Millie said, hating her weakness and the fact her voice was still shaking.

Valerie scoffed. "You know these homes, darling," she said. "All sorts of abuse scandals going on. I'm sure nobody would bat an eyelid if I was to decide it was safer to keep my precious mother-in-law with me full time."

Millie closed her eyes and leaned heavily against the sink. "She's happy there, Mother. You can't–"

"Try me, you little bitch," spat Valerie, her eyes flashing with fury as she gripped Millie's shoulder, giving her a shake. "You just try me."

One second she had a bruising grip on Millie's shoulder, the next Valerie was propelled across the plush cloakroom into one of the overstuffed chaise longues.

"I warned you," Pav growled, "not to put your hands on her."

Millie stared at over six feet of furious Greek male and her mouth dropped open. He looked so completely out of place in the overdone ladies toilets it would have been funny had Millie not been dealing with a panic attack induced by the Mother from Hell.

"How *dare* you," Valerie said, pushing herself up unsteadily from the chaise longue and then dusting her dress off with sufficient drama.

"Come on, Millie," Pav murmured as he took her hand where she was gripping the sink and gently prised her fingers away from the porcelain. "Time to go home now, sweetheart."

"Camilla," Valerie said in a low, dangerous voice, the sound of which would make Millie cower with fear as a little girl. "You leave now and–"

"Just what brand of evil bitch threatens her daughter with her grandmother's well being?" Pav interrupted, his tone almost conversational. "I'm guessing that if the press were to get hold of that little nugget of information, Daddy Dearest wouldn't be seen in nearly the same positive light."

"Nobody would ever believe that–"

"You'd be surprised what people will believe," Pav told her;

then his tone darkened and his eyes narrowed. "Come near her again, contact her again, and you might just find out." With that he pulled Millie to him, tucked her under his arm and walked them both out of the loos and straight to the exit.

RACHEL MULHOLLAND STEPPED OUT FROM BEHIND THE cubicle door as she heard the clicking of Valerie Morrison's heels retreat over the marble and out of the large, ridiculously decadent bathroom. Gossip had always gravitated naturally Rachel's way. It wasn't just that she was an observant person, or that she was skilled in the art of active listening; it was almost as if she attracted the information: it was a gift. So her choice of career made sense. In truth journalism had seemed to choose her. But even by Rachel's standards, the last fifteen minutes had been beyond lucky.

She looked down at her phone and suppressed a small smile. The image of Valerie Morrison gripping her tearful daughter's shoulder, her face twisted in an ugly scowl, was journalism gold. Dirt on David Morrison was not easy to come by. A hard-working philanthropist with a perfect family – his character was very difficult to smear. Rachel herself had always thought there was something off about the guy: his eyes seemed... cold, and his policies as Secretary of State for Energy and Climate Change were pretty despicable. He was about the only climate change sceptic out there and a real barrier to the cold fusion energy revolution. Yes, it was safe to say Rachel despised David Morrison. That was why this story could wait. She would wait and watch. When the time was right and with all the information, she would take that fascist bastard down, permanently.

When Millie and Pav made it outside Michael was waiting for them. He didn't seem to blink an eye that they were without her parents, and proceeded to usher them into the back seat.

Once settled and on the road Millie looked across at Pav and her heart sank. His jaw was so tense that there was a muscle ticking in his cheek and he was taking sharp, angry breaths through his nose. The atmosphere in the car felt thick and Millie's hand snuck up under her coat to her forearm as if acting of its own accord.

"Um..." she started; her voice came out as a croak so she cleared her throat. "I..."

"Why didn't you tell me about them, Millie?" Pav asked in a tightly controlled voice. For once it was *him* not affording *her* the eye contact, and she felt the ball of worry in her stomach rise up to her throat.

How could she explain to him, with his loving, warm, messy but beautiful family, how her parents treated her? In truth she was ashamed of the non-relationship she had with the two people who were supposed to love her more than anyone else in the world. Anwar told her it was their fault that they were unable to give her unconditional love; that it was their shortcoming. But still, after all this time and even knowing it wasn't rational, Millie still had the underlying worry that she just wasn't good enough. How could she explain to this man, brimming with self-confidence and self-belief, that she'd been scared of him knowing the truth about her parents, scared that he might start to wonder what he saw that was so special in her; that he would start to see what her parents saw... somebody hopelessly weak.

"I'm sorry," she muttered, looking away from his angry expression and out of the window instead.

"Hey," his voice was softer now, "I know you're stressed, but don't do that, okay?"

His body shifted closer to hers across the back seat and his warm hands settled on her cold ones, separating them, then pushing her sleeve up to see the red mark she had left. He brought her wrist up to his mouth and gave it a soft kiss.

"And don't say sorry. You don't have to apologise. I just..." He caught her chin and brought her face closer so that his eyes were burning down into hers, "I just want you to trust me. Can you give me that?"

"I..." Millie took a deep breath. If this thing with Pav was ever going to work she had to push past her limits, she had to let him in. "I was ashamed. They..." She looked up at him, meeting his dark, concerned eyes still burning with anger, anger she knew he felt on her behalf, anger for her... because he cared about her, because she was worth caring about. She sucked in a steadying breath and let it out. "They hate me." She felt his hands tighten in hers and saw that muscle tick in his cheek. "Well, maybe hate's too strong a word, too strong an emotion for what they feel for me. I think irritate is better. I irritate them. I was always a quiet child: shy, not interested or even able to impress their friends. They thought that with my intelligence I should be more... competent. But they were... disappointed."

"They made your childhood a misery." Pav stated the truth.

"In some ways, yes. But... they didn't abuse me. Not really. They never hurt me. Mother gripping my elbow is about as physical as they ever let it get with me. I–"

"There are other ways to hurt a child." Michael's angry voice cut Millie off and she turned surprised eyes to catch his in the rear-view mirror. "Ways that hurt more than a few bruises. The way they spoke to you, Miss Morrison, for years. It was... shameful. They're not human."

"Please, Michael, please call me Millie," she told him – something she'd wanted to say for decades. She saw his eyes crinkle in a smile and he gave a short nod.

"All right, Miss Millie." Millie didn't bother to try to get him to drop the Miss, she would be fighting a losing battle. "All I'm saying is that nobody should have to take those sort of relentless ugly words. I wish..." He blinked a couple of times and then cleared his throat. When he spoke again his voice was quieter and a little hoarse. "I wish I had been able to do more, Miss Millie. I should have said something or–"

"You would have lost your job if you'd said anything to either of them. We both know that. And then I wouldn't have had you at all." Michael's encouraging smiles, his kind eyes in the rear-view mirror, the funny faces he pulled behind her parents' back: over the years they had meant more to her than he probably realised.

"Yes, well," Michael said, his voice gruff with emotion as he pulled up in front of Millie's house to park, "it's not right is all I'm saying. You'll not convince me otherwise."

He exited the car before Millie could answer and came around to her side to open her door. As she came out she was surprised to be swept up in a brief but fierce hug. After a moment her arms came up to squeeze him back. When he finally let her go, he held her away from him with his hands on her shoulders and searched her face. Pav had left the car via the other passenger door and came to stand beside them. Michael was staring at her and his eyes looked suspiciously wet.

"I'm okay," she whispered, and managed a small smile. "Well, at least, I'm going to be okay. I think."

Michael's eyes flicked over to Pav who was hovering in wait

to claim Millie. When he looked back at her, his eyes crinkled in another smile. "I know you will," he said, before giving her a brief kiss on her cheek and stepping back. He gave Pav a subtle chin-lift, which Pav returned, and something passed between the two men that Millie didn't quite understand; then he shook Pav's hand and turned back to the car.

Chapter 29

Endorphins

P᷉AV GAVE M᷉ILLIE'S HAND A SQUEEZE AS THEY STEPPED into the marquee. As he was brother of the bride he'd been one of the ushers in the church, and been too busy to make sure Millie wasn't freaking out. He'd only had time to briefly introduce her to Costas, his future brother-in-law, before she took her seat.

Outwardly she seemed to be coping well. In fact outwardly Millie was nothing short of absolutely stunning. El had excelled herself. Millie's dress was cream flowers on a white background, with a wide bright blue belt and matching shoes with impossibly high thin heels. She had some sort of small hat balanced on the side of her head as if by magic, and her mass of golden brown hair secured in an elaborate arrangement on the other side. If you didn't know her you would assume she was a beautiful, confident woman. It was only Pav who could see the tension around her mouth and the pallor beneath her make-up.

Luckily Jamie, Libby and Rosie had been invited to the wedding as well. This was partly because Jamie was Pav's best friend and partly because Greek weddings tended to be huge.

So Millie had been able to sit next to Libby, with Rosie promptly climbing onto her lap, which took up much of her attention as the crowds filtered into the large space.

"Jesus Christ, you've done all right for yourself, mate," Costas muttered to Pav after he'd met Millie, only to flinch as he was smacked around the head by his mother, who was lurking behind him.

"You're standing on consecrated ground, Costas," she hissed. "You cannot take the Lord's name in vain in his house."

Pav stepped back to allow Costas' mama better access to abuse her son, and caught Millie staring at the interaction, her head tilted to the side as she studied them. Costas fended off his mother, then pulled her in to kiss her cheek and give her a bear hug, diffusing her anger successfully although not before he got another swipe around the head for "squashing her hair" (in Pav's opinion Mrs Anastas' hair could have done with a little squashing; just like his own mother, it was hair sprayed out to maximum proportions).

He watched as Millie looked down at her hands, which were gripping her blue clutch bag as if her life depended on it. It made sense to him now: her confusion and anxiety around his loud, casually affectionate family and friends. After meeting her parents he knew that all this was totally removed from any type of family dynamic she had been exposed to before. It had been two weeks since that night and he still had to repress a shudder when he thought of how inhuman her parents had been. For a naturally shy, sensitive girl like Millie, her childhood must have been unbearable.

For the rest of the service Pav had been at the front of the church, only able to claim Millie again after the endless family photos outside. He'd tried to talk to Mama before today and make her see that Millie wasn't the cold, stuck-up woman she came across as. But his mama was stubborn and Pav hadn't felt he could break Millie's confidence about her family, which he knew for some reason was a great source of shame for her. Talia Martakis' stubbornness, combined with Millie's natural reserve, had meant another uncomfortable, standoffish meeting before they left for the reception, and Pav was beginning to think it might have been a mistake to bring Millie at all.

"MILLIE!" AN OVER-EXCITED CLOUD OF WHITE CAME flying towards them and, to Millie's obvious shock, swept her up in a hug, swinging her from side to side. "You came."

Pav wasn't sure what had happened with Millie and his sister at the engagement party but Allegra had been Millie's biggest advocate within the family since – not that it had seemed to make much difference to his mama.

"Er..." Millie's arms fluttered up to return the hug in a rather more hesitant fashion. When Allegra released her and drew back enough to look at Millie's startled face, keeping her hands on her shoulders, Millie managed a weak smile.

"You look fucking fantastic," Allegra cried, giving her a little shake.

"Er..."

"Allegroula mou," Mama hissed as she elbowed her way past Pav to glare at her youngest daughter. "Your yiayia is sitting right there." Pav watched confusion cross Millie's face and he jerked his head towards Yiayia, who was wearing all black (as she had for the last forty years since Pappou passed) and sipping her whisky with a scowl on her face.

"Yiayia swears more than me, Mama, and she's stone deaf."

Yiayia threw Allegra a dirty look and muttered some deeply unpleasant insults in Greek.

Pav's mother ignored them both and turned her attention to

Millie, sweeping her gaze from head to toe of immaculate designer perfection, suppressing a lip curl and faking a smile. "So glad you could make it, Camilla," she lied.

Pav watched Millie swallow before she forced her own smile. "Th-thank you for inviting me."

Her voice was tight and expressionless but there were two things Pav knew that his mother noticed: the first was Millie's slight stammer, and the second was how her hand trembled as she extended it out to the older woman. Pav knew this because he saw his mother's expression soften as she took Millie's hand.

"We Greeks," Talia said, her tone now much more gentle than before, "we don't shake hands." Mama used Millie's hand to pull her towards her before letting it go and resting both of her hands on Millie's shoulders. "We do like this." She kissed one of Millie's cheeks and then the other. "Understand?"

Millie's eyes were wide but she didn't flinch away. "Yes," she whispered, her voice heavy with relief and her lips forming a genuine, if tremulous, smile. "Thank you."

"Millie!" a five-year-old ball of fury pushed her way into the group and in between Mama and Millie.

"Rosie..." Libby's warning voice came from behind Pav as she reached for her daughter. "You are being a right–"

"Everyone's going to eat all the chocolate, and there'll be none left for me cause you and Jamie-Daddy are so mean! I wanna stay with my Millie."

Rosie climbed up Millie like a little spider monkey, her chocolatey hands smearing all over the designer dress. When she reached her goal she shoved her face in Millie's neck and burst into noisy tears.

"Oh God, Mils, I'm so sorry," Libby muttered in horror as she surveyed her daughter's handiwork. "Your dress! Your beautiful dress. I–"

"It's just a dress, Libby," Millie told her, as always loving the warm weight of the little girl clinging to her. Before she'd met Rosie, Millie had never been hugged by a child in her life – had never really been on the receiving end of much physical affection at all. There was no way she would ever take it for granted and no way she would let a dress get in the way of it.

Libby groaned. "But you spent days with El picking it out and planning the whole outfit because you were so worried about making a good impress..." Libby trailed off as she realised what she was saying and who was in hearing distance. "Sorry, hun," she whispered.

Pav watched as heat hit Millie's cheeks and his mama's face softened even more. Rosie's sobs had quietened down to a low whimpering now, but she was showing no signs of emerging from Millie's neck.

"What happened, Little Louse?" Millie asked as she stroked Rosie back.

"I'm afraid there was a five-year-old short circuit when she saw the chocolate fountain. We found her face-first, upside-down, trying to ingest the entire thing."

"Everyone does it that way," Rosie's muffled voice said from the depths of Millie's neck. "Tell them, Millie."

"I think," Millie said carefully, "your mother would just prefer you eat some protein and complex carbohydrates before you consume refined sugar."

"Don't wanna eat commix barba–hybate! Want chocwate!"

"A bit of chocolate's fine, Rosie. But long-term consumption of refined sugar can lead to changes in your hippocampus."

Rosie stopped crying and leaned back to look in Millie's face with a frown on her little face. "My hippo–bampus?"

"Your brain. It could stop you reaching your full IQ potential."

"My what?"

"Stop you being super-smart."

"Bu-but I *am* super-smart! You tell me that all the time."

"Of course you are," Millie said, her voice conveying that any other possibility was entirely ridiculous.

"I do my numbers with Millie," Rosie told the group around them. "And we learns bout baccy–eara."

"Bacteria," Millie corrected. "And that's all great. But if you want to fulfil your maximal cognitive potential, then you need to eat what Mummy says."

Rosie tilted her head to the side. "I *do* wanna ill my co-go-live-ential."

"Of course you do because you're–"

"Super-smart!" Rosie threw both hands into the air and then launched forward to kiss her before she wriggled down to the floor. "I'm ready for my lunch now, Mummy," she told Libby, holding out her hand imperiously for her mother to take.

"Yes, madam," Libby muttered, rolling her eyes and mouthing a thank you to Millie.

Rosie might be a cute kid, but once she was in full tantrum mode it was very difficult to bring her back from the brink. Pav had been out with Libby, Jamie and Rosie a few times when they'd had to leave after it had become clear that Rosie was not going to calm down. So he knew how much having Millie diffuse the situation would mean to them.

"I'm definitely signing you up for babysitting," Allegra said, rubbing her small bump under the white dress and smiling at Millie.

Millie's mouth fell open in shock. "I... I would be honoured," she said, her voice slightly hoarse until she cleared her throat. "I hold a paediatric advanced life-support certificate."

"Uh... okay?" Allegra replied with a bemused smile.

"And I have a qualification in dietetics for children and... and a CRB check."

"Sweetie," Allegra said gently. "I was sold after just seeing you with Miss Chocolate Fountain, okay?"

"Allegroula mou, go find your husband," Mama cut in. "Milloula mou–" she moved to Millie, patted her cheek and linked their arms together "– ever drunk ouzo?" Millie shook her head, her startled eyes coming to Pav's amused ones before she was dragged forward to the bar. "Well, you're in for a treat."

"Grappa!" Talia Martakis shouted for what seemed like the hundreth time that night with everyone around returning the call and downing their shots of ouzo. Millie loved ouzo. She loved Greek food. She loved Greek weddings, and she *loved* Pav's family.

Millie had done her research. She'd known the wedding ceremony would be long, she knew that plate-smashing was largely out of fashion, and she knew about the kalamatianos that was traditional at weddings like these. She did not however in her wildest dreams think she would ever be participating in that dance. But here she was, drinking her fifth ouzo, red in the face and out of breath from spinning around the bride in a circle of her family. And, yes, Millie had danced the kalamatianos in the innermost circle of those closest to the bride. In fact she had been holding hands with the bride's mother and father.

The kissing and hugging that had seemed so alien to her was now something she was well and truly a part of. She'd always known that physical affection could give people a rush of endorphins, but she'd never really experienced it before meeting Rosie, then Pav and his family. Something she hadn't even realised was twisted inside of her had relaxed after the first time Talia Martakis added the "mou" to the end of her name. Millie was a big believer in CBT, and of course it had helped her beyond measure, but despite that she knew that just hearing the Greek endearment, just once, from a woman like Pav's mama, had done her more good than half the expensive therapy she'd paid for in the past. She stumbled slightly to the side after downing her shot and was held up by a familiar pair of strong arms.

"I think we'd better get you home, baby," he murmured in her ear, and she giggled. Giggled. Again. Before the last few months Millie had never giggled. To be honest she would never have thought herself capable of it. "We're going to hit the road.., Mama, Papa," he raised his voice to be heard above the music by his parents.

"You're leaving?" His sister's vast dress swirled around them all. She was being carried by her husband for some reason, and he set her down in front of Pav and Millie, between them and his parents. "But I forgot to say thanks for the present."

"Uh... but I haven't..." Pav started to say.

"It means so much to me." Allegra's eyes filled with tears as she turned to Millie. "And thank you. I know it must have been you that told him exactly what I wanted. He would have never thought to look at my Pinterest account. I was amazed you found everything, even the little lampshade and the wall art.

"Allie, I have no idea what you're talking about," Pav told her.

"But... the furniture. My entire nursery furniture set – cotbed, dresser, all the accessories. You had it delivered to my house. I mean, I know you're the surgeon now but I didn't think you'd be able to afford..."

Millie bit her lip as Allegra stepped back from Pav and all eyes came to her.

"Millie?" Pav asked, crossing his arms over his chest and frowning down at her.

"You bought me my *nursery*?" Allegra whispered, her eyes going wide.

"Ha!" Talia shouted, clapping her hands once, then beaming across at Millie. "Paida mou." She pushed Pav and Allegra out of the way and took Millie's arm again. "Yannis! More ouzo!" she shouted to her husband at the bar, who rolled his eyes. "Now, Milloula mou. Have I told you about the new sofabed I have my eye on in John Lewis?" Millie looked into Talia's twinkling eyes and burst out laughing.

Chapter 30

Nothing to do with us

"Oh wow," Millie breathed as she took in the crowded conference hall. Her poster was up in the centre of the presentation area and had gathered a fair amount of interest already. The organisers had eventually relented: allowing Millie to just present a poster and not give a talk to the large auditorium. With a poster all you had to do was prepare an A3 sized presentation outlining your findings and their implications. The only problem was that they wanted Millie to stand next to her poster with Anwar and field questions about it from interested conferences-goers and the judges. This particular conference was at the Royal College of Surgeons and it was a big deal. A very big deal.

"Hey," Pav said gently, taking her hand and giving it a squeeze. "You'll be fine. You only have to stand up with it for half an hour, and Anwar'll be with you the whole time." She directed a weak smile at him and gave a brief nod whilst her stomach turned over dangerously.

"Just concentrate on the techniques we talked about, Millie," Anwar put in, shifting next to them and adjusting his tie. "You're going to have to take all the questions not related to the actual CBT."

"Yo." Kira bounced up to them and shoulder-bumped Millie. "You cats getting your conference on or not?" Kira's smile faded as she took in Millie's pale face. "Hey, what's up?"

"I don't think I can do this," Millie muttered.

When she agreed to go to the conference she hadn't really thought her poster would attract that much attention. She'd been hoping she could just fade into the background and sidle off after a couple of questions. Yes, her confidence was slowly growing over the last few months, but she still had her limits.

She gave Pav's hand a squeeze back and Kira a weak shoulder-bump in return, thinking how lucky she was to have these people now. A lifetime of being alone had been transformed into a life filled with people who seemed to actually care about her. She was starting to really *believe* that they liked her. She spent practically every night with Pav, and the nights when she wasn't with him were taken over by "book group" meetings (this had by and large metamorphosed into cinema trips, pub lock-ins, pole-dancing escapades, regular gay-bar visits). She was so happy... and so completely terrified. What if the bubble burst? What if they grew tired of having the quiet, weird one hanging around?

"You'll be fine, Prof," Kira told her. "Just stay focused on the info. You're great with facts and stats."

Millie nodded and took a deep breath just as Libby approached with Jamie.

"You good to go, honey?" Jamie asked after he'd given her a kiss on the cheek and Libby had hugged her quickly. Millie swallowed. They were all there for her. They'd all come to support her. She owed it to them to at least try to be normal, to at least try to push past her limits.

"Okay, okay," she whispered, taking a step towards the

poster area. She felt a strong hand on the back, guiding her forward, and managed a few more steps before she froze. "I... I can't..." She trailed off and her throat closed over. Her only thought now was escape, but as she turned to leave the hand on her back became an arm around her middle.

"Millie," Pav gritted out, the patience in his tone from before now giving way to obvious frustration. "Come on. I'll stay with you. It's only a couple of questions."

The crowd around her poster was swelling. All the other presentations were being abandoned now for hers. She tried to pull away but he wouldn't let her go.

"I know... I just..."

"Try, baby," Pav coaxed, his attempt to gentle his tone coming out forced. "Just give it a go. There's nothing to be worried about. You can do–"

"I can't," she whispered, pulling back against his arm. That was when his face changed. It was like the mask of calm, patient, easy-going Pav had slipped, revealing a very different man.

"Please just fu... please can you just *try*," he ground out. Anwar was in a low conversation with Kira and edging towards the poster now. "All you have to do is answer a couple of questions. Any normal..." He stopped himself and looked away for a moment as he took a deep breath. "Anyone else in your position would be pleased that their research was stirring so much interest. Some people would kill for the offers you've had to present your findings."

Millie blinked, then stared up into Pav's angry face. Something was wrong. There was something else at play here, but she couldn't think what it was. Not when his fury was radiating off him in waves and her panic had her in a vice grip. That was when it happened. A protective mechanism she'd developed in childhood kicked in. She stopped pulling away from Pav; the fear in her face faded until it was a blank mask, and she straightened where she stood.

"I'll be all right now," she said, her voice devoid of the terror from before, in fact devoid of anything at all. Pav loosened his arm and she stepped back from him. "I don't need you to come with me," she told him, shaking his hand off hers. Without looking back at him she walked towards her poster with Anwar in tow. Numbness settled over her as she turned to face the group that had formed around it.

"I..." Her throat threatened to close over but she took a deep breath in and started again. "I'm Camilla Morrison and I'd be happy to answer any questions."

There was a long pause and then the barrage began. One gentleman she recognised as the Chairman of the Royal College of Surgeons had a particularly long list of queries. Once she was in the swing of it, Millie found it wasn't so bad. Technical questions had never really fazed her and there was so much curiosity around the study that there never seemed to be a lull in which she could become nervous. She noticed Pav, Kira, Libby and Jamie out of the corner of her eye, but steadfastly ignored them all. When the questions finally subsided, she realised she'd been fielding them for nearly forty-five minutes. That, she decided, was enough. She made her excuses and slipped away to the nearest bathroom, ignoring Pav, who was calling her name.

∾

"You okay, love?"

Millie jumped slightly and looked away from her reflection to see a lady in a cleaning uniform behind her with a concerned expression on her face.

"Yes, yes – fine," Millie said. "Er... thank you. I'm fine."

"It's just you've been staring in that mirror for a good ten minutes without moving a muscle," the cleaner told her.

"Have I?" Millie blinked and stepped away from the sink.

"Bad day?"

Millie blinked again, then looked back at her reflection in the mirror. The numbness was lifting. She frowned as she remembered Pav's tone, his angry words. Something was different. Something didn't make sense.

"Yes... yes, you could say that," she muttered, giving the concerned woman a brief smile. "Thanks for asking though." She straightened her shoulders and walked towards the door. Her whole life she'd been restricted by her limits, running away from problems. Well, this time she was going to get some answers. She wasn't going to run away. Once out in the corridor she collided with Kira.

"Hey," Kira said, steadying Millie with both hands to her upper arms. "You okay? Well done out there. That was some sick–"

"Where's Pavlos?"

"I... uh, I think he's sorting something for tomorrow."

Pav was giving a big presentation in the main hall tomorrow morning. Millie had been helping him prepare for it for weeks. She knew it off by heart herself. Kira linked her arm through Millie's. "Hey, let's go and cause some trouble at the bar now you've smashed your poster."

Millie was being led down the hallway when she heard Pav's voice around the corner. Something niggling at the back of her mind told her to stop, and she came to an abrupt halt.

"Without my help she wouldn't even have attended the bloody conference," Millie heard him say. "So don't–"

"Yes, yes, we're grateful to you for convincing her, but–" the deep voice of an older man started to say.

"It was a lot more than just convincing, Duncan. It was a

good few months of *painstaking* coaxing. You've no idea the effort my friends and I have put into this. She was totally patho-logical before we got involved and loosened her up."

"Well, I guess she did at least present something," the deep voice said. "But that doesn't mean you automatically get twenty minutes to talk. Cut the presentation down. Allow some time for questions."

"Look," Pav's voice held all the frustration and anger of earlier. "You may have only let me into the presentations because I agreed to get Dr Morrison here, but you have to admit my findings have real merit. I need at least fifteen minutes."

Millie slowly turned to look at Kira and it was the first time she'd ever seen the other woman anything less than totally at ease. In fact Kira's face was frozen in horror. Millie tried to take a step back but Kira grabbed both her hands.

"Listen to me, Millie," she said, her voice almost frantic. "It wasn't like that. I mean, okay, at the start Pav wanted us to try to get to know you partly because of the conference, but mostly because he was worried about you. We were all worried about you."

"Pathological," Millie whispered, looking up to see Pav's normally tanned face now ashen and staring at her from down the corridor. He must have heard Kira's voice and come around the corner. Everything made sense to Millie now. *Of course* these people didn't really want to be her friends. *Of course* there was an ulterior motive. How could she have been so stupid?

"But now," Kira moved into Millie's space, blocking her view of Pav. "Now Professor X, you're our friend. None of that is about this stupid bloody conference. Since when did I give a badger's arse about Pav's surgical career."

"What's going on here?" Libby walked up behind Millie

and touched her lightly on the shoulder, but Millie flinched away and took a few steps back.

"I'm going to go," she whispered. "I can't... I've got to..."

As she backed away Pav seemed to snap out of his shock and started moving towards her.

"No," he said, his voice hoarse. "No, don't leave. Please, baby, you know that this was never about the bloody conference. You know that, right?"

Millie kept backing away but gave a quick shake of her head. She felt numb again. The pain would come, but now she was numb.

"Okay, I'll admit," Pav went on, his voice frantic, "I wanted you to agree to come here. I wanted to be given that slot. But that has nothing to do with you and me." He moved to her and cupped her face in both his hands, leaning his forehead against hers. "Are you listening, Millie? That has nothing to do with us."

Millie stiffened, then put both her hands on his chest and pushed him away, jerking her face away from his hands. She took another few steps back and wrapped her arms around her middle to try and control the shaking.

"Leave me alone," she managed to get out in a hoarse whisper. "Just..." she backed away further "... just leave me be."

As she turned and walked away, Millie realised why she'd lived within her limits before, despite the crippling loneliness. After her childhood, she'd assumed that she'd become used to rejection, become hardened to feelings of loss. But, as she was discovering now, the pain was just as bad as an adult, and if she'd lived within her limits she would never have exposed herself to it.

Chapter 31

Boundaries, schmoundaries

PAV DRAINED THE LAST OF HIS BEER AND STARED DOWN AT the empty bottle hanging loosely in his hand. He tried to concentrate on his next move, on being constructive, but, as seemed to happen continuously over the last month, other thoughts crowded his mind: Millie's pale face and her horrified voice whispering "*Pathological* . . ."; the accusation in Don's eyes after she'd come back to work a shell of the person she'd started to be; even worse, the fact that that accusation transformed into worry and even fear, as Millie withdrew completely into herself, working such long hours and with such ferocity that she'd cleared the entire reporting backlog for the department; then the way she looked through Pav when he tried to approach, and the obvious stress etched on her features that those approaches caused.

It was an impossible situation. Millie was determined not to engage with either him or any of his friends, even though they were *her* bloody friends too now, dammit! And she'd know that, if she'd just *listen*. Nothing they tried worked. She blanked all communication: she wouldn't answer his calls, she wouldn't answer the door to him, wouldn't let him into her office, and was polite but ice-cold when she saw him or the others in the hospital. So Pav was stuck. He felt like his chest had been ripped open and his heart removed. In fact he felt like his heart was working away in the radiology department, losing weight and becoming more depressed every day, and there was not one bastard thing he could do about it. Frustration washed over him and in a sudden movement he drew the hand holding the bottle back and threw it across the room to smash in the fireplace.

"Jesus," he heard muttered from the doorway, and spun around to face Jamie with a scowl.

"I didn't give you that key so you could prowl about my house like some sort of stalk..." Pav trailed off as a small figure stepped out from behind Jamie. Eleanor was staring between Pav and the shattered glass nervously.

"Don't worry, El," Jamie told her, rolling his eyes. "He's always been a drama queen; it's all that Mediterranean blood – rather undermines any attempts he makes at a British stiff upper lip."

Pav ignored Jamie the Dick and focused on El instead.

Of course.

Why hadn't he thought of that sooner? Of course El would be the best way to get to Millie. There was no reason for Millie to cut El out of her life.

"How is she?" he asked, moving around the sofa towards them.

El straightened her shoulders, pulling herself up to her full height and mustering a decent glare at Pav, despite her obvious nervousness.

"Well, she's crap," she told him. "But I expect you know that. Whether you give a toss remains to be seen."

"I–"

"What happened? One minute she's coming out of her

herself, she's my friend, I'm finally getting the real Millie: the funny, dry, kind woman I'd only seen flashes of before, and the next she's totally shut down. She's bloody worse now than she was when I first met her."

"I... I let her down," Pav said, his voice heavy and his chest constricting. He'd been angry with Millie at first for not listening to him, but over the last two weeks he'd realised that he was the one at fault. He should have been honest with her from the beginning. He should have taken care of her like he promised. The way he spoke to her... he let his ambition and frustration get the better of him, and he snapped. It was inexcusable.

"Oh–" El broke off and her posture relaxed slightly on seeing the dejection wash over Pav's features. "Oh... right, well, at least you admit it. Do you... do you still–"

"I love her," Pav cut in. "If she would just let me explain, then I..."

"Thank God for that," El breathed, finally cracking a relieved smile. "I knew you weren't a total wanker."

"Uh... thanks, I think."

"Pav, mate," Jamie said, drawing both of their attention. He was currently in Pav's kitchen area, making a huge sandwich for himself. Pav rolled his eyes.

"Make yourself at home," he said as he watched the greedy bastard slap the last of the ham on top of the brie he'd been saving for later.

"El came over to see Libby 'cause she's worried," Jamie told him, talking around a brie-and-ham-filled mouth. "As you're in self-involved-broody-mode your bloody phone was off so I had to bring her round here."

"I think..." El paused and tilted her head to the side. "I don't know how much you know about Millie's parents?" Her expression was guarded and her eyes had narrowed. She was obviously torn between her concern for her friend and her desire not to betray Millie's confidence.

"I've met them," Pav reassured her. "I promise I know *all* about them."

El blew out a relieved breath. "Right, great, well, you'll know that it's not a great idea for Millie to have any contact with them."

"Yes," Pav replied with conviction.

"She came to me this week asking for an outfit she could wear to a press conference."

"What?" Pav exploded; if he'd been holding another bottle it would have gone the same way as the first.

"I think it has to do with her father," El paused. "I tried to get more information out of her but she clammed up and... well, I didn't want to push her, she seems... fragile: really pale, thin, and she said the outfit had to have long sleeves. I caught sight of her forearms when I was adjusting one of the jackets and..." El trailed off and bit her lip, glancing between the two men, obviously unwilling to betray another confidence.

"What about her arms?" was Jamie's barely interpretable reply as he continued to plough through his massive sandwich. Pav ignored him; he was struggling not to punch something, hard.

"I'll sort it," he told El through gritted teeth and with his trademark confidence, which at the moment he was very far from feeling.

"Uh... I'm just heading out so..."

Libby narrowed her eyes at Millie and put her hands on her hips. Hilariously Rosie mimicked her gesture exactly, but with an added five-year-old foot-stomp. Beauty just gave a big hurrumph as she pushed her nose into Millie's crotch in greet-ing. Lurking behind them all was an apprehensive-looking Kira.

"I haven't seens you in *ages*," Rosie's grumpy voice whined from the doorstep. Millie's cool expression softened signifi-cantly as she looked down at the little girl.

"I know," she said, her voice holding more than a hint of strain and her hand dropping unconsciously to the top of Beau-ty's head. "I'm sorry, Rose-Pose. I just..." She trailed off and swallowed, then surprised Libby by taking a step back to open the door so they could all step through. Libby could smell cleaning fluid in the air, and as she followed Millie through to the living room she frowned when she saw the meticulous throw cushion arrangements and immaculate space. Libby knew that Millie cleaned and organised when under stress; judging by the state of her house her current anxiety levels must be through the roof.

"Rosie, Kira," she said as she walked over to the sofa. "Go take Beauty into the garden for a minute. I need to do some grown-up talking with Millie."

"Great idea, Libs," Kira said, backing away towards the garden door. "Grown-up talk's not my forte."

Rosie however scowled at her mother before skipping to Millie and giving her a hug. Beauty lumbered that way as well and sat her massive backside down on Millie's feet. Millie looked startled for a moment, then a tiny smile broke through her strained expression. She laid one hand on Rosie's head and the other on Beauty's.

"Rosie," Libby said in a warning voice. Rosie huffed but released Millie after another few seconds.

"*I* needs to do grown-up talkins with Millie too," she said indignantly as she flounced to the back door with Beauty in her wake to grab Kira's hand. Once they were out of hearing distance Libby took Millie's cold hand and pulled her down to sit on the sofa. She could feel Millie stiffen under her fingers, but Libby had waited long enough to confront her, and she wasn't going to back off just because she knew it made Millie uncomfortable.

"Right, now then," she started. Millie had withdrawn her hand and was avoiding her gaze, preferring to look at the coffee table instead. "We're going to get a few things straight."

Libby saw Millie frown in confusion and flick her a quick, bemused glance before looking away again. *Progress*, Libby thought. Anything that broke through that bland, ice-cold expression was progress.

"Since you won't answer your phone to me or reply to any messages anymore, I've come to see you in person. I'll get straight to the point: I'm bloody furious with you."

That got Millie's attention. She sat up in her seat and looked away from the coffee table and straight at Libby.

"*You're* furious with *me*?" she asked, total confusion and a little anger in her expression now. More progress, Libby thought.

"Yes." Libby clipped, and then softened her tone. "I thought we were friends, Millie. You can't just cut people out of your life. That's not the way this works."

"But... but I..." Millie trailed off and her eyes darted away again. Libby sighed.

"I was friends with you before you even started seeing Pav. Before the idea of this bloody conference came up.

Millie bit her lip and shook her head. "I didn't... I mean, I offered to help with Rosie and..."

"And you thought that was why I spoke to you? You thought I was using you to – ?"

"No," Millie interrupted, shaking her head more vigorously now. "No, I never thought that. I was lucky to spend time with

Rosie. I knew I was lucky. Now you're doing a medical attachment you don't need me to help so..."

"Oh, Millie, what am I going to do with you?" Libby groaned. "Of course we still need you. Rosie's missed you, *I've* missed you; the bloody dog has missed you. We care about you. You were never just convenient childcare. And you know that I never gave two shits about any bloody conference so there's no excuse for cutting me out."

"Oh... I..." Millie pressed her lips together and swallowed again. "Okay," she said, her voice slightly hoarse, "I'm sorry... I just didn't realise that you'd want to..."

"Pav told me about the money." Millie flinched and stiffened again, which almost made Libby regret bringing it up, but she wanted complete honesty with her now. "He told me last week when he was drunk at our place doing his sad-case, heartbroken routine – which by the way I also blame you for. The last thing I need is a six-foot moping Greek man getting in my way of an evening."

Millie blinked at Libby and her mouth dropped open in shock. "Moping?" she whispered. "You think he's moping... over me?"

"Well of course it's over you," Libby snapped. "I'll tell you what's given that away: you dumping him coinciding perfectly with the start of said moping and the fact that he bangs on about you continuously. I think that's pretty strong evidence."

Millie turned away from Libby and stared into the middle distance for a long moment.

"Right, that's enough about Moody Greek Boy," Libby said briskly. "I'm here to talk about you and me." She leaned forward and took Millie's hand, softening her tone. "Why did you set up that fake grant, Millie?"

Millie started in obvious shock and bit her lip. It was a good minute before she could reply.

"You needed it." Millie shrugged. "You deserved it."

"When you started the payments you barely knew me."

"Libby," Millie said, turning towards her and this time making direct eye contact, "I barely *know* anyone. If you hadn't noticed I'm not exactly a social butterfly. I could see you struggling. I admired how you were coping and what a good mother you were despite everything. I have… I have a lot of money." She shrugged. "It made sense to me. It was logical."

Libby huffed out a frustrated laugh. "You can't just start transferring large amounts of money into somebody's account because it fits in with your brand of logic. That's craz–"

"Did you know that the first hug Rosie gave me was the only spontaneous gesture of affection I'd had since my nanny left me when I was seven?" Millie told her. Libby took in a sharp breath and she squeezed Millie's hand tightly.

"Looking after Rosie meant something to me, Libby. Your friendship meant something to me."

Libby swallowed and blinked back the stinging in her eyes. "Right," she said, her voice gruff with emotion. "Well, let's stop playing silly buggers then. I'd like you to talk about our friendship in the present tense if you don't mind. And I will be paying you back all the money I owe you."

"Libby, I–"

"Every penny, Millie. And you have to stop the payments."

Millie bit her lip.

"Millie," Libby said slowly in a warning tone. "You should know that Jamie's feeling pretty emasculated since he found out you've been supporting his wife. It's almost worth it for that, to be honest."

Millie smiled and Libby finally felt like she was getting somewhere. She took a deep breath and tried to ignore the ache in her chest when she thought of an affection-starved seven-year-old Millie.

"Now, I'm a hugger, Rosie's a hugger, and Kira is *definitely* a hugger. We'll have to set up some sort of cuddle schedule because you've got a lot of making up to do."

Millie let out a startled laugh and Libby decided that was all the green light she needed. She lurched forward and snatched her up in a fierce embrace, which, to Libby's relief and after a long second, Millie returned.

Another set of arms engulfed them both in a crushing grip. "Group hug!" shouted Kira, who had thrown herself bodily onto both of them on the sofa. "I knew you'd see sense, Professor X. As if I give a crap whether Dick-Boy gets to talk at his willy-fiddler conference, you loco lady."

"What's Dick-Boy?" a small voice asked as Rosie's body launched over the back of the sofa into the middle of the enforced group hug.

"Ki-Ki, can you please at least try not to load her up with the type of ammunition that gets me called into see her Reception teacher?"

"No promises, my lovely, no promises."

Rosie's small hands found their way up to Millie's cheeks and she proceeded to squeeze them. "I missed your face," she told Millie.

"I missed your face too, little louse," Millie whispered.

"Ki-Ki," Libby said.

"Yes, my beautiful friend."

"This is becoming uncomfortable now. Remember we talked about boundaries." If anything Kira's grip tightened and she kissed Libby, then Millie, and then Rosie on the cheek.

"Boundaries, schmoundaries," Kira said, swaying the whole group from side to side. A loud woof interrupted her swaying and a wet nose pushed under their arms. Once Beauty's huge head had worked its way on top of all their laps she closed her eyes and started to shake it from side to side, her drool flying into the air around her and causing everyone to spring apart.

"Way to spoil the moment, Beast of Bodmin," Kira grumbled, wiping a globule from her cheek. Libby gave Millie, the clean-freak, an apprehensive look but to her surprise she was still smiling. Then Millie buried her face in Beauty's fur and her body started shaking with muffled laughter. Libby took her hand and gave it a squeeze and this time – this time – she squeezed back.

Chapter 32

Every word, dear

"Push me faster, boy," Gammy shouted from her chair.

"Any faster and we will literally break people's legs," Pav told her through gritted teeth. "We're nearly there anyway."

"No thanks to you and your dawdling."

Pav rolled his eyes and turned the corner into the entrance of the hotel. He wasn't exactly sure what Gammy meant by dawdling. If racing over to her residential home, explaining the situation at supersonic speed, then loading her and her wheel-chair into his ill-equipped car and nearly breaking his back in the process was dawdling, he'd like to see how fast Gammy usually travelled to her weekly outing at the day centre. Pav doubted that the overweight minibus driver he'd seen earlier lifted Gammy bodily into his vehicle, or that he drove at double the speed limit through London. The foyer was full of people holding cameras and sporting lanyards with *Press* written on them. Pav powered through to make it to the information desk.

"I need to see the Morrisons," Pav told the stressed-looking receptionist, who just rolled his eyes.

"You and every other bugger in town," he said. "I'm afraid that the–"

"Young man." Gammy's commanding tone cut through the noise of the foyer as she pushed herself up to a wobbly stand next to Pav, who supported her arm, taking nearly all her weight. "Firstly, you are a representative of one of the oldest hotels in London. I hardly think that the word 'bugger' should be present in your vocabulary."

"I–"

"Secondly, I am certain there will be a problem if you do not allow Mr Morrison's *mother* to support him before this *very* important press conference."

The receptionist's eyebrows went up in challenge.

"Pavlos, my handbag," she said. Pav jumped into action, grabbing the huge leather bag from the back of the chair. Gammy snatched it from him and began rummaging in its depths. "Ha!" she shouted after a good few minutes and a number of questionable items, including some ancient-looking boiled sweets, five pairs of reading glasses and what looked like a dead cat, which shocked even Pav until he was assured that it was in fact a hat, had been dumped in front of the less-than-pleased receptionist. "There you are." Gammy's wrinkled, papery hand was brandishing a piece of paper so old it wouldn't have looked out of place next to the *Magna Carta*. "My marriage certificate."

The receptionist took the paper tentatively from Gammy and examined it. "Right, yes," he mumbled, still unsure how to proceed.

"You've met my son I assume?" Gammy asked.

"Er... well, yes, he..."

"Arrogant, demanding, awkward bastard, isn't he?" The other man's mouth fell open. "Well, if you think he was bad before, imagine how upset he'll be when he hears that his

elderly mother was kept waiting in her delicate condition."
Nothing about Gammy appeared in the least bit delicate in that
moment, but the receptionist seemed to make a decision and
picked up his desk phone. A few minutes later, and with
Gammy back in her chair, they were efficiently whisked
through a conference room and into a large waiting room.

"What on earth... ?" Valerie Morrison's sharp voice cut
through the low murmuring in the room. Pav stopped in his
tracks, his eyes swept through David Morrison with his two
advisers, and he focused in on Millie. She was standing next to
her mother, dressed in an immaculate cream suit, with her hair
in one of the elaborate but severe styles that Pav disliked and a
piece of paper gripped in one of her hands.

Gammy, obviously not in the mood for any more
"dawdling", ignored her son and daughter-in-law, addressing
the only person in the room she cared about.

"Millie, child," she said in a commanding voice. "We. Are.
Going."

Millie blinked, her eyes flicking from Pav to Gammy and
back again, her face creasing in confusion. "Gammy, what are
you doing here?"

"Taking you home, you ridiculous girl," Gammy told her.

"But... but..."

"Mother," David Morrison's exasperated voice cut in, and
Gammy finally deigned to look his way. "I'm about to do an
extremely important press conference. May I ask, respectfully,
what the bloody hell you are doing here?"

Gammy rolled her eyes. "Boy," she said, and Pav
suppressed a laugh. Mr Morrison must have been in his late
fifties at least, and about as far from a boy as humanly possible.
"You wouldn't know what was 'extremely important' if it
smacked you around the face and called you Mary."

"Mother M.," Valerie Morrison started in a sickly sweet

voice, a painful, forced smile on her face. "Isn't this wonderful. Why don't we have a lovely catch-up just after David has finished talking to the pesky press people."

"Oh do shut up, you poisonous excuse for a woman," Gammy snapped, refocusing on Millie and softening her tone. "Come on now, child. Time to go with Gammy."

"But..."

"They lied to you, Millie," Pav put in, reading the worry and confusion in Millie's eyes. "They can't take Gammy out of that home. Even if she loses the capacity to make her own decisions, she has made an advance directive that only you are allowed to make medical and financial choices for her."

"Did you really think I would put these idiots in control of my future? I may have made some mistakes bringing up this one," Granny M. made an impatient gesture towards her son, "but that doesn't mean I didn't learn from them."

"Well, I–"

"Honestly, why not just come to me about it?"

"I didn't want to worry you, Gammy," Millie said, snapping out of her frozen shock to move forward, around her father, and then kneel in front of Gammy's chair.

"I'm not a helpless doddery old fool," Gammy said, softening her tone and laying her good hand on Millie's cheek. Millie leaned into the hand, closed her eyes and nodded. "Always wanting to make everything better, keep everyone happy; ever since you were a child. Time for *you* to be happy now." Millie opened her eyes and to Pav's shock they were glistening with tears. One escaped and fell onto Gammy's hand. "That's it," Gammy muttered, wiping the tear away. "You live your life now. You let yourself *feel*." Millie nodded again and then fell onto Gammy in a fierce hug. When she finally released Gammy, Millie drew back and her eyes caught Pav's for the first time.

"Camilla." Valerie's abrasive voice cut across the room but Pav and Millie didn't break eye contact. "I'm sure we're all pleased to see your grandmother, but family reunions can wait. I want you to get up and come with us into that conference room, like we agreed." Millie started to rise from the floor, her eyes unreadable but still fixed on Pav.

"*Camilla.*" Valerie's voice was sharper now. "Will you–"

"Leave her a–" Pav started, but stopped abruptly at Millie's frown and the shake of her head. She turned to her mother and lifted her chin, her hands bunching into small fists at her sides.

"How *dare* you try to blackmail me," she said, her voice clear and surprisingly loud.

"I don't know what you're talk–"

"I used to think I was a weak person," Millie went on, taking a threatening step towards her parents and even raising a finger to point in their direction. It was only because Pav was standing so close that he could see the fine tremor in her hand. "But I'm not weak. To survive a childhood with two soulless people who do not give one single shit about me–" Pav blinked at the swear word, then smiled. He knew Kira would rub off on her eventually "– and come out the other side... to even function. Well... I'm not weak, I'm... I'm bloody brave actually. And you can both go get... get stuffed." Pav would have preferred that she told them to go fuck themselves, but made allowances for her profanity inexperience. Next time.

She spun around as her parents both spluttered out various protests. Pav ignored them all, stepped around the wheelchair, grasped Millie by the shoulders, and gave her a hard fast kiss on the lips. This predictably ramped up her parents' annoyance, but both Pav and Millie had tuned them out. When Pav pulled back and searched her face she looked shocked for a moment; then a slow, wide smile emerged.

"Forgive me?" he whispered, and she laughed.

"I think finding Gammy, racing around London and saving me from having to be on television supporting my..." she took a deep breath and straightened her shoulder again before raising her voice slightly, "total *arsehole* of a father–" this drew shocked gasps from around the room which only served to widen her smile even further "– I think that might have earned you enough brownie points in the forgiveness stakes." She lowered her voice again. "And I think I'm ready to believe that maybe... maybe you like me, just a little."

Pav rolled his eyes. "If risking life and limb to interrupt your Gran's chair-acrobics session doesn't prove how much I love you, then–"

"You... you love me?" For the second time that day Millie's eyes shone with tears. The awe and wonder in her voice was nearly enough to unman Pav as well. Luckily, just as he felt the suspicious stinging sensation at the back of his own eyes, Gammy cut in.

"Of course he loves you, crazy girl," she said, huffing impatiently and using her umbrella to give Pav a poke in the leg. "Now let's get out of this place. My son and his screaming banshee are starting to give me a migraine. I'll have to resort to taking my hearing aids out in a minute." Pav let out a short bark of laughter and moved to grip the handles of the wheelchair.

"Fine, get out," Valerie shouted, her true colours emerging as she sensed defeat in the air. "You always were a spineless, ungrateful brat anyway. Your father can win this election without your help. The public aren't going to care whether a nobody like you shows up or not."

"Well..." All eyes swung to a small figure standing near the doorway that Pav was approaching. "As far as *I* know, your husband is only a candidate for leader of his party, not for the election. Not yet." The woman stepped forward into the room and smiled at Valerie and her husband, both of whom had gone a rather alarming shade of white. "I'm Rachel Mulholland by the way, political correspondent for the *Herald*. I must say if this is how the Morrisons go about their business I can't wait for the press conference." She turned to Pav and Millie, gave them a wink, and then slipped out of the door ahead of them.

By the time they had negotiated the doorway and corridor with the chair, leaving the muted, panicked tones of Mr and Mrs Morrison and their campaign team, Rachel had faded back into the depths of the press pack.

"How much do you think she heard?" Millie asked as they made their way to the exit.

"Every word, dear," said Gammy from her chair. "She was watching us in the reception and followed us there. I don't know. You young people really are the most unobservant sort. You would never have survived the Blitz. Come along." She tapped Pav smartly on the shin and he winced. "If we start back now I might catch the last few minutes of the residents' meeting, and I want to complain about the downstairs toilet again. Betty spent a good thirty minutes looking for the loo roll the other day. Madness."

Chapter 33

All she ever wanted

"Can't I just slip out now?" Pav grumbled as Kira and Libby crowded him into his seat in the lecture theatre. "I'll come to the next one, I swear."

"You say that every time," Kira said, shoving him towards a seat in the front row.

"And why do I have to sit in the bloody front?" he hissed. "I can't even check my phone here."

"You are not sixteen years old, Pavlos," Libby said as Jamie strode over to them with a wide smile on his face. Why were all these lunatics so excited about another boring Grand Round? He rolled his eyes and fell into the seat in front of him. Kira sat on one side, and for some reason she was bouncing and tapping her foot, but then again Kira was weird in a variety of ways. Jamie and Libby sat on the other side, and he saw Don shuffle in to join them. It was the first time he'd been to a meeting in a long while. With Millie now able to work with the rest of the department better, he'd been semi-retired over the last few months.

As the theatre began to fill, Pav frowned. What was he

missing? Yes, you could get your mitts on the odd cheese sandwich at Grand Rounds, but that was never enough of a draw to get the whole hospital turning out. Then he turned to the entrance and blinked. El, Claire and Tara were walking into the large space together. El gave his group a small wave before scanning the crowd and biting her lip with what looked like worry.

"What on earth...?" he muttered, noticing that the others seemed to think that three random women strolling into a hospital lecture theatre in the middle of the day was no big deal. He was about to say something to Jamie when the side door opened and a hush fell over the crowd. Millie stepped forward, then froze in place and blinked as she looked up at all the people. Pav half rose out of his seat to go to her, but Jamie's strong arm pushed him down.

"Leave her be, mate," he muttered under his breath. Pav shot him a filthy look and refocused on the stage. An image of Millie's pale face before she crumbled into a heap and the sound of her head cracking against the wooden surface bloomed in his mind with perfect clarity. Leave her be, his arse. He wasn't about to let her put herself through that again. He shook Jamie's arm off and shoved him away, but was distracted by a sharp poke in his arm on the other side.

"Stand down, Double D.," Kira told him in a harsh whisper. Over the last few months Pav had morphed from Dick Doc to Double D., which seemed to amuse Kira, as she already called Jamie Triple G. Pav had been most put out to find out that Triple G. stood for Gorgeous Grantham the Gasman. He'd proposed a comprise of Triple D. to Kira so that she could include adjectives such as "dishy" but she laughed in his face, telling him his head was the size of a small planet already and that the last time any man was called *dishy* was in bad nineteen-sixties sitcoms. "She does not need you to go all Conan the Barbarian on her and drag her off the stage. Let her do this."

Pav frowned but settled back down into his seat, raising both hands in defeat. But he remained tense and ready to jump up should Millie's eyes show any sign of rolling back into her head again.

MILLIE SCANNED THE CROWD ONCE MORE AND TOOK another deep breath in through her nose and out through her mouth. She focused on Anwar in the audience, who gave her an encouraging smile and a small thumbs up. The breathing techniques they had practiced were just to get her up on stage; other techniques would get her through actually speaking. But standing here and not shaking like a leaf still felt like an enormous victory in itself. She moved forward towards the microphone and gripped both sides of the lectern. Between them Anwar and Millie had decided that she should start with the PowerPoint presentation, and she clicked on the projector, which was already set up with her first slide. When her eyes met Pav's she even managed to smile. He looked so cross and worried that she felt like climbing off the stage and kissing him right on the mouth in front of everyone. The fear that fuelled that worry for her was because he loved her.

Millie was loved.

Had she believed it right away? Well, no. Years of conditioning were tricky to undo all in one go. But gradually she'd started to trust. Yes, he'd said the words, and often, but it was more the way he showed her it was true. The way he stole her toothbrushes and her knickers to keep at his place so that she couldn't use that as an excuse not to stay over. The way he wanted to be with her, even going as far as reading *The Vagina*

Monologues so that he could come with her to book group – much to Kira's annoyance. The way he came with her to visit Gammy every time if he wasn't working, remembering to bring a bag of Werther's Original and submitting to the new name of "Paul", as Gammy found Pav "a bit too European for me, darling".

So much so that last night Millie even said it back. It might have been a whisper and it might have been in a post-sex cuddle when she thought he was asleep, but when his arm tightened around her, and judging from his smug grin this morning, she knew he'd heard her.

"So I'm not sure how many of you were here for my last talk," she started, her voice cracking a little. She cleared her throat and pushed on. "I'm hoping this time around things will be a little less dramatic."

There was a light wave of encouraging laughter and Millie risked a small smile. After she'd been through the slides, explained the next upcoming article in the *Lancet* about her results, there was a barrage of questions. They'd practiced this, Libby, Kira and her. She knew what to expect. Even a snide remark from a jealous radiology trainee couldn't put her off her stride. Once the questions had dried up she looked down at the lectern for a moment and took another deep breath before raising her eyes and fixing on her friends in the front row.

"I wanted to finish by..." Millie paused and closed her eyes briefly. An expectant hush fell over the hall. When she opened them again she focused on the people in the front row again: *her* people. After all these years Millie could finally say that she had her own people, ones who cared about her, even loved her.

"I know that I haven't been an easy person to work with or even..." Her eyes dropped to the lectern for a moment before she looked up again and straightened her shoulders. "... or even a human being. I've heard the nicknames." There were a few uncomfortable murmurs in the crowd and she could see some of the audience shifting in their seats.

"I'm not accusing or blaming any of you. I know none of you meant for me to hear, and I know I have lived up to my name "Nuclear Winter". I've upset people, it wasn't intentional but it has happened. I just... I didn't want to be that way, but I was stuck; stuck within my limits, scared all the time." She took a deep breath and then stepped around the lectern and forward towards her friends.

"Anxiety and phobias can rule your life if you let them. I know I'm not the only one who's been crippled by it – even in this room there'll be others; maybe not as extreme as me, but people whose lives are restricted, even if it's just in small ways. What I wanted to say is that you can push through the limits you put on yourself. So... I'm sorry if the Nuclear Winter has upset you in the past. And I can't promise she's gone, not completely. But I want you all to know I'm working on it. CBT has always helped me, but what really made the difference was *people*. People who made me see I didn't have to live within my limits, that I didn't have to stay stuck where I was. That there was a way out." Millie fell silent and the entire lecture theatre followed suit.

"So... thank you, Don, El, Kira, Libby, Jamie, Anwar, Claire, Tara and, of course, my Pavlos. At least... at least I hope he's still my... oomph!" She was cut off as Pav launched from his seat and nearly winded her in a hug that took her off her feet.

"I love you," she whispered in his ear once she was able to fill her lungs again with much needed air. He pulled away just enough that he could look down at her, and grinned before kissing her, right in front of the entire lecture theatre. She smacked his arm and when he pulled back her face felt on fire.

"I've still got *some* limits," she hissed. Pav laughed in the face of her residual rather-not-swap-spit-in-front-of-entire-hospital limits, and they were promptly swamped on all side by Millie's friends. At least with the ensuing group hug she was shielded from the crowd, and Pav was distracted from doing anything even more inappropriate than he already had.

It was Don who started the clapping. When Millie finally emerged from the arms of her friends she saw the audience on their feet. A year ago having so many eyes on her would have sent her into a flat panic, but now, with her hand in Pav's, Kira administering a sloppy kiss on her cheek, Don's hand on her shoulder, Jamie, Kira, Tara, El and Claire flanking her, now she just felt... loved.

And really that's all she ever wanted, anyway.

Epilogue

Loved, unconditionally

"We're willing to overlook the appalling way you've treated this family, Camilla, if *you're* willing to be sensible."

Millie waited for the familiar shame and guilt to swell up inside her. Years of dealing with her parents had made it almost a conditioned response. But after a minute she realised that she just felt... annoyed. Not even angry. Not upset – just a little bit pissed off. She glanced over at her soon-to-be mother-in-law and sister-in-law's red faces, and realised that, whilst *she* might not be furious, the rest of the room was spitting mad.

Millie sighed. She needed a moment so she turned away from her mother and towards the full-length mirror on the wardrobe in front of her. El had been in seventh heaven since the moment Millie told her she was getting married and that she would need dresses. Lots of dresses. The number of brides-maids she had settled on was ridiculous, even for a Greek wedding. But in the end she *had* to have Kira, Libby, Rosie, El herself, Pav's sisters, Tara and Claire.

The old Millie would have worried that it wasn't normal to

Susie Tate

have that many bridesmaids, that people would think she was weird, that it wasn't precisely right. The new Millie was so over the moon to even have women she could ask to walk up the aisle with her that she didn't give a badger's arse (one of the many Kira expressions she used now with some regularity) what anyone thought.

Her dress was cream lace over fitted, strapless satin; her hair fell around her shoulders in its natural soft waves (Pav's request), and she wore just a single flower in it, stolen from the bouquet after Rosie pitched a fit that Millie had to wear a tiara; the flower appeased her somewhat, but the six-year-old was still in grumpy mode. She'd only just stomped out of the room a minute ago, a second before Millie's parents' unexpected arrival.

"And by sensible you mean... ?"

"I'm going to walk you down the aisle," her father put in. "Then there's a photographer who'll–"

"No."

Millie's hands clenched into fists at her sides so hard she could feel the nails cutting into her palms.

"No way."

"This rift has gone on long enough," her mother coaxed. "I don't know what you think we've done to deserve this kind of treatment, darling."

Valerie Morrison was playing to her audience now. Millie could count on one hand the number of times she'd used an endearment with her before.

"All we've ever done was want the best for you. I can't understand why you would turn your back on us. We didn't even know you were getting married today. We had to find out from the matron of Mother M's nursing home last week, and that was only because Matron assumed we would be transporting your grandmother to the wedding and she wanted to

298

sort out timings. It probably didn't occur to a sensible woman like that, that the bride had excluded her own parents from the guest list."

"You've *never* been my parents," Millie said, her voice low with suppressed anger.

"What a ridiculous thing to say. I–"

"Before you needed me for the campaign we hadn't spoken in over two years."

Valerie narrowed her eyes at Millie and clamped her mouth shut. A tic at her mother's left eye heralded a probable loss of control.

"You took a naturally shy, introverted child with a special gift and forced her through the education system so fast she was doing her A-levels at thirteen years old. You belittled her and ignored her until she was an anxiety-ridden adult with social phobia so severe she had trouble even ordering a coffee."

"Don't blame us for *your* deficiencies, Camilla." Her mother's voice had changed now. Gone was the disingenuous façade of hurt and concern. Anger turned her tone ugly and derisive. "You always were a bloody embarrassment. What sort of child can't even attend a few simple functions without practically collapsing from stress. You're weak; weak and pathetic and I–"

The slap resounded around the large space and the room fell into shocked silence. Millie hadn't even seen her mother-in-law-to-be move, but now Talia was standing in front of Valerie, breathing heavily after the exertion of leaving a livid handprint across the other woman's face.

"How dare you!" shouted Valerie, clutching her cheek and shaking with outrage.

"My God," David said, going to take his place near his wife, but in typical cowardly fashion he stood just behind her instead of at her side. "What on earth –?"

"Get. Out." Talia said, her voice trembling with rage.

Susie Tate

"Now just hang on a damn minute," David blustered, but still took a small step back in the face of Talia's rage. "This is between our daughter and us. I'll not have some–"

"She is *my* daughter now," Talia said in the same low, dangerous voice as she reached back and gave Millie's hand a squeeze. "Unless you want your face to match your wife's I suggest you both get out of this room right now."

"Are you threatening me?" David scoffed. "I should call the police, that's what I should do. This is outrageous." The idea of her father calling the police on tiny Talia Martakis almost made Millie smile. Almost.

"Call them," Millie said as she moved forward to stand next to Talia and squeezed her hand back. "I think I've still got Rachel's number in my handbag. I wonder what *that* headline would look like?"

The week after her father's abysmal press conference where Millie had been a very obvious no-show, Rachel Mulholland had published an article on the Morrisons. Somehow she'd dug up all sorts of sources from Millie's past: ex-nannies fired for complaining, teachers concerned about the way Millie was being treated, school contemporaries who thought it was unfair for Millie to be with children much older than her.

But even more damning than that was the up-to-date information about Millie's estrangement from her parents, coupled with the photographs. It seemed that Rachel was skilled in the art of covert photography. To be honest Millie thought that the images she'd published had probably been the deciding factor for the public. There was one in the bathroom at the Savoy. Valerie Morrison was gripping Millie's arm, her face twisted with fury; Millie's back was to the camera but you could see her face reflected in the mirror above the sinks. Her expression was so achingly sad and resigned that even Millie had been a little shocked by it. Various other photographs had been taken that night and on the day of the press conference – one of them with Gammy and Pav in between Millie and her parents when those ugly words had been exchanged, all of which Rachel had recorded. As it turned out, the public don't like parents who neglect their child, or ones who would blackmail them by threatening an elderly relative.

Millie had not been over the moon about the articles. She had been bluffing when she said she had Rachel's number – she would never have wanted that story out there. The woman had contacted her for comment of course, but Millie chose to say nothing. Yes, her father didn't deserve to be the leader of his party, but not because he was a crap father: his politics were flawed and he was a lying, manipulative bastard who would do anything to get the power he craved.

Millie had once gone to a lecture about personality disorders. The psychiatrist drew a graph with power on one axis and love/dependence on the other. Average people were plotted in the middle of the graph with some power being important to them (like earning money and their career) but also family and love being of equal importance. Millie knew straightaway where to plot her parents: up the top of the power axis with very little love, right along with the serial killers. The difference with her parents was that they didn't achieve power by killing people; they achieved it through more conventional means and needed a conventional family in order to do that. Having Millie was never about love; it was about being more credible. And having a gifted child was never about helping Millie achieve her dreams; it was about using her to gain more power.

Millie was a firm believer that there were CEOs, high-profile politicians and world leaders who were *not* like her parents and serial killers. Not everybody in power was a psychopath. So, yes, she was pleased that the press had exposed her dad, as now someone better could step into his shoes. But there was no way Millie would ever do anything to garner more press attention. For a few weeks things had been uncomfortable. Had she not had the support she did, she knew she wouldn't have been able to bear it. But judging from her parents' pale faces and horror-filled expressions, they did not realise this at all. It only went to show how little they knew her.

"You wouldn't dare," whispered her mother, but her voice had lost its edge as it broke with uncertainty.

Millie did something that she had never done before, something she'd seen Kira and Libby do frequently in an argument: she put her hands on her hips.

"Try me."

Valerie Morrison's eyes dropped to her daughter's attitude-filled stance and surprise crossed her face before she carefully blanked her expression. "Fine," she said, retreating with her husband and sweeping the room with a contemptuous look as they moved to the door. "Have your pathetic little wedding and live your pathetic small life without us. I hope you and your new, ridiculous, mentally unstable family will be very happy." The door slammed after them both and Millie smiled.

"We will," she whispered as she turned back to the people that mattered to her.

~

NINE YEARS LATER...

"How old was Gammy when she died, Mummy?"

Millie's breath caught in her throat as she saw her little man standing in the doorway in a smart shirt and dark trousers. Unlike her other two children, whose outfits had already undergone two changes since breakfast in an attempt to keep them clean for the funeral, Leon's was still immaculate. She smiled and walked over to him, then crouched down so she was at his eye level.

"She was ninety-eight, darling," she told him, smoothing his dark curls away from his face.

He frowned and stared over her shoulder for a moment. "Does that mean that I've got ninety more years alive?"

"Well... uh... I'm not sure how–"

"Because that doesn't seem like a very long time at all." He was speaking more quickly now, his words tumbling out in his anxiety. Trust Lee to worry about his own mortality before most of his friends had even learnt their times tables.

"Lee, my darling," Millie said, shaking her head and pulling him in for a hug. His arms came up around her neck and he buried his face in her hair. It was down, just as her husband liked it, and it was covered in all manner of stuff transferred from little hands that morning: a few cornflakes, chocolate, some glitter. Appearance would always be important to Millie, but she had learnt to let go of the obsessive perfectionism over the years. When Leon drew back his expression was calmer; he needed that affection to anchor him when his little brain went into overdrive. His brother and sister might be more pushy and outgoing about... well, everything really, but it was Leon who really thrived on regular hugs even though he was the least likely to ask for them.

"But... but I can count to ninety," he whispered, looking down at his shoes, which were shiny from the polish he'd insisted on applying that morning. "What if I don't *want* to die then?"

"I'm not going to lie to you, Lean Bean. Everyone dies at some point. But it doesn't have to be a sad thing. Look at what we're doing today. Gammy didn't want us to stand around being sad, so we're going to play bingo and eat sausage rolls before we scatter her ashes. She had a good life and she was ready to go. She wants us to be happy too."

"I miss her."

Millie blinked as her eyes started to sting; she kissed Leon on the nose. "I miss her too, baby," she whispered back. "But we couldn't keep her forever. She's got other stuff to do, up in heaven."

Leon looked off into the middle distance again; she could almost hear his mind whirring away. "About heaven and God, Mummy..."

Millie laughed and pulled him in for another hug. "Let's leave the theological debate for another day, shall we?" she said as she swung him from side to side. Two sets of thundering footsteps gave her a short warning before the two compact bodies collided with her and Leon from either side. Millie drew back enough to get a look at them all and started laughing again. Costas' face was streaked with mud and Tallie's dress was covered in a mixture of paint and glitter, whilst one of her bunches sat up on the side of her head and the other hung down rather forlornly, with the ribbon only just holding on to the silky mass.

Tallie moved into the centre of the enforced group hug and rugby-tackled Leon, the low centre of gravity of her little body taking his longer and leaner one down to the floor. Once there she sat on his chest and tickled him. Costas broke away from his mother to join in and soon the three of them were rolling around the floor of the kitchen together. Death and theology discussions thankfully put on hold, as Leon's laughter, mixed with his siblings', filled the kitchen.

"What was that about?" Pav's low murmur sounded in Millie's ear as his strong arm came around her middle to pull her back into his body.

"Just the usual Leon worries," Millie said, turning in his

arms to look up into his handsome face. "You know: death, mortality, God, the meaning of life. Standard stuff."

Pav frowned. "He's taken Gammy's passing hard."

"He'll be okay," Millie said, sliding her hands up into the slightly-too-long dark hair at his collar and kissing the underside of his stubbled jaw. She would leave the nagging on both counts to Talia – who, over the years, Millie had discovered was far better at it than her.

"Yeah," Pav muttered, looking over at the children, a frown still marring his forehead.

Millie reached up and put a hand to his cheek, moving his face back to look at her before she smiled. "He *will* be okay, you know," she told him. "He just needs a little more time to process things."

"Inherited his mum's big brain," he said as a grin emerged from his frown and he tapped the side of Millie's head. "Too much going on up there."

Leon had always been different. He'd already done GCSE-level maths (tricky for the school as his parents refused to let him have any classes with older children), and Pav had caught him reading the *Guardian* the other day – he'd had to put a stop to it as Lee was getting himself worked up about the potential economic ramifications of the UK's exit from Europe on the farming industry. The poor child had fallen asleep that night murmuring to himself about EU subsidies.

Millie rolled her eyes and slapped Pav's arm. "He'll have a higher IQ than me."

"Hmm," was Pav's noncommittal response as the frown returned.

"Do you know how I know he'll be fine?" Millie asked, pulling Pav's face to hers. "Because he's loved, unconditionally. Because he has you and his brother and sister shining their light on him and never letting him slip into the dark. Because he has a huge Greek family as well as the adopted aunties and uncles that fuss over him. Because his life is filled with laughter and happiness."

Pav's face softened as he looked down at Millie, reading the meaning behind her words. She was talking about Leon, but he knew she meant herself as well. He knew how much all of those things meant to his wife. She made that clear every day.

They held each other's gaze for a moment before Pav closed his mouth over hers and her senses were swamped with everything Pavlos: firm lips, rough stubble, clean, woodsy scent, broad chest, until...

"Gah! *Kira*." Millie wiped the side of her face that was now wet, and turned to a grinning Kira who was brandishing a water-gun and rolling her eyes.

"Sorry," she chirped, not sounding sorry at all, and Millie got another face full of water, this time from a giggling Leon; the other two were concentrating on their father. "But there are children present. I was saving you two from corrupting young minds. Married people should not be allowed to suck each other's faces."

"But Auntie Kira," Tallie piped up, aiming her water-pistol at Kira and soaking her dress. "You're married and you kiss Uncle B. all the time."

"I kissed that man once on my wedding day as any proper wife should."

"That's a lie!" Costas shouted. "You're even more gross than Mummy and Daddy."

Kira gave her Super-Soaker a couple of pump actions and aimed it at Costas, who gave a yelp and turned tail to run. The others followed suit and soon the four of them were tearing through the house into the garden. The carefully selected outfits getting soaked.

But Leon's laughter made it worth another outfit change.

Yes, he would be fine.

They all would.

More than fine.

They would be happy.

DAVID MORRISON SLIPPED INTO THE BACK OF THE MASSIVE hall and stood in the shadows. She'd already started her talk and had everyone's attention. As she would. The rest of the presentations were just filler: she was the main event. Every person in that room was on the edge of their seat to hear what she had to say, her quiet voice amplified through the microphone explaining how she had revolutionized her area of medicine. An idea so simple it should have been glaringly obvious to anyone, but it took a mind like Camilla's to really see it.

Within the medical profession, even outside of it, Millie was known across the world. People listened when she spoke. His shy, watchful, anxious daughter was a world leader in her profession.

He always knew she was beyond intelligent but dismissed her as weak. In David's world you had to push yourself forward to get things done, to get to the top of the heap. Her low-key approach of simply solving the problems with her brilliant mind and sending the results out for the world to make of them what they would was totally alien to David's personality. He peered over to see if *he* was in the front row: her urologist husband. He was a success too: some new surgical technique they used for prostates or whatever. Not in Millie's league, but the bastard seemed happy with that. Happy for her to have the limelight. David shook his head; he couldn't comprehend it. But then again, maybe if he had ever tried to be happy for *his* wife, or encouraged *her* ambition instead of clinging to his own, maybe she wouldn't have turned into such a raving bitch. Maybe he would have spoken to his daughter once in the last ten years, met his grandchildren. Whereas now, after everything, he was just a washed-up old man. Failed political career behind him... Not even his harpy of a wife at home to complain to.

He gave Camilla one last long look before he turned to leave and saw the Greek get up from his seat as the applause rang out through the hall. Pavlos Martakis was smiling as he stood, sparking off a standing ovation. His proud, smug face beaming over at Camilla as she rolled her eyes and gave a low wave to the crowd.

David tried to muster some pride in the fact his genes had helped create her. But he knew, in the end, none of her success was down to him. It was in spite of him.

Had he been a better man he would have stayed, he would have tried to reach out to her, to apologize. But David was not a better man and she was better off without him. She was better off living her life, enjoying her success, being with the family she'd chosen for herself.

The one that made her happy.

The End

Acknowledgments

I'll start by saying a massive thank you to my readers. I never dreamt that people would take the time to read the stories I have thought up in my freaky brain, and I am honoured beyond words. Your feedback and reviews have made all the difference to the books and is the reason I've been able to make writing not just a passion, but a career. Special mention for Susie's Book Badgers - you are wonderful humans and your support means the world.

Thank you to my agent, Lorella Belli, for your support and encouragement. Yet again Martin Ouvry has done a fantastic job editing this book. Thanks also to Steve Molloy for such a wonderful cover design, which exceeded all my expectations and I know will help the book beyond measure.

Jane and Alexa – you are both so kind to run your eagle eyes over the manuscript for me; I am so grateful. Susie, Jess, Ruth and Curly, thanks for your wide and varied opinions and invaluable feedback; you have made Millie's story better than I could have on my own.

Thanks to Elisa from Living in Our Own Story: thank you for reading my books and inviting me to the RARE signing in London which was fabulous.

Last but not least thanks to my very own romantic hero. He's been married to me for fourteen years now and he supports me unconditionally. I love you and the boys to the moon and back.

A Word on Anxiety

I see many patients with anxiety and depression in my work as a general practitioner. If you've never suffered with any mental illness it is difficult to understand how crippling and isolating it can be. In my story Millie's main issues are social anxiety with some obsessive-compulsive traits. She chooses to tackle these with cognitive behavioural therapy, but there are many varied different options out there in terms of treatment.

At least a third of my consultations in general practice involve mental health. So, if you are suffering with these problems, in whatever form, please know that you are not alone. It may take time but you can feel better, given the right help. Below are some of the charities with great online resources and signposting:

UK based: Mind.

US based: National Alliance on Mental Illness

Canada based: Canada Mental Health Association

Australia based: Sane Australia

About the Author

Susie Tate is a contemporary romance author and doctor living in beautiful Dorset with her lovely husband, equally lovely (most of the time) three boys and properly lovely dog.

Susie really appreciates any feedback on her writing and would love to hear from anyone who has taken the time to read her books.

Official website:
http://www.susietate.com/

Join Facebook reader group:
Susie's Book Badgers
-
Find Susie on TikTok:
Susie Tate Author

Facebook Page:
https://www.facebook.com/susietateauthor

Printed in Great Britain
by Amazon

44151714R00182